I0572847

BARELY A CONVENIENCE

SUMMER LOVIN'
BOOK 3

RACHAEL OGLE

Barely a Convenience © 2025 by Rachael Ogle

The Library of Congress Cataloging-in-Publication Data is available upon request

ISBN: 979-8-9919576-4-9 (paperback)

CONTENTS

AUTHOR'S NOTE

As I'm learning in my author journey, I can never leave anything alone. Teagan's story was never supposed to exist. Hell, I even wrote Callahan's cousin Maddie's story (book 4) WAY before I ever even thought of writing Teagan and Joel.

I guess that's a spoiler, huh? That Maddie's also getting a book? Well, she is! Next year. But I digress.

As I said, Teagan's story wasn't supposed to exist. But something about her friendship with Jonas in books one and two (*Fake it to Forever*), intrigued me. Not that anyone ever has to have a reason for not wanting to settle down and live the "Great Big American Dream" of getting married, having two-point-five children and the picket fence, but I needed to know why she didn't want it.

Turns out, she did, just maybe not in the conventional sense.

Enter her grumpy AF single-dad neighbor, Joel. Not to spoil anything, but these two REALLY shouldn't work. He's all Broody McBrooderson and she's Sally Sunshine. Sure, grumpy-sunshine is a trope for a reason, but these two couldn't be more opposite.

But maybe that's why the *do* work.

Because I'm me, this story wouldn't be one of mine without really putting my characters through it. Teagan and Joel are no exception. Some subjects and themes in this story may be triggering for some readers, so always proceed with caution and take care of yourself.

As I always say, no book—not even mine—is worth your peace or mental health.

Some of the themes in this book include:

- Infidelity (not main characters)
- Divorce
- Miscarriage and infertility (off-page, historical)
- Pregnancy (not main characters)
- Death of a parent and family member (off-page, historical)
- Depression
- Internalized rage that results in one incident of minor property damage
- Severe postpartum depression (not main character)
- Grief
- Unintentional sexual involvement with a minor (off-page, historical)

Shitty parents don't worry that they're shitty parents. If you're worried, you're doing better than you think you are.
This ones for all parents. Those by birth and those by choice.

CHAPTER ONE

TEAGAN

The legal-sized manilla envelope with the logo for the law offices of Hornsby, Conners, and Cavendish taunts me from its position on the coffee table. I knew it was coming, but sometimes even knowing something beforehand doesn't make its actualization any less jarring. Especially when it's all there in black and white.

The words might as well be in flashing fucking neon.

I always knew Tootsie was a bit eccentric. It may have even started when she insisted everyone call her Tootsie instead of the much more conventional "Hannah". But I, along with everyone else, heeded her desires and she was Tootsie my entire life.

This goes past bohemian eccentricity. This is downright nutty, bordering on certifiable. This is unrealistic and unbelievable and shocking. This is...insane. Yeah, that's the only word for it.

I pour myself another shot of tequila as I eye the offending legal document. Downing the liquor, I wince with the burn, poking at the thick paper with one finger as if it may spring to life and attack me. The idea is absurd, but so is this.

I'm so caught up in my thoughts about Tootsie's post-mortem ultimatum, I don't even hear the ringing of my phone until it nearly rolls to voicemail. Snatching it up, I think for sure it will be one of the lawyers telling me this is all some elaborate prank and I'm in the clear. I don't bother looking at the screen before swiping my thumb and lifting it to my ear.

"Hello?"

"Miss Tee, Jethro's in the pool again."

I groan inwardly. "Okay. I'm on my way." Sighing, I rise from the sofa, shooting a glare at the envelope. I grab Jethro's leash, slipping on my flip-flops before heading out the side door leading into the yard.

Sure enough, the excited barks and splashing of my chocolate lab, Jethro, filter over the fence. I've paid a shit-ton of money in order to keep the dog out of our neighbor's pool, but apparently, his love for the water can't be contained.

Gus, my ten-year-old neighbor and the person responsible for the phone call, stands on the concrete pool deck with his hands on his hips, surveying the scene. As I open the gate to jog the extra twenty feet to my neighbor's gated pool, he offers me a glance. "How many times does that make this week?" he asks.

For some reason, he likes to keep track of how many times Jethro escapes in a given week.

I step up beside the boy. For ten, he's tall, and by this time next year, he's probably going to be taller than me. He's also tan, dark-haired, and stocky like his father, but has his mother's green eyes. We don't talk about his mother. No one in the neighborhood does. At least, not within earshot of Gus or his father, Joel. I make it a point not to talk about her at all.

"Three, I think. I still don't know how he's getting out. He's figured out where the blind spots are on the cameras and must be using them to make his escape." I whistle for my dog, who pauses in his paddling to look at me. I could almost swear he looks contrite. He begins to swim toward the steps, so I turn to look at Gus. "Where's your dad?"

He jerks a thumb over his shoulder toward the garage, and I extend the leash to him. "When he gets out, can you hook him up? I'll be right back."

The boy nods, accepting the leash. "Yes, ma'am."

As I enter the garage, I hear the unmistakable sound of a socket wrench, followed by a muttered curse, and the clanging of metal against concrete. I stand just inside the door and simply watch Joel for a moment. His legs—long, thick, tree trunk ones currently encased in worn, stained denim—stick out from beneath his ancient Chevy truck.

"Did Gus call you?" His words are a bit muffled from being under the truck, but I guess it means he heard me come in.

"Yeah. Sorry about Jethro. I swear, I don't know how he's getting out of the yard."

"It's fine," he says as he rolls out from under the vehicle. As he stands, he swipes a shop towel over his hands. "Although I think he availed himself of the pool a lot less when there wasn't a fence at all." As usual, his tone is matter-of-fact.

My mouth falls open at the sight of his face. "What the hell happened to your cheek?"

His hand reflexively rises to his left cheek, and he winces. "Huh. I didn't think that did anything, but I guess it did."

He has a small gash on his cheek, and it's pouring blood; most of which looks to have run down toward his beard and sideburns. Pulling his fingers away, they come back a bit bloody. "Dropped the socket wrench, and it smacked me in the face."

"You need to clean that up or it could get infected," I warn.

Rolling his eyes, he tosses the dirty towel toward the

corner, where a basket full of identical soiled blue towels sits. "I'm good. If I need someone to mother me, I'll let you know."

I open my mouth to tell him to not be such a grump when Gus comes into the garage with a dripping Jethro. "You want me to put him back in your yard, Miss Tee?"

Giving the boy a friendly smile, I nod. "That'd be great. Thanks, bud."

He jogs off toward my yard, so I turn my attention back to Joel. His eyes are narrowed. "You've been drinking."

"What are you, the temperance brigade?" I ask, incredulous.

He folds his huge arms over his broad chest. "No, but you smell like tequila and you don't normally hit the hard stuff on a Tuesday night. You want to talk about it?"

Ignoring the shocking fact that he's actually asking if I want to talk about anything other than mundane day-to-day chitchat, I shake my head. I definitely don't want to talk about why I'm half in the bag on a work night.

"No, I don't want to talk about it. You want to talk about why, in addition to that gash on your cheek, your knuckles are all banged up?"

He flexes his hands but doesn't bother looking down to confirm how red and raw his knuckles are. "No."

"Good."

"Good," he parrots.

I glance over my shoulder to make sure Gus is still out of earshot. Watching him toss Jethro's tennis ball to let him retrieve it, I can't help but smile. But when I return my gaze to his father, my expression is neutral. As it always does when our eyes meet, my heart gives a tiny lurch.

Joel has heterochromia, so one of his eyes is this rich brown, while the other is a bright blue. It's striking, and I'm not sure I'll ever get used to it. I'd be lying if I said they weren't the most beautiful eyes I'd ever seen.

Not that I'd ever tell him—or anyone—this. Despite knowing Joel since before Gus was born, we aren't exactly friends. Even with the effort I've put into trying to be his friend, we're not there. Friendly, yes. Coworkers, yes. Pals, buddies, besties, no.

I also ignore how incredibly hot he is. At forty, he's the epitome of ruggedly handsome mixed with nontoxic masculinity. I'm not ashamed to admit that I may have admired the way those faded jeans he tends to favor on the weekends fit his thighs and ass.

Not that I'd ever—in a million years—do anything even remotely close to flirting with him. Not while he was married, and certainly not now that he's single.

Despite the fact that his divorce is final, I'd never make any sort of overture; if for no other reason than I like his kid. If I made a pass at Joel and he didn't reciprocate, he might decide that I can't hang out with Gus anymore. And that's the last thing I'd ever want.

Gus is the absolute best and no longer being able to spend time with him would be a blow I'm not sure I'd recover from. God knows I'm not having kids of my own and since I'm an only child, it's not like I'll ever have any nieces or nephews; at least until Jonas and Callahan pop out a few adorable tiny humans. For now, Gus is the closest thing I'll ever get to being to someone what Tootsie was to me. I'd never do anything to lose that.

So what Joel and I can, at best, be called are friendly neighbors. We borrow sugar and coffee from one another, he occasionally comes over to fix stuck doors or look at my car when it's making a funky noise, we all sometimes have pizza and watch a ballgame, and my dog sneaks into his pool. On exceptionally rare occasions—usually when there's been more than a little alcohol consumed—one of us will confide in the other. I can probably count on one hand in the past decade how often that's happened, and every instance has been in the past year.

"How's he doing?" I ask.

One thing Joel will discuss, though, is Gus.

His eyes flit to my yard, and his expression softens into one of paternal affection. "I think he's okay." He looks down at his feet, arms still folded, his dark brown hair falling over his brow. "He's going to stay with Brooke next week."

My eyebrows shoot up my forehead in surprise. "What? Since when?" I realize my voice is high pitched and shrill, so I lower it. "Does Gus know?"

He sighs. "Yeah. It's only for a few weeks, but I'm not thrilled about it. Obviously."

"I'm sure. Where is she living now?"

He absentmindedly scratches his beard. "In this tiny town in Tennessee. About an hour north of Knoxville. But I have to fly in with him."

"How are you feeling about it just being you for a few weeks?"

He's quiet for a moment before he clears his throat, leveling me with a gaze. "I'll thank you to not try to psychoanalyze me, Teagan."

I return his stare. "It wasn't an attempt to psychoanalyze you, Joel. It was an attempt to be your friend. I'd think you'd recognize it by now. I've only been at it for ten years."

He gives me a smirk. "Yeah, yeah. You're persistent, I'll give you that. Have you eaten? We ordered pizza and still have a few slices left."

"I'm good, thanks. I'm going to go try to figure out, yet again, where Jethro is escaping from."

"Alright. Send Gus home when you get tired of him."

I give him a quick nod, turning to go, but I pivot right before stepping outside. Joel looks at me, expectant. "If you ever did want to talk, I would be happy to listen, you know. I can't begin to fathom how all of this feels for—."

His expression hardens. "Have a good night, Teagan."

Holding my hands up in an attempt to placate him, I nod. "Okay. But the offer stands."

Later, after Jethro is snoring happily on the other end of the couch and I've downed a few more fortifying shots of tequila, I eye the envelope again, blowing out a breath. Reaching for it, my hand shakes. But even with trembling hands and a pounding heart, I finally pick it up, turn it over, and slide my finger along the flap.

Pulling out the sheaf of papers, I lay them in my lap and blink in surprise when I see a smaller envelope—a standard, everyday one like you'd send a letter in—on top of the document. My breath hitches when I see my name in Tootsie's handwriting. Not exactly feeling like getting emotional tonight, I set the envelope to the side to examine the document.

The words "Last Will and Testament of Hannah Elizabeth Maynard" are the first thing I notice. Swallowing, I scan through the first page of boilerplate until I get to the second page. Even having heard her lawyer read this out to me the day after her funeral, it's surreal to read the words myself.

To Teagan Hannah Roth, I leave all of my worldly possessions and assets. Those are as follows, with the necessary conditions listed therein.

1. *The Jacksonville, Florida house on Sailfish Drive, where she has resided for the past eleven years.*
2. *The Del Mar, California house on Caminito Pointe Del Mar.***
3. *My 10,000 shares of Amazon stock.***
4. *My 5,000 shares of Apple stock.***
5. *My 5,000 shares of Berkshire Hathaway stock.***
6. *All monies and assets currently held in my accounts at Bank of America***
   A. *Account ending in 5784, total balance: $125,374.36*
   B. *Account ending in 2748, total balance: $84,945.28*
   C. *Account ending in 9210, total balance: $210,412.45*
   D. *Account ending in 4987, total balance: $225,022.12*
   E. *The contents of safe deposit box number 516 at the Neptune Beach branch.*

I pick up the tequila bottle again to take a few healthy swallows as my eyes drop to the line with the two tiny asterisks that detail the *conditions* of me receiving my inheritance. *What the hell was going through Tootsie's mind when she made her will?* It's not the first time I've asked myself that question; I also seriously doubt it will be the last.

I've always suspected my aunt was well off. I never knew exactly how apparently filthy rich she was. Okay, maybe not *filthy* rich, but the lawyer told me the Del Mar house was last appraised for over two million dollars. The stocks I have no clue about, but they'd be a tidy sum as well. Then there are also the bank accounts and safe deposit box to consider. This type of money isn't something I've ever been able to fathom.

I'm a high school guidance counselor. I drive a ten-year-old Honda, and don't spend frivolously. I have a fair amount put back in savings, and my student loans are paid off, but I'm not swimming in it.

As the will currently stands, the only thing I'm actually entitled to at this moment is my house. I suppose I should be extra grateful for that, and I am.

I steel myself to read the stipulations. Or, rather, *stipulation*. There's only one, but it's a fucking doozy.

***In order to receive these conditional assets, beneficiary Teagan Hannah Roth must be legally married within one year of the deceased's day of death. If said beneficiary fails to meet this stipulation during the specified time period, all conditional assets will be liquidated and distributed to the charitable organizations listed on pages 10-12 of this document.*

Married. Married? Fucking *legally* married? What the hell was Tootsie thinking?

CHAPTER TWO

JOEL

I watch Teagan walk back through her yard to ruffle Gus's hair as she passes him, and I can't help but wonder—not for the first time—why she's single. Not that I'm wanting to dive into anything with her; I'm simply curious.

Teagan is...amazing. Not that I've ever told her that or anything. Because Joel Briggs doesn't use the word "amazing" to describe people. That's a flowery word that I reserve for—well, to be honest, I'm not sure when I've ever even uttered the word "amazing" in my entire life.

But Teagan is. She accepted a job as the guidance counselor at the same high school where I work as the auto shop teacher, then moved in next door when Brooke was pregnant with Gus. She's always been a good neighbor. She's friendly, and on many occasions, had babysat for us so Brooke and I could have date nights. In the months since my life imploded, she's checked in on Gus. I know he talks to her, but I don't ask him what about. I trust that if there's something Teagan feels like I need to know, she'll tell me.

She's also stunningly beautiful. She's around five-three and curvy, with wide hips and an ass that I must admit I've stared at a time or two. It must be said, though, I never did any staring while I was married. That's not to say I haven't always seen how pretty Teagan is, because I have. You can't miss how good-looking she is. I'm just saying there were no blatant stares or imagining what it might be like to take a perfect, round globe in each hand and pull her—.

I digress.

While I get a lot of compliments on my eyes, for the most part, I think it's the novelty of seeing one brown eye and one blue. Most of the time, I wish I had "normal" eyes that were a standard color; like Teagan's. Not that hers are what I'd call *standard*. They're this dark blue with a gold ring around the pupil. Pretty cool if you ask me.

Her hair is a dark, nearly black, brown with some reddish undertones, and is cut to just below her shoulders. Over the years, I've seen it range from a platinum blonde pixie to a solid black sheet hanging nearly to her elbows, along with countless iterations in between. With her olive complexion and good bone structure, she's able to pull off just about any hairstyle she tries. I think this darker shade might be the closest to her natural color, though.

I definitely don't hate it. It wouldn't matter if I did, but I can still admit how well it suits her.

But tonight she asked me if I wanted to talk about my *feelings*. I don't talk about my feelings. Especially not with someone like her; someone with whom I've developed a somewhat begrudging friendship. I don't share feelings with friends. Truth is, I don't have a lot of friends anymore. Any really. Not that I've ever been Mister Popularity, but I had a tiny circle. Not anymore, though.

Tonight, I almost caved. I almost wanted to bitch about the fact that I'll be taking my kid seven hundred miles away. I nearly wanted to vent about having to leave him with the last people I ever want to see again. I was *this* close to letting all of my frustrations fly from my mouth instead of taking them out on the garage wall with my bare hands.

The law's the law, though, right? I don't really have a choice. I guess I should just be thankful I was granted full custody after Brooke decided to uproot her life and move to Tennessee.

But because I don't share my feelings, I couldn't bring myself to tell Teagan how anxious I am that I'll be without my kid for twenty-one days. I'm anxious about spending any time without him. My anxiety nearly doubles thinking about him being so far away and there not being a damn thing I can do about it.

I have no clue how I'll occupy myself while he's gone. I could go on a vacation, but taking a solo trip has never appealed to me. A thought occurs to me. Maybe I should book a place within reasonable driving distance of where Brooke is currently living. She wouldn't have to know, but at least that way, I'd be close in the event Gus sent up a flare or something.

The more I think about that, it sounds right. I'm on summer break—perks of being an educator, I suppose—and it's not like I have anything keeping me here. If nothing else, I can stick around for a few days and make sure he's good before I head back.

Navigating to the search engine on my phone, I spend a half-hour attempting to find a vacation rental for the first few days after I hand Gus over to Brooke. It might not be a bad idea to have some quiet time for myself away from home, too. If I'm here, I'll just dwell on missing Gus. If I'm somewhere where there aren't constant reminders of him, I might not go as stir crazy as I fear I might here.

Finally landing on a cabin that sits on a lake in the mountains—but with verified wi-Fi—I book the trip and change my return flight to the day I check out from the cabin.

Feeling less frantic than I have since learning that Gus would have to go to Brooke's, I breathe a sigh of relief.

"Dad, did you remember to pack my iPad? And Mom's house has wi-Fi, right?" Gus asks as he taps his foot, nervousness radiating off him as we wait to board the plane for Tennessee.

I nod. "Yeah. I double checked your bag. You're good to go."

He nods, still not relaxing. I open my mouth to tell him that everything is going to be fine, and he has everything he needs when his eyes widen with delight as they move to somewhere over my shoulder. "Miss Tee!"

Whipping my head around, I'm shocked to see Teagan walking toward the terminal, carry-on suitcase rolling behind her.

She seems just as surprised to see us. "I didn't realize y'all would be on this flight." Jerking her head to the seat next to mine, she asks, "This seat taken?"

"Have at it," I offer and she drops into the empty chair. "What are you going to Knoxville for?"

"I'm going to a wedding; I think I mentioned it a few months back. My friend, Jonas? His fiancée's family has a big lake house, and that's where they're having the wedding."

"Jonas? As in—." She nods, not needing me to finish the sentence. "And his fiancée is cool with you being there?"

Teagan laughs. "Definitely. Callahan's cool people. Plus, it's not like I ever wanted a long-term claim on him. And it was clear after they met that he was gone for her."

I'm about to open my mouth to ask if it's not weird to watch a guy she's slept with for years get married, but Gus says, "I get to go to Dollywood next week."

She turns her attention to my son, her smile warm. "From what I hear, it's a pretty cool place. You'll have to tell me how you like it when you get home, okay?"

He nods. "I will. So if you're going out of town, where's Jethro?"

"He's staying with some other dogs at a kennel. It's kinda like sleep-away camp for dogs."

"Do you think he's going to like it?"

She gives him a reassuring smile and I simply watch their exchange. I'd be lying if I said I don't like how close Gus and Teagan are. She's helped him maintain some semblance of stable normalcy in all the upheaval this last eighteen months has brought and I'll never be able to adequately convey my gratitude for it.

"He loves it. Plus, the kennel has cameras set up, so I can check them anytime I want to see how he's doing."

"That's cool. Do they have a pool for him to swim in?"

She chuckles. "They do, actually. It was one of the biggest reasons I booked it."

Seemingly satisfied with the information she's given him, he picks up his backpack, searching through the pockets until he finds his iPad and headphones.

Teagan nudges me with her elbow, and I give her my full attention. "Is he nervous about the flight?" she asks quietly.

I nod. "I think so, but he hasn't come right out and said it."

"And how are you doing?"

Not wanting to discuss how I am, I shrug. "Fine." Pivoting the subject away from me, I say, "Hard to believe you're going to Jonas's wedding."

She frowns. "Why? He's my best friend."

"Yeah, but weren't you dating?"

Snorting in amusement, she shakes her head, lowering her voice so Gus won't overhear our conversation. "I hardly think drinks at the bar and no-strings hooking up constitute dating. I always knew Jonas would eventually find his forever, and I always knew it wouldn't be me."

"You don't sound too torn up about it."

"I'm not. Jonas and I were just friends. With benefits. That's all. I'm happy for him. Like I said, Callahan's great."

"So, you guys never talked about evolving your relationship or anything?"

She lifts a brow as she narrows her eyes. "Why, Joel Briggs, are you actually wanting to talk about *feelings*?" Her tone is playful, and the corner of her mouth pulls into a smug sort of half-smile.

I scoff. "I think you know me better than that. It's just morbid curiosity, is all. Does his fiancée know about the two of you?"

Nodding, she pulls a bottle of water out of her bag and takes a long drink. "Of course; they don't have secrets."

"And you really feel nothing for him?"

"Nope. He was simply an outlet. A safe, reliable outlet."

For the briefest of seconds, I wonder what having an *outlet* like she's describing might be like, but then I shake the thought away. I've never been one for the hookup scene. Even now, when I'm no longer hindered by any legal or moral tether, I can't bring myself to do more than simply entertain the idea of sex with a stranger. Or, as the case may be, *not* a stranger.

CHAPTER THREE

TEAGAN

Joel's quiet for a long moment after I explain exactly what Jonas was to me. And then he gets this faraway look in his eyes that I'm unsure how to interpret. My gaze snags on the tiny scratch still on his cheek from last week. It only makes him look roguish, the handsome bastard. I'm contemplating asking him if he's even been on a date since everything happened with Brooke—his lack of desire to discuss feelings be damned —when our plane is called and everyone rises to walk to the gate.

"What seats do y'all have?" I ask as we make our way to board.

"C2 and C3," he answers.

I blink in shock. "Shut up."

He frowns. "What?"

"Are you joking?"

His frown deepens, his dark brows drawing down over those striking eyes. "Why would I joke about seat assignments? That's absurd."

Heaving a sigh, I roll my eyes. "It's a figure of speech; typically said when what was just said was nearly unbelievable. Ask me what my assigned seat is," I prompt.

"What's your seat, Miss Tee?" Gus obediently chimes in.

I smile. "C1 for me, boys. Looks like you're stuck with me for the next couple of hours."

"Lord help us," Joel quips good-naturedly.

"Really?" the younger of the Briggs males asks in wonder. "Can I sit beside you?"

I offer him a friendly smile. "Of course. Although, if you've never flown before, don't you want to be able to look out the window?"

He seems to seriously consider my question before turning to his father. "Dad, can Miss Tee sit in the middle so I can sit beside her and look out the window?"

Joel shrugs. "It's fine with me." Turning his gaze on me, he asks, "Are you up for that?"

"I think I'd survive it."

"Alright, then. Gus, looks like you've got the window seat."

Thankfully, the flight is smooth and Gus is afforded a good first flying experience. Joel pulls out a book two seconds into the flight and I take that as my cue that he doesn't wish to talk—he probably knows I'd ask him how he's feeling about Gus going to Brooke's—so I put my earbuds in to listen to music, lay my seat back, and try to nap.

When we're about to land, Joel nudges me. "Sit up, Tee. Don't want your seat being reclined those extra four degrees to be the cause of some major disturbance to the landing gear." I roll my shoulders and raise my seat, covering my mouth as I yawn. "By the way," he says in his usual matter-of-fact tone, "you snore like a congested chainsaw."

I scoff. "I do not snore."

Gus lets out a soft laugh. "Sorry, Miss Tee, but Dad's right. Not about the chainsaw part, but you totally snore. It sounds more like a weed whacker that's running out of gas."

Narrowing my eyes as I fold my arms over my chest, I shake my head. "Nope. Never happened."

Joel shrugs. "If I were you, I'd make an appointment with a sleep specialist. That sort of breathing pattern can't be normal."

I frown, growing a bit concerned, and lower my voice. "Was it really that bad?"

He snorts an amused laugh as he looks past me to Gus. "Told you she'd fall for it."

Pointing at them both and narrowing my eyes again, I swivel my head back and forth, giving them glares. "That was mean. See if I'm nice to either of you ever again."

They both laugh as the plane descends. Joel grins. "We both know you're still going to be nice to us. If for no other reason than my kid is one of your favorite people. And no, you don't snore." His expression softens. "You do, however, mumble in your sleep."

I nod. "I've been told that before."

"It's cute."

I can't help but smile. "That might be the sweetest thing you've ever said to me."

He rolls his eyes. "Mark it down. It probably won't ever happen again."

"You know, I don't think you're as much of a bear as you like people to think you are. And when you smile, it almost makes you look downright approachable."

He lets out a small snort of laughter. "Approachable is never something I've strived to be. I have quite the reputation of being the surly auto shop class teacher and hard-ass baseball coach. Can't intimidate my students and players if I'm *approachable.*" The last word comes out like a curse and I laugh.

"You know, sometimes, it's nice to let people think you're actually human. Don't pretend you're not. I've seen you with Gus. You're a big teddy bear with him, not the grizzly you are with students."

"We can't all be like you and foster everyone's dreams and imaginations. I live in the real world and there are a lot more grizzlies than teddies out there. I'm just preparing them for what's ahead."

I dismiss his cynicism with a wave just as the plane touches down. "Yeah, yeah. Whatever you say. I prefer optimism and hope, thank you very much."

"We made it," Gus says, obvious relief lacing his tone.

Joel's lips curve into a small smile. "We sure did. Now we just have to wait for them to let us go."

"Did Mom say where she'd be waiting?"

He tenses briefly at Gus's mention of Brooke, but not so much that his son picks up on it. "By the exit," is all he says, his demeanor seeming to flip like a switch. Any sense of relaxed humor—well, humor for Joel anyway—vanishes, and I watch as he almost visibly shutters any sort of emotion other than indifference.

It's hard to watch. Even though Joel hasn't and won't open up to me—or anyone, I suspect—I'm sure his emotions surrounding this trip are messy.

The thing is, I've seen him playful and laughing with abandon and completely carefree. But not in a couple of years. And even if we've never been besties, we've always been friendly. These days, even that feels like it's hard for him. It's as if he's angry at the entire world and tries so hard to keep it boxed up so it doesn't affect Gus. While it's admirable, it's most definitely not sustainable, so I'm nearly holding my breath, waiting for everything to spew like a shaken soda bottle.

A moment later, they allow us to rise and exit the plane and Gus walks a few feet ahead of us. "So, when is your return flight?" I ask.

"Not for a few days."

I frown. "I thought you were just dropping him off and going right back home."

He shrugs. "I wanted to be close for a few days. Just in case."

I lower my voice, even though I know Gus is far enough away that he can't hear us. "Does Gus know? Does she?"

He shakes his head. "No. Don't bring it up?"

I nod. "Of course."

I'm about to ask him where he's staying when all the color drains from Joel's face at the same time Gus says, "Mom!", his eyes wide, as he takes off at a run.

Following Joel's line of sight, my mouth nearly falls open when I see Brooke, who is heavily pregnant, and not alone as she embraces her son. I swallow around the sudden lump in my throat. Even though I have no dog in this race at all, anger simmers in my chest at her nerve.

It's one thing to cheat on your spouse and move seven hundred miles away. It's a completely different thing to do it with your husband's *father*.

Joel's eyes don't move from his son, and he doesn't even acknowledge Brooke or his father, Clive. I, on the other hand, can't look away from the pair of them. One of the most shocking things is, Joel looks just like a younger version of his father. I guess I can see the appeal, but seriously, his *dad*?

I would imagine the men have similar taste in women and honestly, I don't want to think about that. All I mean is, Brooke has similar coloring and build to Joel's late mother. She's naturally tan with dark-blonde hair and green eyes. At thirty-nine, her face is still unlined. Although she typically wears quite a bit of makeup, I've seen her without it plenty, and know she has great skin. In pregnancy, she's even prettier than normal. There's a reason they say mothers-to-be glow, because she's gorgeous.

She finally lifts her gaze to Joel and registers my presence, frowning in surprise. "Teagan. Didn't know you'd be coming with Joel to drop Gus off."

I clear my throat and lift my chin, ignoring the slight accusation in her tone and simply reply, my tone flat, "Brooke."

After a beat and her eyes flitting from me to Joel and back, she drops her gaze to her son. "Go tell your dad bye, okay? You can call him when we get home."

Home. Really?

Gus's *home* is back in Jacksonville.

I can't imagine what this must feel like for Joel. I'm ready to claw Brooke's eyes out for hurting someone I want to consider a friend; even if he doesn't seem inclined to want friends. How much worse must this be for him?

But Joel doesn't say anything and neither do I as Gus runs back over and hugs his dad, who bends to whisper something I don't hear into his ear. A second after they separate, Gus launches himself at me, hugging me around the waist. I immediately return the embrace, unable to keep the warmth from spreading through my chest. "Have a good visit, okay?"

"I will." He lowers his voice. "I bet Dad would let Jethro swim in the pool all the time if you asked."

I snort a laugh. "I'll do that." Ruffling his hair as he steps back, I offer him a smile as he pivots to rejoin his mother and grandfather. Jesus, the drama.

Clive, who's been silent the whole time, grins down at Gus

as the trio turns to walk out the doors. "What do you think, Champ? Ready to go home?"

It's probably by some miracle that I even hear Joel's breath hitch. The airport is bustling and noisy, but the sound of his quick inhale registers in my brain and I steal a cautious glance at him. His face is a mask of seething anger and even more pain, but he blinks, clearing his expression when he notices I'm looking at him. I open my mouth and he shakes his head, not making eye contact with me. "Don't ask me if I'm okay. Don't ask me if I want to talk about it. Don't ask me about my fucking feelings, Tee."

I shake my head. "I wasn't. I was going to ask if you wanted to get a drink."

His eyes finally meet mine, his gaze full of barely concealed anguish. "If I start drinking, I'm not sure I'll stop."

I nod, a pang of sympathy hitting me in the chest with the rawness of his voice. "Alright. Where—." My phone rings in my hand and I blink. "Don't leave yet, okay?"

Uncertainty flits through his gaze, but he finally shrugs and leans against a nearby wall as I swipe my phone's screen after registering Jonas's name on the ID. "I have some bad news," he says in greeting.

I frown. "What? Is the wedding off or something?"

He scoffs down the line. "No, nothing that dire. The cabin we rented for you, Elliot, and Russ to share burnt down last night."

My mouth falls open in shock. "Shit. Was anyone hurt?" Joel stands up straighter and glances at me.

"No," Jonas replies, "but we haven't been able to find anything else close for y'all to stay at. Since it's Memorial Day weekend, everything's booked."

"Okay, so doesn't that house have, like, forty rooms or something? Stick me in a corner somewhere. You know I can sleep anywhere. Where are Elliot and Russ staying?"

"Russ has a friend who actually lives nearby, believe it or not. They're crashing with them. I asked if they had room for you, but they're already going to be sleeping on a pullout."

I rack my brain. "I mean, like I said, I can sleep anywhere. What about the media room?"

"Callie's mom has turned that into a secondary ceremony space since there's a chance of rain. It's already decorated."

"Okay," I say, resigned. "I'll figure something out. Don't worry about it. You know me, I'm resourceful."

"I'm sorry, Teag. I tried to call you earlier, but I guess you were already in the air. Callie's dad said he's going to keep trying to find something."

"I'm sure Callahan's parents have enough to worry about with the wedding. They don't need to add me to that list. Like I said, I'll figure something out."

"You can stay with me," Joel says quietly. I whip my head up and he shrugs. "I'm not sure how close it is to them, but you won't have to sleep in your car." He lifts a brow as if he knows that's exactly what I was considering doing.

I open my mouth to protest and Joel takes my phone from my hand. "Jonas? Hey, it's Joel, Teagan's neighbor...Total coincidence, actually. But I'm in town for a few days; she's going to stay with me...No, that's not necessary. Really..." His cheeks puff up as if he was about to say something that I'm sure Jonas is making an argument for or against. Blowing out a breath, he slumps. "Sure. I'll be there." He disconnects the call and holds out my phone. "Thanks to you, I now have to go to a wedding."

I furrow my brow in confusion. "What? It's not my fault. No one asked you to come to my rescue. Don't put yourself out on my account," I retort, planting my hands on my hips.

He rolls his eyes. "Oh, please. You were standing there, all resigned to your fate like some sad puppy. Like I—or anyone with some semblance of decency—would let you sleep in your damn car."

"You're so chivalrous I can't stand it, Joel," I deadpan.

"I'm not that chivalrous; you're sleeping on the couch. A simple 'thank you' would suffice."

"Thank you," I say, my tone sincere.

He shrugs. "It's fine. But I need to get my rental car, and apparently have to get wedding clothes. I'm making you shop with me. I hate shopping." As if all the matters at hand are settled, he pivots and begins walking toward the rental car counter.

I nearly have to jog to keep up with his longer strides. "Did you agree to this simply so you wouldn't have to think about Gus? Because it would give you a situation to 'fix' or whatever?"

"So what if I did? You going to complain when I've actually done a nice thing? Might as well mark this down, too."

Shocked he's actually admitted that he wanted to fix something he can versus dwelling on something he can't, I nod. "I will."

CHAPTER FOUR

JOEL

What was I supposed to do, let her sleep in her car when I know my cabin has a couch she can crash on? I'm not that big an asshole. Plus, this is a situation I can do something about. Gus being here with Brooke and *him* isn't something I can do anything about at the moment.

As we wait in line at the rental car counter, Teagan asks, "So, where is the place you rented?"

I pull out my phone and navigate to the app to show her the reservation. Her brows rise in surprise. "Damn, that's right down the street from Callahan's family's lake house. Or, judging by the address, it seems to be. It's on the same road."

"The coincidences keep coming, huh?"

She nods. "I guess. Why don't you cancel your car? It doesn't make sense to have two cars if we're going to the same places, right? I'll extend my reservation and you can drop it off when you fly home. Of course, you'll have to bring me back to catch my flight, but other than that, you can drive it."

"Wouldn't it make more sense for you to cancel yours?

Mine's already booked through my entire stay. I can still bring you back for your flight."

She splays her hands. "I was just trying to pitch in. But if you want to keep your car, it's fine; I have no issues canceling mine."

"Okay," I say with finality.

"So, what's the dress code for this thing? Is it tuxes and ballgowns and shit?" I ask as we make a detour on the way to my cabin. We're headed to the outlet malls in Sevierville in the hopes of finding me something decent to wear to a wedding I have no desire to attend.

Teagan shakes her head as she ushers me into the Gap outlet store. "No, no tuxes. The whole thing is pretty laid back. They're doing corn hole at the reception and they're going to be married on the boat dock. Jonas isn't even wearing a blazer or anything. You could get by fine with a pair of chinos and a button-down."

She strides over to some racks and immediately begins pulling articles of clothing, shoving them in my direction. She's done it so quickly, I don't even have time to register what items I'm holding. "Try these. I guessed at the sizes, but if you need a different one, I can grab it. I'm sure you usually go with a more relaxed fit on the pants, but I think this slim cut will look more put together."

"Okay," I answer, my tone wary as I make my way to the dressing rooms. Teagan follows behind me, dropping onto a nearby bench as I step into one of the rooms.

"What sort of shoes did you bring? Anything other than the sneakers you have on?" she calls as I strip down.

"No. I wasn't planning on being anywhere but at the cabin. Why would I need more than one pair of shoes for that?"

"I was just checking. Jeez. What about a belt; do you have that?"

"I'm wearing a belt right now."

"Is it black or brown?"

"It's reversible," I say with a sigh, hurriedly slipping into the clothes she picked out. And other than them being a bit more form-fitting than I'm used to, the size is right.

"Alright. How's it coming in there?"

I give myself a final once over as I tuck the light pink shirt into the navy chinos. "Seriously, pink?" I ask, opening the door.

She smiles when she sees me. "I can't believe I got the sizing right." Standing, she tilts her head, appraising my appearance. "And yes, pink. It goes with both your eyes. I was so right about the cut. I knew they'd look a lot better than those grandpa pants you wear at work."

Her eyes trail down my frame, and I'm not sure what to do with the appreciative way her gaze lingers on my arms and thighs. "My eyes are up here, lady," I finally say, just to watch as a blush creeps into her cheeks.

Well, that's new.

She snaps her eyes up and blinks. "I think you're good. You just need shoes."

"Thank God. I'm shocked you're not making me try on everything in the store."

She snorts a laugh. "What can I say; I've got a good eye." As I'm redressing in my original clothes, she asks, "Are you hungry? Because I don't know about you, but I'm starving."

"I could eat," I agree. "Steak? Didn't we pass a place on the way here?"

"Yeah, but from what Jonas said, there's a great steak place on the way to the lake house. He raves about it."

"Works for me. Do you know if this is a dry county, or do they have liquor stores?"

I open the door, and she takes the items I didn't even try on to hang on a nearby rack. "I don't think there are any here in Sevierville, but they sell beer and wine in the grocery stores."

"Good enough for me. We should probably stop to get some breakfast stuff, too, right? What time is the wedding?"

"Six. They're doing pizza and cupcakes and there will be an open bar. One thing about Callahan's parents is, they're loaded." Some emotion flits through her gaze, but I can't decipher it because it's gone just as quickly. "Jonas said her mom balked at how low key they wanted everything to be, but her dad is stoked because all he had to do was mow the yard and buy the booze."

"Sounds like my kind of shindig."

After shopping, stopping to eat, and pickup the groceries we'll need for at least a couple of days, I'm exhausted by the time we get to the cabin. Even with the GPS, we nearly miss the turnoff, but I breathe a sigh as I shut off the engine. I simply want to unpack and crawl into bed.

The cabin is fairly basic; a single bedroom and bathroom, natural walls and floors, a simple eat-in kitchen and living room. There's a fireplace in the corner with a television mounted over it. There's a deck out back with a beautiful view of Douglas Lake, complete with a porch swing and a couple of rocking chairs. "Pretty amazing you could get this, considering everything was booked," Teagan says as she stashes a case of beer in the fridge.

"Yeah. I basically just picked the first one that was open.

Not gonna lie, the view is nice. And you said the place where Jonas's wedding is being held is close?"

She nods as we move around the kitchen, putting away groceries. "Yeah. We passed it on the way in. I'm not sure exactly where, because he said you can't see the house from the road, but it's back the way we came."

"Do you have to go to a rehearsal dinner or anything?"

"No. They were only doing a dinner with the immediate family since they don't really even have to rehearse." She holds up a bottle of red wine. "Want some?"

"God, yes."

Huffing a laugh, she opens drawers until she finds a corkscrew. As she opens the bottle, she doesn't look at me. "Thank you for letting me crash with you. I'm sure you'd rather be alone to stew, but I really appreciate this."

I accept the glass she extends my direction and level her with a gaze. "Let's not make it a big thing, okay? I just didn't want you sleeping in your car. You'd end up getting murdered or something, then Jethro would be an orphan. I'd probably be forced to take him in, and I'm just not up for all that dog hair being all over my house."

She rolls her eyes as she shoves the cork back into the bottle. "Nice to see it was for purely altruistic reasons."

"Definitely," I deadpan.

Wordlessly, she takes her glass, along with the bottle of wine, walking over to the back door to step outside. And even though I don't really feel like talking, I've never minded sitting in silence with Teagan, so I follow her out to the deck to join her on the swing. "It's not too humid. I was expecting it to be a lot worse, honestly," she offers and I simply nod.

I keep my gaze focused on the woods as the swing sways beneath us in the waning light of the sun on our backs. I could turn and watch it go down, but it would mean I'm acknowl-edging the fact that my kid isn't spending the night with me.

"What would you do to be able to live an entirely carefree life?" she questions sometime later.

I don't bother looking at her as I drain my wine glass and refill it. "Define carefree."

She sighs. "A life where you didn't have to work. A life where your days were whatever you wanted them to be. You might still choose to work, but it would be with the knowledge that at any point, you could say, 'take this job and shove it', and your lifestyle would never have to change. You could travel or find passion projects or whatever. A carefree life," she repeats.

To my mind, a carefree life would mean that my kid is under my roof all the time and I never have to worry about Brooke coming back into our lives in any capacity. Is that fair to my kid? I can't say. He loves his mother and despite the things she's done, I know he's happy to see her. I simply wish I felt nothing at all. It would make things easier for me. But I don't feel nothing. I still feel everything. Even if I don't talk about it.

"I would probably do a lot," I admit. "Probably not murder, but my morals might be a bit flimsy depending on how *carefree* we're talking."

"Set for life," Teagan responds.

"Would I have to do anything illegal?"

She huffs a laugh. "What happened to your flimsy morals?"

I shrug. "I'm just curious about the parameters of this quandary you've posed. If I, say, had to rob a granny on a fixed income, I'd probably say no. If you said, 'if you take all these diamonds that fell off the back of a truck and sell them on the black market and you'll never get caught and we'll give you ten million dollars', that's a different story. If you said, 'kill this puppy,' that'd be a hard pass. If you said, 'chop off your pinky toe,' I'd at least consider it."

She's thoughtful for a long moment. "Your pinky toe, huh?"

"It is the least necessary toe," I explain.

"No, nothing illegal," she answers. "But it would be something big."

"Big like what; shaving my eyebrows or moving or making a fool out of myself on live TV?" She sighs, and I get the feeling she's legitimately asking this sort of question, and I finally look at her. Sure enough, she has a pensive, anxious look on her face, so I give her an honest answer. "If the payoff would be that my kid would have a good future and no one would get hurt, I'd probably do just about anything."

Nodding, she drains her glass and holds it up. I pour the remainder of the bottle into it. "That's kinda what I figured."

"Why do you ask?"

She blinks as if clearing her head and waves off my question. "Just making conversation. But it's nice to know your morals become questionable, depending on the possibility of money."

CHAPTER FIVE

TEAGAN

I'd posed the question, but I could've predicted his legitimate answer. If it was for Gus, Joel would do almost anything. But he's his dad, so I guess that's kind of expected. Because Joel is a good dad.

As the sun descends behind the trees and the light grows dim, we sit in companionable silence while we sip our wine. The swing sways and crickets and frogs begin to make themselves known as we continue to sit.

It strikes me that this is the first time we've ever been alone. Truly alone. Usually Gus is just around the corner or we're all hanging out. But we're alone and the image of Joel walking out of the dressing room flashes through my mind and what an image it is. Damn, he's good looking. And we're going to a wedding together. Okay, not *together*, but still.

"Why are you single?"

The question takes me by surprise and surely I've misheard because Joel doesn't talk about stuff, but he's asking this? I ask him to repeat himself. He does, and nope, I didn't mishear.

I blow out a breath. "I mean, I'm only thirty-one, so it's not like I'm decrepit." He rolls his eyes and I nudge him and smile. "But I've never considered that I was cut out for long-term monogamy. Jonas was probably the closest thing I've ever had to a relationship, and we were never exclusive. Not for ten years. And it never bothered me. I would think if I was ever going to develop feelings, they would've manifested way before then. Granted, Jonas never showed interest in any sort of relationship with anyone until he met Callahan. Well, I take that back. He was engaged in college and it went bad and he's always felt responsible, so he never let himself want anything."

"Okay, but that's him; not you. Why are *you* single?"

I look down into my nearly empty glass. Hey, if he's actually wanting to talk, I might as well, right? "I can't have kids. And kids weren't ever something I was dead set on having, but—."

"When it's not even an option, it feels like you were robbed," he supplies, his tone gentle.

"Pretty much. And honestly, I had boyfriends in high school and college before I went the strictly hookup route. I don't think I ever loved anyone, so I'm not sure it's something I'm actually capable of."

"But you think because you can't have kids, it's a reason to not settle down?"

I shrug. "In my experience, most men want to procreate. Isn't it some kind of biological *urge*? I mean, you wanted kids, right?"

He considers my question for a long time. "Yeah." His lips pull up into a sad half-smile. "I wanted a ton of 'em. Gotta admit, though, Gus is pretty great all on his own."

I nod. "He's amazing," I agree. "Best kid ever." Tossing out a question I have no hope he'll actually answer, I figure the most he can do is tell me he doesn't want to talk about it. "Did you and Brooke talk about having more after Gus?"

Joel's jaw clenches, and he gets a faraway look in his eyes. "Yeah. She didn't want more." He downs his wine in one long gulp. "She was so adamant, in fact, that I had a vasectomy."

I swallow at the bitterness in his voice. "I'm sorry."

He rises. "I'm going to bed. I'll put some blankets on the couch for you."

When he's almost to the door, I call his name, and he pauses, his posture rigid, but doesn't look at me. "Goodnight, Teagan."

"Night," I echo, knowing he's done talking for the night. I shouldn't want him to keep talking about his pain, but honestly, I want him to talk about everything and having just bits and pieces of him over the years only makes me want that much more. Even if it's only to be a better friend to him.

I give him plenty of time to do whatever he needs to in the bathroom and go into the bedroom before I head inside. True to his word, there are a couple of blankets and a pillow on the couch. No light spills from under the bedroom door, so I quietly go about washing my face, pulling on my nightgown, and readying the sofa for me to sleep.

Lying down, I feel a bit out of sorts. It could be that Joel and I are under the same roof to sleep. And really, that's a bit strange, but I'm pretty sure it's that I'm still thinking over our conversation where I'd asked him what he'd do to be set for life.

I still have time to figure out what I want to do. A year is a blip in the grand scheme of things and it's already been a month, but I still have time. It's not as if I'm opposed to the entire institution that is marriage. Honestly, I'm indifferent about the whole thing.

Callahan asked me when we met why Jonas and I never became more than just friends with benefits. I told her I never wanted to get married or have kids and I knew someday, Jonas would want that. I love Jonas—as a friend. And our ten years of sexual history notwithstanding, I'm no longer attracted to him. Seeing him actually fall in love with someone killed any desire for him I had.

In truth, Joel is the first person, aside from my parents and Tootsie, who knows that I *can't* have kids. People are less likely to probe deeper when you say you don't want them. Most of the time, they either say I'll change my mind or they accept what I say at face value. I'm not sure what made me tell Joel; especially because I've never even told Jonas.

And maybe it's manipulative to think that if I share parts of myself, Joel will want to do the same, but I don't care. I've known the man for over ten years and can tell you what his favorite food is—a medium-rare steak with a fully loaded baked potato. I can tell you how he takes his coffee—two sugars and a splash of milk. I can tell you his birthday, his favorite book, movie, and type of music—February fourth, *The Outsiders*, *Fight Club*, and 90s grunge. I know he's allergic to bees and hates mushrooms. I know his dad used to be his best friend, and he was head over heels for Brooke. I suspect he's still heartbroken over losing them both. I know his kid is the most important thing in the universe to him and this time apart from him must be killing him.

I don't know how to reach him, even though I want to.

I'd be lying if I said I wasn't attracted to Joel. How could anyone not be? He's ruggedly handsome; so tall, broad, and stocky it could make someone as petite as I imagine fantasies about being scooped up and ravaged like some helpless damsel out of smutty fiction. And except for his current inability to share his feelings, he radiates masculinity of the non-toxic variety. Honestly, though, I think that has more to do with how he's still reeling from Brooke and Clive than any real shortcomings in that area.

But like I told him; I don't think I've ever been in love.

That's weird, right? To be thirty-one and never felt like you loved someone? So what could someone like me ever hope to offer someone who loves as big as Joel? Plus, there's his kid to consider. Even if I don't know what romantic love feels like, I love that kid. I'd never want to do anything to jeopardize my relationship with Gus.

So, no possible hooking up with his dad. Nope. Never. At least, not until he's in college and has his own life. Then maybe. Of course, by then, Joel might be all healed and moved on to someone he loves. And I'll still just be me, the woman who doesn't know what love is.

———

I'm jarred awake by the sound of grunting and heavy breathing. It's almost obscene and I open my eyes halfway to see what's making the noise. I mean, I have a suspicion judging by the deep richness of the sound, and it's making all kinds of non-platonic thoughts fly through my brain.

How long has it been since I got laid? Thinking back, it has to be at least a few months. Too damn long ago, that's how long. It's a situation I need to remedy post haste when I get home.

Peering out from under my covers affords me the view of Joel doing bicycle crunches on the living room floor, only four or five feet away. Shirtless. Judging by the sweat glistening off his entire upper body, he's been at it a while.

He rolls over, beginning to do pushups without even pausing, and I'm greeted with the sight of taut back muscles and a round, firm ass you could bounce a quarter off of.

I shut my eyes against the onslaught of this torrid visual and groan. "You know, some of us enjoy our summer break. Can't you do that in your room?"

He huffs a laugh. "Can't you find someone else's couch to

crash on? Oh, wait, there is no other couch," he says between labored breaths.

"Deal with it. Plus," he grunts as he pushes up and I try not to think about other instances when he'd grunt like that, "it's almost ten. Get your ass up."

"Why?" I whine.

"So you can fix me breakfast," he replies, a smile in his voice. I pull my pillow out from under my head and throw it at him. It hits him with a thud and he laughs. "While you're at it, I'll take some coffee."

"Fuck off," I retort, rolling over.

This only makes him laugh harder, and I've got to admit, it's nice to hear. I haven't heard it in a while.

"Seriously, get up. I'm about to get a shower and unless you want to go pop a squat in the woods, you'll want to go pee before I'm done with this set."

I groan, dramatically kicking off the covers before stomping to the bathroom to pee. After I come out, I stand beside the sofa and fold my arms across my chest as I glare at him. "Happy?"

Joel executes a burpee and jumps to his feet, sweat pouring down his face. He plants his hands on his hips as he drags in a lungful of air. "Ecstatic."

His eyes land on my bare legs and linger, and I nearly blush. "My eyes are up here, you know."

I'm shocked when I see color fill his cheeks and he blinks, whipping his head to look anywhere but at me.

Did that really just happen?

Caught off guard, I do the only thing I can think to do and fold up my blankets, dropping them and the pillow on a nearby wing-back chair. When I turn around, Joel is gone and I hear the shower starting just after the bathroom door slams.

CHAPTER SIX

JOEL

I swear, if I had to watch her bend over in that minuscule night gown to pick up blankets again, I was going to run the risk of busting out of my boxers briefs. Fuck me.

And *that's* what she looks like first thing in the morning? Jesus, help me. Her hair was all mussed and her skin was all flushed from sleep, the short nightgown she wore hanging nearly off one shoulder , falling to just below her ass. I was vividly reminded how long it's been since I've had sex. Way too fucking long, that's for sure.

After a cold shower—because although my right hand and I have gotten intimately reacquainted over the last eighteen months, it certainly hasn't been with mental visual aid of my gorgeous neighbor—I pull on a clean pair of shorts and a T-shirt. As I exit the bathroom, I smell sausage cooking. Music emanates from Teagan's phone on the counter as she shimmies from the stove to the coffeemaker to pull her cup from under the Keurig's spout.

I'm transfixed as she sings along with Otis Redding. She's thrown her hair up into a haphazard mass and doesn't seem to know that I'm watching her, so I continue to do exactly that. At least until my conscience and good sense make me walk across the room to fix myself a cup of coffee.

As soon as I get my mandatory two sugars and splash of milk into the mug, she extends the spatula she's been using on the sausage in my direction. "You can finish cooking. I'm going to go shower."

I accept the utensil with a nod. "Over medium, right?"

"Yep," she calls over her shoulder, taking her coffee with her to the bathroom.

Twenty minutes later, she returns to the kitchen just as I'm pulling the toast from the oven to butter. "I didn't expect you to still be listening to Otis when I got out. I figured you would've changed it to Nirvana or Pearl Jam," she says and refills her coffee.

"Everyone loves Otis. And if they don't, they have no taste."

"True," she agrees.

I drop toast on to both plates before pivoting to hand her one. She accepts it with a smile and tucks her damp hair behind her ear. We wordlessly take our seats at the table, and I've just taken my first bite when my phone buzzes with a text. I pull it out and examine the screen. It's a text from Gus with a photo of his room at Brooke's.

> Gus: What do you think about my room?
> Mom and Gramps said I can paint it whatever
> color I want and they're taking me to pick out
> my own bedding. Can I paint my room at your
> house?

I swallow around the lump in my throat and blow out a breath. I don't want to think about my son having a bedroom anywhere but at the only home he's ever known. And although I knew Brooke and my father were living together, it's still a shock to the system to hear Gus refer to them so casually. Like all of this isn't fucking surreal.

Not wanting to leave him on read, I type out a quick response.

> Joel: It's great, bud. I'm sure you'll pick something awesome. We can definitely talk about painting your room at home when you get back.

As soon as I hit send, I toss my phone on the table, disgusted. It's definitely with more force than is necessary, and Teagan eyes me over her coffee mug. "Everything okay?"

"Fucking peachy," I mutter, shoveling food into my mouth.

"On a scale from 'I stubbed my toe' to 'I want to spit nails', how angry are you right this minute?"

I push away my plate and fold my arms. "I'm at 'my kid is excited about his bedroom at his mother's house and oh, by the way, she lives with my father and is having his kid'."

"That good, huh? Are you having *feelings* about no longer being an only child?" I know she's trying to lighten the mood, but when I glare at her, she winces. "Too soon?"

"Pretty sure the kid could be in college and it'd be too soon, Tee."

"Sorry," she says sheepishly. "I make bad and inappropriate jokes at the worst moments."

I nod. "I know. My favorite one was right after I told you Brooke left. You said that at least she wasn't a cliché since she hadn't traded me in for a younger model," I deadpan.

She groans. "Oh, God. I still can't believe I said that. I was just in such shock, it was the first thing that came to mind and sometimes, my brain-to-mouth filter gets completely bypassed."

I shrug. "If all of this were happening to someone else, I'd probably think it was fascinating. As it stands, it just—."

"Sucks all the ass," she supplies and I nod, resigned.

"Yep."

"I know. But listen, just because he has a room at Brooke's doesn't mean anything. His home is in Jacksonville; that's not going to change. She's probably just trying to buy some good grace. Someday, he'll understand everything and realize how noble and classy you've been during this whole thing."

"I'm not feeling very classy right now," I admit.

"I'm sure. Any chance you'd want to come watch a baseball game? The Smokies are playing today. Might get you out of your head a little."

I frown. "How do you know there's a game?"

She gives a nonchalant half-shrug. "I looked up stuff to do in the area when Jonas said they were getting married here and saw they have a baseball team, so I looked at the schedule. The tickets are pretty cheap and there's a game at noon, so if we wanted to go, we'd be back in plenty of time for the wedding."

I consider her idea, and she nudges my knee under the table with her own. "Come on, you live, sleep, and breathe baseball. It's a nine-inning vacation, right?"

"That's really cheesy."

She scoffs. "I didn't make it up; I just repeated what I'd read." Pulling out her phone, she levels me with a gaze. "We're going."

"Damn, bossy much?"

Lifting a brow, she drops her eyes to her phone screen. "I prefer assertive. Doesn't change the fact that you'll go."

***

Although the game's already started when we walk in and I don't know anything about this team except that they're a farm team for the Chicago Cubs, it's still baseball and I relax the moment we're in our seats. Teagan has her hair braided in adorable pigtails and we share an order of nachos and sip over-priced beers as the game progresses. And even though she understands plenty about the game of baseball, she still lets me explain certain plays and stuff. I suspect it's simply, like she said, to get me out of my head.

We're forced to leave before the game is over to make it back in time to get ready for the wedding, but as we pull out of the parking lot, I shoot her a grateful smile. "Thanks for talking me into coming. It was fun."

She grins, her nose and cheeks a bit red from being in the sun. "Hey, anytime you need me to tell you what you need to do, I'm happy to oblige," she quips with a wink and then sobers. "But I'm glad it helped. And I know you don't want to talk about your shit, but I just want to say that I am here for you, Joel. Because this is a really shitty situation and no one should have to deal with it; least of all you. What Brooke and your dad did was monumentally fucked up, and I can't imagine what all this must be like for you." I roll my shoulders, uncomfortable, and she holds up her hands defensively. "That's all I'm going to say. Promise."

"Okay," is all I say.

***

We have just under an hour to get ready for the wedding and I let Teagan grab a shower first. As she comes out of the bath-room, dressed in a robe, we nearly collide with how fast she's moving. "Careful there, Speedy. Save the stepping on my toes for the dance floor."

She rolls her eyes. "Lucky for you, there is no dancing."

"Well, hot damn, this really is my kind of party."

I hurriedly take another shower . As I come out of the bathroom, I'm adjusting my belt and brushing a piece of lint off my pants. When I look up to find Teagan, she's sitting at the bar applying her makeup, her hair falling in soft waves over her shoulders.

The dress she wears is flowy and black, with some sort of sheer floral overlay. It also has a slit that shows a lot of tan, toned thigh and is currently unzipped in the back, and she doesn't appear to be wearing a bra. I remind myself that these pants are way too tight to hide a hard-on, so I need to keep it the fuck together.

Her eyes connect with mine in the small mirror she's using, and she grins. "You look great. I'm almost ready, but I think my zipper's stuck; can you see if you can get it?"

"Sure, if you can roll my sleeves for me? I usually do it before I put my shirt on and forgot and whenever I try to do it after it's already on, it always looks sloppy."

After a final swipe of mascara, she tucks away her makeup and hops down from the stool. "No problem."

I close the distance between us, bending to examine the zipper. After some careful jiggling, it slides up her back and I watch as the muscles in her back flex as I tug up the zipper. I have the absurd thought that I want to know what that skin feels like under my fingers, but I push away the dangerous notion.

As she turns to face me, my heart lurches at the sight of her. She's stunning. The dress hugs her waist and is cut low in the front, showing off quite a lot of what I can only imagine might be the world's most perfect tits. With however she's applied her makeup, it's made her eyes look bigger and even more blue. All I can say is, "Wow." The word is out of my mouth before I can bite it back.

"I'm going to choose to believe that's a good 'wow'," she says with a chuckle, a pleasant blush filling her cheeks. She tugs on my sleeve and I blink, raising my arm to allow her to roll it up.

"It was," I confirm. "You look beautiful, Tee."

She bites her bottom lip, suddenly shy, and spares me a glance. "Thank you, Joel."

She finishes rolling my sleeves and steps back, examining my appearance. "And you, my friend, look exceptionally hand-some," she says with a bit more sass than a moment ago. "Let's do this thing, I guess."

"Let me grab my keys and phone." Jogging back into the bedroom to grab the items and returning a few seconds later, I hold them up. "Although honestly, I think these pants might be too tight to put them in my pockets. Seriously, how do people function with pants this tight?"

She snorts, stepping up to pluck my phone from my hand to drop it into her small purse. "There. And I'll hold the keys once we get there." Stepping even closer, she reaches up toward my face and I stiffen, unsure what she's doing. "Your collar is funky in the back. I noticed it when you went back to the bedroom; just fixing it," she offers as an answer to my unasked question.

But her arms draping around my shoulders have me thinking about other reasons she might be that close. Images swirl through my mind; ones of dancing, kissing, hugging, and a super brief flash of her on top of me, while she still wears this dress and no panties.

I mentally groan as I shake the thoughts away and send a reminder to my dick to behave, because now is not the time to make a scene.

"Ready?" Teagan asks, slipping on a pair of wedge sandals before gesturing to the door.

Clearing my throat, I nod. "Yep."

CHAPTER SEVEN

TEAGAN

As we make the turn onto the winding drive that leads to the lake house, I hurriedly apply a bit of sheer gloss before shoving the tube back into my purse. I steal glances at Joel who, exactly as I told him, looks exceptionally handsome.

Okay, that might have totally been an understatement. He looks downright hot and my mind is concocting dangerous and sexy scenarios that it has no business showing me.

The clothes look amazing on him, and dear sweet baby Jesus, in those pants, his ass makes me want to grab on with both hands and do things we can't take back. The shirt made his eyes—and the muscles of his arms—pop. While he normally looks fine for work and working around the house, I've never seen him outside of jeans and T-shirts or ill-fitting khakis and baggy button-downs.

I know he has regular visits with a barber and the cut works for him. It's shorter on the sides and longer on top and normally, the top kinda just flops around or down over his forehead when he moves. I've definitely never seen him put actual product in his hair. Tonight, though, he's used some gel or styling cream or something, because it's messy, but you can tell it's intentional. He's also trimmed his beard and cleaned up around the edges.

Joel Briggs cleans up real good.

We both seem to inhale quickly as the house comes into view. "Holy shit," he mutters.

"Yeah," I agree.

"I thought this was a 'lake house'? This isn't a house."

"Right? I mean, Jonas said it was a big house, but damn."

He pulls into a designated parking area and there aren't that many guests in attendance, which I knew would be the case. Jonas and Callahan both said they were keeping the guest list to only family and close friends.

Just before he shuts off the car, I put my hand on his arm and he looks at me. "If you get really bored or are having a terrible time, we can leave, okay? I know this wasn't what you saw yourself doing this weekend and you've been roped into this, but I'm only obligated to stay for the ceremony. So, if you decide you're done, we can leave anytime after that."

He frowns. "I'm not going to do that to you, Teagan. Jonas is your best friend. I'm good. It's only one night. I'll still have days to wallow and stew. Besides, you look too good to only stay for the ceremony. And so do I," he quips with a cocky grin.

I can't help but laugh. "That is true. Okay. I just wanted to toss that option out to you."

He shuts off the car and extends the keys to me. "I'm good. Let's go to a wedding."

Nodding, I take the offered keys and drop them into my purse as we step out of the vehicle, and once again, I'm struck at the sheer opulence of the house.

It's two stories and white, with giant stacked-stone columns and a beautiful large porch that runs the length of the ginormous house. Gorgeous rosebushes, full-to-bursting with fragrant blooms, fill the flowerbeds in front of the porch.

A clear path has been designated to the side of the house, with lanterns leading down toward the lake. And although there's still plenty of sunlight left, it will provide much needed visual aid to guests as they depart later. We make our way down the path and I'm forced to hold the front of my dress with one hand to ensure that I don't trip. Joel also stays close and at one point, when I do actually stumble a bit—short woman plus long dress equals potential disaster—he reaches out to steady me, planting his hand on the small of my back. It doesn't leave that spot until we take our seats down by the boat dock, and I don't want to admit to myself how nice it feels.

There's no real decor to speak of, save some lights that have been strung throughout the branches of the mature hardwoods that are scattered through the yard. The view of the lake and surrounding greenery are plenty. Truthfully, I wouldn't expect anything different from Jonas. He's a simple guy, and although Callahan comes from a lot of money, she's not stuffy or ostentatious.

Jonas stands at the end of the dock with the officiant and my best friend looks mighty handsome in a pair of slim-fit khakis, a light blue button-down and a dark gray tweed vest. He's declined to wear a tie and simply leaves the top two buttons of his shirt undone. His dark curly hair is perfectly messy, and his intentional stubble is neatly trimmed.

He looks over the crowd, and as our eyes lock, he gives me a warm smile that I can't help but return. His gaze slides to Joel, and he nods, impressed, and I roll my eyes, making him laugh.

There are only a few people I actually recognize at the wedding. Jonas's mother and grandmother sit toward the front. I know his mom being here is a huge deal since they've recently reconnected—after fifteen years of estrangement, she recently got sober and is trying to stay clean. Callahan's best friend, Elliot, and his boyfriend, Russ, sit just behind them. In truth, Elliot is responsible for Jonas and Callahan getting together in the first place. But that's a whole other story.

I also recognize Callahan's cousin, Maddie, whom I've met a few times while she was living with Jonas and Callahan following some issues within her marriage. Sitting next to her is a man I know must be her wayward husband. Maybe they've made amends?

The remainder of the crowd, I know must be some of Callahan's family, simply by deductive reasoning. Some of them look like Maddie while Callahan favors a woman with stiff posture sitting in the front row.

"So, how many people do you actually know here?" Joel asks in a whisper. His breath brushes my neck, sending tendrils of awareness snaking down my torso. Not to mention, he smells woodsy and a bit herbal. It's fucking delicious, and forever and ever amen, this scent will always be *him*. I force myself focus on my breathing as I answer his question.

I point out the people I know and who I suspect the others are, and he nods, listening intently. "This is simple, but really beautiful."

I shrug. "That's Jonas and Callahan. Neither of them are too flashy. Don't get me wrong, they both clean up really well, but a huge wedding wasn't ever going to be something either of them wanted. From what Jonas said, Maddie's wedding was this week-long blowout with, like, a million guests. They were adamant they didn't want something like that."

He looks around. "Yeah, I think simple is better. You can really focus on what matters and not on what you're going to feed two hundred people."

Wondering if he'll talk about anything, I ask, "What was your wedding like?"

He considers my question, and for a second, I expect him to not answer it at all or tell me he doesn't want to discuss it, but he rolls his shoulders. "Full catholic mass with five bridesmaids and groomsman. Huge reception at the country club with a four-course meal and a five-tiered cake. Fucking champagne tower and dance lessons for weeks."

"I didn't know you were catholic," I say, hoping it's a safe topic.

He snorts. "I'm not; Brooke is. Or, rather, her parents are. She goes on the holidays and wanted to have Gus christened, so we did. I grew up methodist."

"Was it the kind of wedding you wanted?"

His expression morphs into something decidedly more sad and a pang of sympathy hits me in the chest. "I didn't care about the wedding. I would've married her in a garbage heap. I only wanted her."

I'm about to apologize for even asking the question when music begins to stream from the trees and the officiant motions for everyone to stand. We all do as Callahan makes her way down the makeshift aisle to a beaming Jonas out on the dock.

After we're seated again, I don't register their vows or even much about the bride's dress, although it's beautiful and so is she. The only thing I'm able to think about is what Joel said.

I would've married her in a garbage heap. I only wanted her.

What must that kind of love be like? It's not that I don't know what love is. I know my parents love me—even if they were content to ship me to Tootsie's every summer. Not that I'm complaining about that because I loved Tootsie; we were kindred spirits. I also know my parents love each other. And like a dutiful daughter, until recently, I'd gone to see them once a month, and we'd all have lunch. Last year, they even stopped asking me if I was ever going to settle down. For that, I suppose I should be thankful.

But how much do you have to love someone to not care about the circumstances of marrying them, so long as you're married? It's clear that Jonas and Callahan love each other that way. And when he pulls her to him for their first kiss as husband and wife, I don't feel what one might expect me to, considering Jonas and I were in a physical relationship for nearly a decade. I feel happy for him and them. I'm overjoyed for him. Really.

But if Jonas, who from the time his engagement ended in college to when he met Callahan last year and was one of the most hedonistic, self-centered, unromantic people I've ever known, can find his forever, shouldn't there be hope for me, too?

I'm sure it's just some sort of biological thing. When single people attend weddings, it makes them begin to ponder what things like that might be like. Even if you've never entertained those sorts of thoughts before, surely the romantic nature of nuptials makes even the most cynical commitment-phobe wonder, right?

It probably has to do with Tootsie's conditions on my inheritance. I mean, I'd be nuts to not want it, right? Even if the condition is marriage, though? Plus, the stipulation doesn't state how long I have to be married, just married. Maybe for a cut, I could find someone to enter into something with for a specific period of time.

My eyes slide to my companion, but I immediately discard the thought. Nope, that's not a feasible idea at all.

Okay, then who? I don't have a lot of friends and even fewer who'd I trust to not try to swindle me out of every penny Tootsie wants to leave me. One of them just said, "I do" and—. Yeah, he's pretty much it. Again, my gaze involuntarily shifts to Joel. Okay, maybe Jonas isn't the only person I trust that much. But again, I shake the thought away.

I'm brought out of my musings when Joel nudges me. "Earth to Tee."

I blink rapidly. "Sorry, I spaced for a minute. Ready to eat?"

He smiles. "Definitely. Pizza and beer at a wedding are the way to go."

Rising, we follow the crowd over to a tent that's been setup for the food and bar area. Unlike most other reception tents I've been in, there is no designated dance floor. And while there is music playing, there's no DJ. String lights crisscross the space, giving it a romantic glow and even if this isn't some fancy event, it's still nice.

Joel and I go through the food line, grabbing some beers, and take a seat to dig in. We're both about a slice in when Jonas and Callahan stop by our table. I stand, and after receiving a quick hug from his wife, my best friend pulls me into his arms. "Thanks for coming."

I return his embrace with a big grin. "Please. I had to see this for myself. You look good, friend."

He pulls back and eyes me before his gaze slides to Joel. "You, too. Y'all look...cozy."

I roll my eyes. "Not cozy," I reply, keeping my voice down.

His brow furrows. "Really? I figured—."

"No," I say firmly. "I do know how to keep it in my pants. Unlike some people." I give him a knowing look and he cracks up.

"Yeah, yeah. But for real, I'm glad you could make the trip. I'm sorry about the cabin thing." He turns his attention to Joel and the two men shake hands. "Thanks for putting Teagan up."

Joel shrugs, the gesture nonchalant. "Of course. I was glad to be able to do it. Thank you for inviting me. Ten out of ten on the pizza front."

Jonas smiles. "Definitely. Callie and I were determined that this would be a party we'd enjoy. No stuffy canapés or champagne toasts or anything like that for us. I hope y'all got some cupcakes, too, because they're awesome."

"We will," Joel promises. "Congratulations."

The other man nods. "Thank you. I guess we'll let you get back to supper. Play some corn hole with us later?"

"Maybe," I answer, not wanting to commit Joel to something he might not have an interest in.

"Sure," he says at the same time.

Okay, I guess we're playing corn hole later.

True to Jonas's word, the cupcakes are indeed amazing. Joel and I split one each so we could try a couple of different kinds. We make small talk as we drink our beers, and my companion eyes me after a couple of drinks seem to have loosened his tongue. "So this really doesn't bother you?"

"What, Jonas and Callahan?" When he nods, I shake my head. "No. You can't see how in love they are?"

He nods again, taking another long pull from his beer bottle. "Yeah, I just wondered if you had any kind of jealousy or anything."

"No," I say automatically. "Jonas was never 'mine'." I put the word in air quotes to emphasize my meaning. "Like I said, he was simply an outlet." He gives me a look that says he's not sure he believes me, and I narrow my eyes. "What, you never just hooked up with anyone? Nothing without feelings or strings or commitment? Every *encounter* you've ever had was within an actual relationship?"

"Yes," he answers, his tone matter-of-fact.

"Yes to which question? I believe there were three of them."

Color creeps into his cheeks as he downs the rest of his beer. "Yes, they were all within actual relationships."

I frown, surprised. "Really?"

He nods. "Yeah. I had a couple of girlfriends in high school and then Brooke and I met sophomore year of college."

"So you've never done anything casual?" I ask, incredulous.

"You say it like it's absurd to contemplate. Have you ever done anything *not* casual?"

"No," I admit.

"Why not?"

I lift a brow. "I could ask you the same thing."

"I asked you first," he counters.

I debate giving him some bogus answer about how I don't want commitment or I'm not built for it or something, but I tell him the truth. And honestly, I'm not sure that before this moment, it's something I've even admitted to myself. "I'm not sure I would be enough for someone all on my own. Telling someone I can't have kids and knowing they might decide it's a deal breaker and bail makes me not want to risk it. I know there are probably men out there who don't want kids, but most of them do. And I'd have to be in a place that I can trust them fully before I even tell them about the no kids thing. By then, I'd probably already be really invested and I'm not sure I'm built for getting my heart broken." I take a pull from my beer and lift a brow. "Your turn."

He sighs and plucks my beer from my hand and drains the rest. "I wanted what my parents had." His tone is resigned and sad, making a weight fall into the pit of my stomach.

I look down at my hands, but Joel nudges me with his elbow, so I look back over at him. "For the right person, who you are—exactly as you are—will be enough. I don't think you give yourself enough credit. You're pretty amazing all on your own."

Warmth that I have no clue what to do with floods my chest and I swallow around the sudden lump in my throat. "You're pretty great, too, you know. Brooke is an idiot."

He nods, offering me a sad smile. "Want another drink?"

"Sure. Thanks."

He rises, and a second later, Callahan drops into his seat and looks at me, expectant. "Please tell me there's something actually going on between you two because damn, lady, you can feel the tension all the way on the other side of the tent."

I roll my eyes and huff a laugh at my best friend's new wife's insinuation. "No, there's nothing going on. We're just neighbors. And friends."

"But you can't tell me you don't want him. If I lived next door to that, I'm not sure I would've been able to keep from sneaking into his bedroom window."

I lower my voice. "We're friends. Strictly friends. He's got a kid and I really like his kid."

She nods knowingly. "Oh, I see. You're afraid if you make a pass, it'll screw things up with having a relationship with his kid."

"Yeah, I—." My words are cut off by a buzzing sound emanating from my purse, and I snatch it off the table and fish out the vibrating device. Joel's phone screen reads "S. Sato—Lawyer" and my heart lurches.

I quickly excuse myself from my conversation with Callahan, who gives me a friendly nod. I hurry over to where Joel stands at the bar, and extend the device in his direction. "Your phone's ringing."

He takes it, and after glancing at the name, steps away, immediately swiping his thumb over the screen, his posture rigid. I try not to eavesdrop, but want to stay close in the event he—by some uncharacteristic miracle—needs support. I can't make out his hushed words, but there's no mistaking the outrage and venom in his tone.

CHAPTER EIGHT

JOEL

Seeing the word "lawyer" on my phone screen on a Saturday night can not be good. Sure enough, the words out of Selena's—my lawyer and an old friend from college—mouth are anything but good. "Brooke is suing you for full custody."

"But *I* have full custody. Plus, she lives in Tennessee. Don't custody proceedings have to happen in the state where the child is a resident? Gus has lived in Florida his whole life. Wouldn't she have to be living in Florida for her to even be able to attempt this?"

She's quiet for a long moment and I know the other shoe's about to drop. "Your father still has a residence in Florida."

"Okay, that's him; not her. She lives in Tennessee. She moved when we separated because she got a job."

"I reminded her lawyer of this fact, and he informed me that Brooke actually splits her time between Tennessee and Florida and she and your father go between the two residences because her job allows her to work remotely half the time."

For now, I put aside the outrage I feel knowing that Brooke is physically in the same state as our son at least half the time and has only chosen to see Gus a handful of time since we split. I can think—stew—about that later. I feel like she's trying to tell me something other than just what she's said, and I pinch the bridge of my nose. "Selena, just spit it out. What are you trying to tell me? Because you told me when she moved that I was pretty much safe because Gus's legal residence was in Florida and she'd have to be living in Florida to pursue full custody."

"She and your dad got married, Joel. So *legally*, she has a residence in Florida."

I think my heart actually stops for a full five seconds. "Married? Since when?" She clears her throat and blows out a breath, but doesn't say anything. "Since fucking when, Selena?" I spit out, my chest aching and head spinning.

"A year ago. According to the filing date, it was a week after your divorce was final."

I inhale sharply as bitter, unwanted tears burn my eyes. I try to calm down because I'm not somewhere I can freely explode at this moment. "Okay, what can I do?"

"We'll fight it, of course, but listen, Joel, her lawyer has brought in an associate who is ruthless. And not that I'm not happy to go toe-to-toe with them, but these things can sometimes come down to who has the most money to drag it out the longest. It would appear that your father is going to be backing Brooke financially. And with them being married, he can do that."

When she speaks again, her voice sounds pained. "You know I will do whatever I can to help you, but I'm just me and something like this would require that you be my only client for the foreseeable future."

"I get it," I answer automatically. "I know you can't work for free and I'd never expect you to. I'll figure something out."

"Joel, I know you already took out a second mortgage for the divorce. I—."

"Selena, I said I'll figure it out. You just worry about keeping my kid where he belongs."

"Okay. I'll get to work." The call disconnects, and I hang my head, trying not to freak out. I will myself to take deep breaths, calm the fuck down, and not spiral.

A hand on my arm startles me, and I whip my head to see Teagan, her expression concerned. "I told Jonas and Callahan we had to go."

I shake my head and intentionally relax my posture. "No, it's okay. I'm good."

She holds up a bottle of tequila and a zip-top bag of lime wedges. "And I'd bet this bottle of Patrón that you're full of shit. Come on, I'll make you a drink at the cabin."

Too tired to argue, I follow her back to the car. She slides behind the wheel, and I wordlessly get into the passenger seat. She doesn't speak and neither do I for the ten-minute drive. Inwardly, though, I'm seething and bitter and I want to murder someone, starting with my father.

When we walk in the door, she tosses the keys onto the kitchen bar. "Go change into something comfortable and meet me back in here."

I don't question it. I simply walk to the bedroom to peel myself out of the wedding clothes before pulling on a pair of worn sweatpants and a T-shirt with the sleeves cut off. When I return to the kitchen, Teagan already has two drinks poured, and she sits on a stool, shot at the ready. She's changed into a pair of jogging shorts and a tank top and has her hair thrown up in a messy ponytail. Joining her, I pick up the shot and down it without hesitation and fill the glass again.

"Okay, so that's how it is, huh?"

"It's super shitty is how it is," I mutter.

"I'm sure. Want to talk about it?"

"Not really."

She sighs, downing her own shot, and sucks the lime wedge with a wince before blowing out a breath. "I'm sure. But hearing from your lawyer on a Saturday—over Memorial Day weekend, no less—can't be a good sign."

I down another shot and another and wait for the edges to dull. I don't share shit with anyone. Occasionally, when I'm really buzzed, I have been known to divulge bits and pieces. Maybe subconsciously, though, I actually want to share this with Teagan. Despite how much I say we're not really friends, she's possibly one of my best friends. She's witnessed the entirety of how everything has fallen out. Maybe I just need the tequila to give me an excuse to spill it all.

She doesn't prod, but simply does her shots more slowly and stops altogether after her third. Probably good if one of us stays at least semi-sober, right? After my fifth shot, she corks the bottle, sliding it away, and I glare at her. She glares right back. "You're, like, twice my size. If you pass out, I don't even know that I can roll you over so you don't choke on your own puke. I need you to at least be able to walk with assistance. Now, I'll ask you again, do you want to talk about it?"

"Brooke is suing me for full custody. Apparently, she and my father got married a week after our divorce was final and because he still has a house in Florida and they split their time between her place here and his place there, technically, she can legally fight me for custody.

"My dad hired this big shark of a lawyer and Selena—my lawyer—said that this kinda stuff usually comes down to who has the most money. Selena's good, but she's just one person. I already took out a second mortgage just to be able to buy Brooke out of her half of the house and fight for what little I got to keep in the divorce."

I huff a sad laugh. "My father is a fucking surgeon and has more money than he knows what to do with. I'm a high school teacher with the salary to match. If it comes down to money, I'm going to fucking lose, Teagan. I'm going to lose Gus and I'll be one of those dads who only sees his kid every other Christmas and a few weeks during the summer.

"Yeah, I could move. And if she wins, I'll have no choice, but why should they get to win this? I already lost everything that ever mattered to me. I lost my mom, my relationship with my dad, and my wife left me. All I have left is Gus." The last words come out choked as tears burn behind my eyes and I swipe my thumbs over my lashes to ward them off.

Teagan's expression is full of compassion and sadness. She uncorks the tequila bottle, turning it up, and I blink in shock. I'm pretty buzzed, but not fully drunk, and watching her guzzle liquor isn't something I've ever seen her do. When she finally sets the bottle back down, she wipes her mouth with the back of her hand and rolls her shoulders, nodding as if coming to some sort of conclusion about something.

"I asked you yesterday what you'd do to have a carefree life."

Confused by her sudden change in topic, I frown. "Yeah, I remember. I'm not that buzzed."

She examines my face and her expression is possibly the most serious I've ever seen, and I'm not sure what to think about it. "It wasn't a hypothetical."

"What do you mean?"

"My aunt—the one who died a few months ago?" I nod, remembering her having to go to San Diego for a funeral. "She left me everything. Her estate was...substantial."

"Congratulations," I say, unsure why she's telling me this, and the word comes out more like a question.

"I asked you what you'd do to have a carefree life. You said as long as it wasn't illegal and no one would get hurt, you'd do just about anything. Did you mean that?"

I frown. "Yeah, I guess. Tee, I'm tired. Why are you telling me all this?"

"Marry me," she blurts out.

Shocked, I physically recoil at her words. "What?"

Color rises to her cheeks, and she takes another swig of tequila. "Tootsie—that's my aunt—left me everything. And like I said, it's substantial. Several million dollars substantial." My mouth falls open at the figure, and she presses forward. "But there's a stipulation. As it stands right now, I'm only truly entitled to my house, which was technically her house and where I spent all my summers growing up, but that's not the point.

"To get everything else, I have to get married. I'm not sure why, but it's the condition she set in place for me to receive my inheritance. You need money to fight for Gus; I would have plenty of it."

I open my mouth to tell her she's insane, but she holds her hand up. "I know it's a crazy suggestion, but I was already entertaining the idea of marrying someone and possibly giving them a cut. Hell, if Jonas and Callahan weren't together, I probably would've married him just to get it."

Her expression softens. "Gus is the best kid ever, and I don't want you to lose him. I don't want to lose him. Let me do this for you. I don't need all that money, but if I don't accept the conditions of the inheritance and take it, it'll be divided among a bunch of charities. I'd rather it go to helping someone I know and care about than some faceless organization who, while I'm sure does great things, isn't my favorite kid.

"Nothing has to change—I don't think—except legal status. I wouldn't think we'd have to live together or anything like that. I think as long as we had the marriage license and maybe, like, some photos of a ceremony or whatever, the lawyers would be satisfied. Once I have the inheritance and you win custody of Gus, we can quietly dissolve things."

Still reeling, I blink rapidly as I try to absorb everything. Although my brain is a little foggy, the wheels are turning, and I shake my head. "I can't ask this of you, Teagan. It's absurd."

Her jaw clenches, her eyes turning flinty. "No, what's absurd is that you'd let your pride get in the way of fighting for your kid with whatever weapons you can have at your disposal. You don't ask people for help. You don't tell people when you're dealing with shit. You'd rather be stoic and grumpy and suffer in silence. Besides, you didn't *ask*; I offered."

I shake my head again. "It would never work."

"Why?"

"Because her lawyers will dig up whatever dirt they can and if we got legally married but weren't living like a married couple, it would look suspicious." I blow out a breath against the pain that settles into my chest. "I don't know who Brooke is anymore. She is a completely different person than the sweet girl I met in college. She's ruthless now, and I have to believe that if she thought something like this was an act, she'd figure out a way to use it against me."

She nods, considering. "Okay, so what if, in public, it looked real? We've known each other—and worked together—for ten years, so it wouldn't be a huge leap for people to assume that we could get together, right? It doesn't have to be real behind closed doors, but you were the one who said you'd do almost anything if it meant your kid would have a good future and no one got hurt."

She bites her lip. "I don't know how to be someone's wife or anything, but I love your kid, Joel, and I want to do this for him. And I know you don't want help, but accepting it when it's offered doesn't make you weak, it makes you smart. You're not stupid, so don't let your pride make you look like you are. If it needs to look real, we can pretend." She snorts a laugh. "I can get pointers from Jonas and Callahan."

I frown. "Why would you say that?"

She dismisses my question with a wave. "Don't worry about it." Her eyes flick around the space as she thinks, and then she stands, pacing as she speaks. "We've been friends for years, so when Brooke left, you confided in me. We got closer and spent more time together—which we do. We watch games and hang out in the yard with Jethro and Gus and I hang out all the time. We happened to be on the same flight, and after you dropped Gus off with Brooke, I invited you to come to the wedding with me. We can say we hooked up and got all swept up in the wedding fever and eloped."

Her saying things like *hooked up* and *eloped* has my brain swimming and I drag in a lungful of air. She stops pacing and comes to stand in front of me. "It's not like we don't know each other well enough that we couldn't pull this off. Hell, we could probably pass one of those newlywed questionnaires." Her eyes search mine. "And I know it would be complicated with Gus and everything, but I promise I won't let him get hurt in this."

"You can't promise that, Teagan."

She nods. "Yes, I can, Joel. Because as long as he stays the priority in this whole thing—which he will—there's no way he gets hurt."

"Seriously, you realize how insane this sounds, right?"

She squares her shoulders. "You have a better idea? You already said your dad has enough money to drag this out for however long Brooke wants. I have money. Or, I will once you agree to marry me.

"I'll rent my house out and move in with y'all since I know Gus won't want to give up the pool. You've got your office right off from your bedroom; I'll stay in there. After it's all over, we can say we're still friends, but weren't cut out to be married to each other. I'll take the blame because I've never been quiet about my desire to remain single."

I drag my hands through my hair. "This is crazy."

"Crazy smart," she counters.

It wouldn't have to be forever, and I could think of worse people to marry than Teagan. Am I seriously considering this? *If the payoff would be that my kid would have a good future and no one would get hurt, I'd probably do just about anything.* My own words replay in my mind and then I can't believe I'm considering it.

"I would pay you back. Every penny."

Teagan's shaking her head before all the words have even left my mouth. "No, you won't. This would be a gift, Joel. Plus, if I'm renting out my house, I'll be making money during that time. What am I going to do with all that money? I don't have wild dreams of travel or living in some mansion on easy street. I like my job. I like working. I like my life. I like you as a person and I meant what I said; I love your kid. This would be for him. So no, you won't be paying me back."

"Teagan, I don't know," I admit. "What would we tell Gus? He's already had so much upheaval in the last eighteen months. And yeah, he's resilient, but I wish he didn't have to be."

"I mean, he likes me, right?"

I huff a laugh. "You're his favorite person."

She blushes with pride and smiles. "Okay, so I can still be his favorite person. Plus, there's Jethro to consider. He alone is probably worth the whole deal to Gus. Like I said, it's not like we don't spend time together. Gus sees how much time we spend together. And it's not like we'd be affectionate or anything in front of him, even if we had been dating, since that's not something you would do. You'd probably never even introduce your kid to someone unless you were really serious about them."

I shake my head. "I wouldn't."

"I know. And if we're still just friends who happen to be

married and live together, we wouldn't be acting any differently in front of him, anyway."

"Can this really work?"

"Only one way to find out," she says with a shrug.

I try to think of any rational reason I shouldn't consider this and only land on one. "You wouldn't be able to date anymore; not if we really wanted this to look real."

She nods. "I know."

"And that's not going to be too hard for you?"

Teagan shrugs again. "I don't know, but I'm a big girl. I can take care of myself," she replies, lifting a brow.

CHAPTER NINE

TEAGAN

Over the next two days—since the county clerk's office is closed on Sundays and for the holiday on Monday—we shore up our story and plan our elopement. I change my flight to fly home with Joel so that it adds more credibility to everything. I'm also forced to extend Jethro's stay at the kennel, but after checking on him via camera and speaking with one of the staff members, I'm reassured of his continued happiness.

As soon as Joel spilled everything, it was an easy decision for me. Seeing the pain and resignation from everything Brooke and Clive have done to him settled it for me. What choice do I have, really?

And because this is the digital age, we were able to book everything online. We preordered our marriage license and scheduled our wedding that includes a ceremony, officiant, and photographer. All of it should be enough to convince Tootsie's lawyers, right?

On Monday, we return to the outlet mall to find a suitable dress for me, a tie for Joel, and rings. Fucking *wedding* rings. Oy vey. By the third store without something I'd consider acceptable—because if we're going to sell this thing, we should really sell it—we're both frustrated. It's crowded and muggy and we're getting hangry.

"Okay, how about this?" Joel says when we both start to get snippy with one another. "Let's take five minutes to pick out some rings and go find some food. While we eat, we can look online to see if there are any wedding dress places locally where you can buy something off the rack."

I blow out a breath. "Okay. Rings should be easy, right? Since we don't need anything fancy."

"I wouldn't think you'd need too fancy a dress, either, but that hasn't stopped you from turning down every one you've looked at so far."

I elbow him in the stomach as we walk down the sidewalk and he grunts. "If I'm going to do this, I'm still going to look good."

He rolls his eyes. "You could wear a paper bag and you'd look gorgeous, Tee."

Flattered by his compliment, I almost blush. "Be that as it may, if you're wearing the outfit you wore to Jonas's wedding, you're going to look a lot better than me if I 'wear a paper bag'. We'll find something."

Sure enough, the rings take literally five minutes. We basically told the clerk to show us to the simple rings and after figuring out the sizes we needed, we leave with matching yellow gold bands.

After a quick lunch and burying our heads in our phones to look up local bridal boutiques, we make the hour-drive into Knoxville to go to a chain bridal store. Walking into an actual bridal boutique makes my stomach do this strange flip-flop that I'm not sure what to do with. For a good thirty seconds, all I can do is stare at all the white and ivory tulle, lace, and satin.

"Wow, that's a lot of white," Joel says under his breath.

I nod. "Yep."

He points to a sofa near the entrance. "I'm going to sit for a few. I need to check in with Gus and I don't want to hover while you figure out what you want."

"Okay. I'll try to be quick."

He shrugs. "I've had some food, so I'm good now. Take your time."

I tamp down my nerves and nod as he drops onto a plush sofa. Walking over to the racks upon racks of dresses, I find my size and begin sorting through the hundreds of offerings. I immediately bypass any that are bright white, super poofy, or have long sleeves.

About ten minutes into my search, an elderly woman with a name tag comes over to check on me. "Would you like me to start a room for you?"

I glance at her. "Is that allowed? I didn't have an appointment or anything."

"Well, sure," she says with a smile. "And actually, I don't have anyone scheduled for the next hour or so, and I'd be happy to assist you with your search. Is it just you, or do you have any family or friends with you today?"

"My fr—." I nearly say friend, but I guess Joel is technically my fiancé, so I try again. "My fiancé is here with me. We're actually getting married tomorrow. Kinda sudden, I know, but now I'm scrambling to find a dress."

Her eyes light up, her smile warm and friendly, reminding me of Jonas's Nana, Dorothy. The woman is about my height and plump, with cool, dark skin and kind eyes. Her silver hair is cut in an adorable pixie and I immediately feel better having what feels like an ally in this moment. "An elopement, huh? Well, congratulations. My name is Anne Marie. And you are?"

"Teagan," I supply.

Nodding, she surveys the dresses in my arms. "Well,

Teagan, we're going to make sure you have the best experience possible and you leave here today with a dress that will work with your vision and your budget. Speaking of which, do you know how much you'd like to shoot for, price-wise?"

I'd already considered this on the way here and not that I'm unwilling to pay for what will probably be the only wedding dress I ever wear, I'm not yet rolling in it. "Ideally, I'd like to stay below five hundred. I understand that might be a bit low for a bridal gown, but I'm not looking for anything extravagant."

She shakes her head. "Nonsense. We've got lots of great options under that threshold." She examines the rack. "Now, we'll have to make sure it fits off the rack, since you won't have time for alterations. With your height, that might be a bit of a challenge, but can I tell you my super power?" Breathing a relieved laugh, I nod. "I can find the dress the first go-round and stay under budget. Are there any specific style features you'd prefer to avoid or want to include?"

"Not really. Just nothing bright white, overly poofy, and no long sleeves."

"Gotcha. Okay. I'm going to get you into a room with the gowns you've already pulled and I'll work my magic, alright?" She lifts the dresses from my arms and ushers me along toward a dressing room. I look over my shoulder to where Joel is sitting and his phone is up to his ear, but he shoots me a smile when our eyes meet.

"Is that your young man?" Anne Marie asks knowingly.

"Yeah, that's him."

She grins and opens a door. "Well, I'll give you this; you've got good taste. What's your story? How did you meet? I want all the details; it helps me hone my search if I know who you are as a couple."

"Oh, um, there's not much to tell."

She hangs the dresses on a hook as she makes a tutting noise. "Sure there is. How did you all meet?"

"We've lived next door to each other for ten years and we work together."

"Ooh, a slow burn, neighbors-to-lovers story. I love it. Okay, give me more," she says excitedly and I can't help but laugh.

"Alright. Well, he's got this amazing kid—Gus—who I adore."

"Now, Gus is your fiancé, or Gus is the son?"

"Oh, sorry. Joel is my fiancé," I reply sheepishly. "He and his wife divorced about a year ago, and before that, I hadn't spent a lot of time with just Joel. After his wife left, I'd look in on him and Gus. I've also got this dog who likes to escape my yard to sneak into their pool, so I was over there a lot. We started hanging out more and became good friends. A few days ago, we happened to be on the same flight to Knoxville. He was bringing his son to visit his mother and I'm in town for a wedding." I sigh. "I invited him to come with me to the wedding, and I guess we kinda got swept up."

"I see. Well, friends first is a good foundation. Let's see if we can add some pretty window dressing," she quips and pumps her eyebrows. "You try those on and see if any of them are a winner and I'll be back with some other options, alright?"

"Sure. Thank you."

"My pleasure."

Once I'm alone, I blow out a breath before stripping down to pull on the first dress, an ivory silk halter dress with a column skirt. It's beautiful, but too long and the top would require alteration. The second one is a cream-colored satin a-line gown with some beading on the bodice and a high slit that I love, but it still doesn't fit exactly right. The last dress I've chosen myself is short and lacy with spaghetti straps. Although it fits, the waist doesn't sit right and it doesn't feel like *it*.

By the time I've slipped the last dress off, Anne Marie knocks on the door with a few offerings of her own. "Now, I've brought four, but I think this is *your* dress." She gestures to an ivory sheath dress with a plunging neckline and intricate and strategic beading covering the entire, nearly-sheer bodice.

"Okay, let's see if you still have your super powers."

She grins. "Sounds good to me." She turns me away from the mirror and assists me into the dress, which fits so well it makes my heart skip. The length, once I have on heels, would be perfect, and it feels good. She makes approving noises as she steps back. "Honey, I think this dress deserves the big mirror. Do you have any qualms about him seeing you before the ceremony?"

I nearly laugh because the idea of wanting to adhere to any kind of tradition with this thing probably went out the window when I asked him to marry me for money. "No."

"Well, then, we're going out to the main salon, but I don't want you to see. I'm going to get you some shoes and a headpiece so you can get the full effect. Once he sees you in this dress, he's going to want to rip it off you." She does a little happy dance. "Hot damn, I've still got it."

I can't help but smile at her enthusiasm, even if Joel won't react anywhere nearly as excited as she's imagining. "Okay; you're the expert."

She guides me out to a small, platformed curtained-off area with no mirrors and I wait. Less than five minutes later, she returns with some beaded satin heels and a thin crystal headband that she ties into place at the nape of my neck. "Are you ready to see your dress, Teagan?"

"Sure." And although this isn't real in the sense that Joel and I are making some sort of loving commitment to each other, I'm still a ball of raw nerves as she pulls the curtains back. I blink in shock when my reflection is revealed. I look *bridal*, and again, my heart skips.

A soft choking sound to my left has me whipping my head in that direction as Joel stands, his jaw slack, his eyes wide, and my chest tightens because I'm not sure what to do with the look on his face."Teagan, you look—. I mean—. Wow," he breathes.

Anne Marie chuckles, but I keep my eyes on him. "Better than a paper bag, I hope."

He takes a step closer and my breath hitches. "Tee, I don't care if that dress costs more than my truck; you need to live in it."

I snort a laugh. "Your truck is a piece of shit."

He feigns insult, but a soft smile tugs at the corner of his mouth. "Yeah, but it's *my* piece of shit."

I glance at Anne Marie. "I'm almost afraid to ask. How much?"

She grins. "I told you my super power was finding *your* dress within *your* budget. That dress, because it's an altered return, can't be sold on the regular floor. It's ninety-nine dollars. How'd I do?"

My mouth falls open and Joel laughs. "Sold," is all I can say.

The next day, I'm putting the final touches on my hair and makeup. As I slip on the dress in the bridal room of the chapel, things start to feel really, *really* real and my breathing begins to grow short. Although I'm happy to do this for Joel, I'm panicking a little because I'm getting fucking *married*. I'm giving up my house and putting all my belongings in storage. I haven't lived with someone since college; let alone a man and his son. Also, I don't have a fucking clue how to be someone's wife or stepmother. What if I'm bad at it? What if I mess up and make things worse for Joel and Gus? What if something I do affects the outcome of Joel's custody trial? What if—.

A knock at the door jars from my thoughts. "Tee, can I come in?"

I drag in a deep breath that does nothing to calm me. "Yeah," I mumble.

Joel steps in, looking even more handsome than he did at Jonas's wedding. I try not to let on that I'm nervous, but he examines me as he shuts the door. "You're freaking out." His brows rise. "Like, big time."

"A little," I admit, the words coming out barely above a whisper.

His expression softens, and he steps forward to put his hands on my shoulders. "We can call this off; I'll figure out some other way."

I shake my head. "No. I want to do this, I promise. It's just, I'm in an actual wedding dress and this is going to be legal and I don't know how to be married. I don't know how to combine lives with someone or have joint anything." I swallow. "I don't know if I'm going to be any good at this, Joel. I want to do this; please believe me. For Gus and for you, I'm going to do this. I'm just...scared."

"You, Teagan Roth, are scared? I've never seen you afraid of anything. You regularly tell off my grumpy ass and you're half my size."

I huff a laugh. "Yeah, but that's because I know you'd never hurt me like that."

He nods. "No, I wouldn't. And I can't promise I'm any good at this. My first attempt turned out to be pretty shitty and for all I know, it's because I'm shitty at it. But we don't have to do this. Really."

I shake my head and blow out a breath. "I'm good. I just

never thought I'd ever get married and I know I asked you, but it's a little surreal to actually be doing this."

He laughs. "You're telling me." Sobering, he gives my shoulders a squeeze. "Can I let you in on a little secret?"

"Will it make me feel better?"

"Definitely," he promises. When I nod, he drops his hands and pulls up his pant leg, revealing the bright yellow socks with my face on them that I got him as a gag gift last Christmas.

I immediately burst out laughing. "You had those in your bag?"

He shrugs, giving me a sheepish smile. "I've kept them in my suitcase since you gave them to me in case I ever had a road-side bathroom emergency and didn't have any toilet paper."

CHAPTER TEN

JOEL

Teagan wasn't joking about this being surreal. It's fucking absurd, is what it is. But after she finally calms down, I step out to join the officiant. Some instrumental song I can't place begins to play as she comes around the corner into the tiny chapel. My heart trips over at the sight of her.

She is a vision in ivory, her dark hair done up in a soft twist, the beaded headband she wears glinting in the light falling through the stained glass windows. It's only her and me, the coordinator, the photographer, and the officiant, but there could be a thousand people here and I'm not sure I'd be able to see anyone but her. Because Jesus, she's magnificent.

As I've had increasingly non-platonic fantasies about this woman in recent months, her in this fitted, beaded dress is definitely getting added to the file. She is sexy and elegant, and I'm about to marry her.

The rings seem to burn a hole in my shirt pocket and I reflexively pat it to ensure they're still there, but I still can't take my eyes off hers. I'm a tangle of anxiety, but I can't show it, because she's the one who's understandably nervous. She's doing this incredible thing for me and I can't let on that this isn't something I thought I'd ever do again.

Not after how Brooke and my dad blew up my heart.

When she's only a few feet away, I can't resist extending my hand to her. Her gaze drops to it for a split second and she swallows before taking it and coming to stand in front of me. She gives my hand a quick squeeze and nods as I shoot her what I hope is a supportive smile.

The music changes to something softer, and the photographer begins clicking away. I let out a slow breath as the officiant speaks.

"Joel and Teagan, you've come here today to make sacred vows to one another. A vow by definition is a promise of commitment to a calling or role. Today, that promise of commitment is that of marriage. Do either of you have anything you'd like to say to the other before we recite the vows?"

Teagan shakes her head and I glance at the officiant, a short, burly white man in his late sixties with kind eyes and an easy smile. "No, sir," I reply.

"Very well. Do you have rings?" I nod, fishing them out of my pocket. I place mine in Teagan's extended palm as I hold hers in my fingers. "Joel, you'll repeat after me and slide the ring on Teagan's finger, alright?"

I nod again, and he gives me an encouraging smile as he speaks, allowing me time to repeat the vows. I keep my eyes on Teagan's, both our hands shaking just a bit. "I, Joel, take you, Teagan, to be my lawfully wedded wife. With all your faults and strengths, I offer myself to you with all of my faults and strengths. I will help you when you need help, and turn to you when I need help. I choose you as the person with whom I will spend my life."

I slip the ring onto her finger as Teagan's breath hitches, and I give her hand a squeeze.

Our officiant nods. "Wonderful. Teagan, you're up." She repeats her vows, the same as mine. Although her voice shakes with nerves, she manages to get through everything before sliding the ring onto my finger. I give her a quick smile, and she blows out a breath, seemingly relieved to have made it through the vows.

"Good job, Tee," I whisper and she blushes and mouths, *you, too*, and I chuckle.

"As you have committed to one another by reciting vows and with the giving and receiving of rings, by the power vested in me by the state of Tennessee, I now pronounce you husband and wife. Joel, you may now kiss your bride."

Teagan and I both seem to realize at the same time that we've forgotten about the kissing part, but with one glance and a nearly imperceptible nod, we both agree. I step forward and tuck my knuckle under her chin to tip her head back, and while I'm sure it's really quick, time seems to slow as I lean down to capture her mouth with mine.

My heart rate ratchets up to about a thousand beats per minute, and Teagan's breath catches, but she relaxes and kisses me back. It only lasts a few seconds, but I quickly realize that what I've always assumed was simple appreciation for Teagan's looks and personality combined with my recent stretch of celibacy is actually full-blown, find-the-nearest-flat-surface-and-get-her-naked, I'm-totally-fucked attraction.

When we separate, Teagan's cheeks are flushed as she clears her throat and looks at the officiant. "So, we're married?"

I huff a laugh and he grins. "Yes, ma'am. Congratulations." He gestures down the aisle. "I believe the photographer wants to do a few more photos, but as soon as I sign the license, you're all legal."

Once all the photos are taken and we receive a copy of our marriage license, we take a moment to change back into our casual clothes. As I'm pulling on my shorts, T-shirt, socks free of Teagan's face, and sneakers, I can't help but think back over the kiss. It wasn't much, but it was enough to make me want more. And yet, even as the weight of the ring on my finger tells me that legally, I'm allowed to want more, Teagan and I haven't talked about any of that. Hell, we've decided that she's going to be sleeping on the pullout sofa in my office. Not sure you can get much more *not more* than that.

Shaking away the thoughts of what it might be like to kiss her again, I gather up my belongings and step out into the hall to wait for her. I lean against the wall and shove my hands in the pockets of my khaki shorts as I fidget my ring with my thumb. Size-wise, it's probably the same width as the ring I wore when I was married to Brooke, but this one is solid yellow gold, where that one was a hammered titanium. The weight and feel are different; this marriage will sure as hell be different.

With Brooke, I was so deeply, unabashedly, hopelessly head over heels for her, I would've cut off my arm and offered it to her as a wedding gift if she had asked me to. I'm not sure I could ever lose myself that much in a person again. I'm not sure I have enough of a heart left to even contemplate letting someone get close enough to break it. I'm not sure there's more than dust left, anyway.

The door to Teagan's room opens and I stand up straighter as she exits, her dress bag hung over her arm. Gone is the dress, the updo, and the beaded headband. In its place is a still beautiful and selfless woman who, after this, I'm not sure I can ever repay her kindness. She hoists her tote bag full of her hair and makeup tools higher on her shoulder, her wedding band catching the light. I'm reminded that she's my *wife*. I am, once again, married.

"Ready?" she asks with a small smile.

"Yeah. Hungry?"

She huffs a laugh. "I could eat. I'm also getting desert."

I nod, an amused smile pulling at the corners of my mouth. "Yes, ma'am."

***

Through our meal and the drive back to the cabin, we're both more quiet than usual. And while it's understandable, given how introspective we both seem to be, it's weird for us. Teagan and I have never had issues talking, even when it wasn't "sharing" kind of stuff.

By the time we walk in the cabin door, I'm about to come out of my skin. After Teagan hangs up her dress and I store my clothes, I retrieve the bottle of tequila, half-empty from the night of Jonas's wedding, and pour us both a shot. I plunk the glasses down on the bar and as she returns to the room, I jerk my chin down at the liquor.

We wordlessly clink our shots together and down them. She blows out a breath and pours us both another and we down that one, too. A third shot has me corking the bottle and returning it to the freezer. "Okay," she says, "can we talk about it now?"

"I was waiting for you to bring it up," I admit. "You're the one who likes to talk feelings and shit."

She rolls her eyes. "Whatever. Is it weird now? I mean," she lowers her voice, "we've kissed now."

I snort a laugh. "Yeah, we have." And I wouldn't mind doing it again. But I'd never say that.

"So, is it weird?"

"Definitely."

"Oh, thank God. I thought I was the only one still freaking out."

I shake my head. "You are not alone in the freak out." I look down at my hands and can't take my eyes off my wedding ring. "Thank you for this, Teagan. I know it's a lot, and I can never make this up to you."

She puts her hand on mine, so I lift my eyes to her amazing blue and gold ones. She shakes her head. "You don't owe me anything, Joel. I already told you, I wanted to do this. And yes, I'm a little freaked out, but it's not because you and I got married or the reason behind it. It's because I got married at all. Really, I'm happy to be able to help you."

"So, what comes next?" I ask, but I'm not sure if I've tossed the question out so she'll answer it or the universe or what.

She walks around to the fridge and pulls out a bottle of water and jerks her head toward the back deck. I follow her out and we take seats on the swing. As I push us off, she pulls her knees up to her chest, resting her heels on the edge.

"Oh, well, I already called my aunt's estate lawyers—right after the ceremony, actually—and they said they just need a certified copy of the marriage license. I'll probably have to go out to San Diego whenever I sell the house for the closing, but everything else will be able to be handled in Jacksonville."

"Wow, I didn't expect you to have already done that."

She shrugs. "Get the ball rolling and all that. But I guess we also have to get my house cleaned out, stuff put in storage, and rented out. That'll be fun, I'm sure."

I nod. "We also have to tell Gus. Or, I guess, I have to tell him."

"Are you going to tell Brooke?"

The question isn't unreasonable, but it still makes me tense, my jaw reflexively clenching. I swallow against the bitterness that immediately floods my chest. "Why should I tell her? She didn't even give me a hint that she's been married to my father for a fucking year."

Teagan pivots her body on the swing, her toes slotting under my thigh. "Yeah, but you're a better person than she is. If you hide it, it makes it seem like you have something to hide. Obviously, she felt the need to keep the fact that she married Clive a secret for some reason. If the goal is for this to be believable, it probably needs to be public knowledge." Her eyes lose focus for a beat. "I mean, I'm not changing my name or anything, but if we needed to do a whole social media post or something, I don't have objections to that."

"Social media?"

"Yeah, you know that stuff that the kids use where there's all those newfangled things called photos and videos and you can keep up with friends and family. I believe it used to be called letters and emails," she quips.

I nudge her with my elbow. "You're such a smart ass. Yes, I know what social media is. But do you think it's wise to post something before, say, you tell your parents or I tell Gus?"

She looks down at her knees and examines her hands perched atop them. "My parents and I aren't exactly speaking right now."

I frown. "What? Why? Since when?" This is completely shocking news to me. I've always known Teagan wasn't super close with her parents, but this is the first I'm hearing that they're estranged.

Her jaw clenches, and she examines her ring finger. "Since Tootsie left everything to me and my parents said some really nasty stuff at the will reading. My dad assumed she'd leave everything to him and my mom and he got pissed when the will was read. Since I've never been quiet about my lack of desire to settle down, they assume all the money and property will be divvied up to all the different charities. Hell, for all I know, they think I somehow manipulated Tootsie into leaving me everything. Never mind that it was them who sent me to her house every summer from the time I was six until I went to college."

"What, like it's your fault she left everything to you? That's bullshit. If I had a well-off sibling who wanted to leave everything to Gus because they were close, I'd be ecstatic."

Teagan bumps me with her knee. "Hey, you probably are going to have a well-off sibling. And so will Gus," she says with a snort.

And because I'm so emotionally exhausted from the past couple of days, I can't help but laugh at the absurd truth of her statement. "Oh, God. You're totally right. Gus is not only my son, but he's now my stepbrother. Dad and Brooke's kid is going to be my brother or sister *and* Gus's brother or sister. My ex-wife is now my stepmother and my father is Gus's grandfather *and* his stepfather. The baby will also be Gus's aunt or uncle. Where's fucking Jerry Springer when you need him?"

We both burst out laughing and although none of this is actually funny, we laugh and laugh and laugh. But then, my laughter turns to tears and I can't stop them either, so I bury my face in my hands as I sob. It's as if my anguish and grief has chosen this exact moment to pour forth in a torrent of tears, snot, and heaving breaths.

I haven't cried or probably even processed everything that's happened. Every day, I've put one foot in front of the other for my son and I've pushed all the shit with Brooke and my dad down. I'm sure it's not healthy, and this is the product of that avoidance, I guess.

Small, strong arms wrap around me as Teagan pulls me to her. I turn, clinging to her as she simply holds me while I let out every bit of my pent-up sadness. She doesn't tell me it will be okay. She doesn't make soft shushing noises like you would for a small child. She just lets me cry, cradling the back of my head with one hand as she rubs my back with the other.

I have no clue how long it lasts, but it seems to go on forever. When I finally pull back, my sobs subsiding into these pathetic whimpers, Teagan wipes her own eyes and clears her throat. "Sorry about that," I say, embarrassed. "Didn't mean to explode on you there."

She shakes her head. "Anytime. I can handle emotional shrapnel. Isn't that part of marriage?"

"I think it's supposed to be," I agree.

"Well, anytime you need to explode, I can take it, okay?"

I nod, but don't say anything. I mop my face with my shirt and look out toward the lake as we continue to swing. For a long time, we sit in silence as the sun goes down, the insects begin making noises, and an owl hoots in the distance. Still, we swing and don't talk.

At some point, though, Teagan loops her arm through mine, resting her head on my shoulder. It's not sexual or even very romantic, but it's intimate and supportive and it's probably the only affection I've had from anyone who's not Gus in over a year. It's nicer than I want to admit to myself.

"The kiss wasn't weird," she finally says. "This whole thing is weird, but the kiss wasn't."

"No," I agree. "It was a good kiss."

"Yeah, it was." After a beat, she asks, her tone concerned, "Is it weird that it's not weird?"

Despite how wrung out I am, I chuckle. "Did you want it to be weird?"

She doesn't even bother to look up at me as she shakes her head. "I think I worried it might be like kissing my brother."

"You don't have a brother," I remind her.

She huffs a laugh. "You know what I mean. And I did have a brother."

I look down at her. "You did? I didn't know that."

She nods, still not lifting her head. "Yeah. He died before I was born, so I don't know if that actually counts."

"It counts. Brooke was pregnant before we had Gus, but she miscarried early. Sometimes I wonder who that baby might've turned into."

"I never knew that. Although, I guess there's a lot of stuff I don't know about you or your marriage and stuff."

"Probably. I'm sure there's a lot I don't know about you, too."

"Probably," she echos. "Is there anything pressing you want to know?"

"You said you can't have kids. Can I ask why?"

She lifts her head, seemingly surprised by my question, but not offended. "Sure. I was born without a uterus."

"Really? Is that a common thing? I don't think I've ever heard of that."

She wobbles her hand in a so-so motion. "It's, like, one in five thousand girls who are diagnosed, I think. It's something called Mayer-Rokitansky-Küster-Hauser Syndrome. A lot of times, those who have MRKH also have other complications or have to have surgery or go through treatments because they have shortened vaginal canals and can even have kidney and hearing issues and other stuff. I just got blessed with no periods, I guess, because other than the no-uterus thing, I'm 'normal'. I still have my ovaries, but no cervix, either, so no risk of cervical cancer."

"When did you find out?"

"When I was sixteen. My body started exhibiting normal puberty symptoms—I got boobs and body hair and I had wicked PMS. But I never got my period and by sixteen, my parents got concerned, so I went to the doctor. They did an ultrasound and exam and boom, no baby maker."

"I'm sorry. I'm sure that must've been devastating."

She shrugs. "I mean, all I heard was I wouldn't have periods and from what my friends said, they were terrible, so I didn't see the downside. I didn't have to worry about an unwanted pregnancy and even though I've always been safe with my partners, I've never had to go through that 'oh God, I'm late' panic like other people. I've had a lot of time to come to terms with it. I'm okay. It might be worse if it wasn't something I was born with. If I'd had cancer or was somehow injured and lost the opportunity to bear children that way, it would probably hurt more."

"Still, if motherhood via traditional means was ever something you thought about, I'm sorry you can't experience that."

"Thanks. Can I ask why Brooke was so adamant about not having more kids after Gus?"

I sigh. "When she lost her first pregnancy, she wasn't sure she even wanted to go through another one at all. But she ended up getting pregnant with Gus a few years later and she had all of the worst symptoms. She was even hospitalized for dehydration because she was so sick. She also had terrible postpartum depression, and it took a long time for her to come out of it. She didn't feel like she could handle another pregnancy and birth and everything. And she'd gone through everything, so I offered to get a vasectomy."

"I'm sorry that your opportunity to father more children is gone."

"I could get it reversed if I wanted, but I'm forty; I'm not thinking about having any more kids."

"So? Your dad is in his sixties; doesn't appear to be stopping him."

I snort a laugh. "Thanks for the reminder, Tee."

CHAPTER ELEVEN

TEAGAN

The warmth of the late spring air, combined with the buzz from the alcohol, the gentle sway of the swing, and the emotional exhaustion, leaves us both quiet after we share about our respective sterility. I lay my head back on his shoulder and he leans his head on mine and we just sit.

At some point, I must doze off, because when I come to, my head is on Joel's chest, his arm is around me, and he's snoring softly. It should feel weird, but since it definitely didn't feel like I kissed my brother, this is actually kind of nice.

Shifting until I can look at his face, I take him in. In sleep, his face is relaxed, and the semi-permanent furrowed brow he always sports—or, for the last eighteen months, anyway—is gone. In its place is simply a good, if chronically grumpy, man who only wants what's best for his son.

Having seen the way Brooke publicly and needlessly humiliated Joel and broke his heart, it's understandable that he's bitter. I know his goal is not to intentionally separate Gus from his mother, but she hasn't appeared to put in much effort to see him this past year. I know for a fact Gus hasn't stayed with her overnight until now and other than a few visits Brooke has made to town where she'd come pick him up and he'd be back that same day, all of their visits have been via FaceTime. Gus has told me that much himself during our chats over the past year.

As I'm not a mother, I can't pretend to know what I'd do in this situation. I can, however, say that if Gus was my son, I'd have an exceptionally difficult time going days or weeks without seeing him in person, let alone months. And I suppose it's easy to make judgments when you're an outsider, but I feel like I have a better understanding than most in this instance. I honestly have a hard time understanding how Brooke could cheat on Joel with his father, leave him for and marry said father, move over five hundred miles away, agree to Joel having full custody, and then decide to fight for Gus a year later.

It baffles the mind, to be sure.

All I know is, if the idea of Gus being away from Joel—and by extension, me, since I live next door—a majority of the time is causing me to panic and make a rash decision like asking my neighbor to marry me, how must all this be affecting the man himself?

And like that shaken bottle of soda I compared him to, Joel finally spewed. It was hard to listen to the heart-wrenching sobs of pain and helplessness as he cried on my shoulder, but I can only hope it was at least a bit cathartic for him. I also couldn't hold my own tears back as my friend—now husband—poured out his anguish and anger.

I should probably wake him and send him to bed, but like I said, this is kinda nice. So I simply lay my head back on his chest, close my eyes, and listen to the steady thumping of his heart and his breathing, his strong arm still around me. While it may not be a traditional wedding night, this is still pretty good.

A pained grunt rouses me from sleep, and my body shifts as Joel stretches. "We slept on the porch? Jesus, I'm too old for this. I'm not going to be able to move."

Still sleepy, I groan and don't even attempt to move as I squint against the sunlight pouring into the porch. "Too early."

"Yeah, well, you're a lot younger than me. I'm sure your back isn't reminding you of your age." He gently nudges me off him and stands with a hiss, groaning as he plants his hands on his lower back, and bending this way and that, attempting to loosen up.

"You know," I say with a yawn, "those sounds you make are nearly obscene. Do you need to be alone with yourself?" In my pre-coffee fog, it doesn't hit me that I've actually said the words until Joel freezes and chokes on air. I drag my hand down my face as my cheeks heat. "Ignore me. My filter's not active yet. As you were."

He laughs. "Note to self: avoid the scandalous noises prior to Teagan's morning coffee."

I stand as I roll my neck and shoulders. "Aww, how sweet. Already starting lists for our cohabitation. Probably smart." Scratching a mosquito bite I've received sometime in the night, I ask, "What do you want to do today?"

He turns to face me, absentmindedly scratching his chin. "Do we have to do anything? If we just got married yesterday, wouldn't it be weird if we were out and about?"

I feign curiosity. "And why's that?" I try to keep my smile hidden, but I'm not sure I do a very good job.

He rolls his eyes. "Are you so immature that I need to spell it out?"

My smile breaks free and I nod, amused. "Absolutely. Why,

dear *husband*, would we want people to think we stayed in the day after our wedding?"

His eyes narrow as he stands up straighter, and I'm not sure how to gauge the change in his posture or expression. "Because, *wife*, if this was a 'real' marriage, as soon as we walked in the door last night, I would've tossed you over my shoulder and carried you to bed. I would've fucked you within an inch of your life and you'd be too tired to do anything but sleep today."

My mouth falls open and I no longer need coffee. He lifts one brow. "Sorry; guess my filter's not working, either. Do we have stuff for biscuits and gravy?"

"I think so," I reply, my voice coming out a bit breathy.

"Good." He pivots to walk into the cabin. I'm left still reeling, an uncomfortable ache settling between my legs.

Danger, Will Robinson.

Guess I need to start my own list. Note to self: don't poke the bear.

Thankfully, the cabin has cable and wi-Fi, some decent books, and even a deck of cards, so Joel and I aren't bored over the next couple of days. There is no more porch sleeping or poking of the bear or scandalous morning noises. There is, however, a lot of quiet porch sitting, cooking together, and generally learning more about each other. Because although we've lived next door to one another for a decade, there's obviously quite a lot that we don't know.

I tell him about my summers with Tootsie. That because she was a great listener, it made me want to become a guidance counselor. He tells me about how he felt the first time he held Gus in his arms. He doesn't talk about Brooke or his dad or Brooke *and* his dad. He talks about his mom and how much he misses her. I talk about how my estrangement from my parents has made me feel as though I've done something wrong, even if I know that's not the case.

We discuss how to tell Gus about us getting married and handling my moving in—we'll wait until he returns from Brooke's and he'll sit down with him and I'll move in after that. At that point, he'll also inform Brooke.

We talk about designating one of the savings accounts that Tootsie left to me as a legal fund. Joel objects to this suggestion, but in the end, he goes along with the idea since that's the whole reason we've done this thing to begin with.

We send emails to our school board, informing them of our marriage and although there shouldn't be any issue with two staff members who work at the same school getting married, we're trying to make things appear as legitimate as possible.

Does the idea of being married still freak me the fuck out? Absolutely. Is it because I'm married to Joel? Not in the least. He's a good man and if I had to shackle myself to someone for anything less than true love, I can think of much worse candidates than him. I only hope it all won't have been in vain by the time everything is said and done.

As we're exiting the plane, walking toward the parking lot four days after we get married, Joel stops in his tracks, slapping his forehead with his palm. "Shit."

I freeze and turn to him, confused. "What?"

"I don't know why I didn't realize it until right before this second."

"What is it?"

He tugs me out of the path of foot traffic as he lowers his voice. "You're going to have to move in before Gus gets home."

I frown. "Why?"

"Because. If Brooke finds out we got married and I suddenly have no financial reasons why I might struggle to go toe-to-toe with her, she's going to start digging. If it's discovered that you inherited a shit-ton of money if you got married, and I turn around and use that money for the custody battle, there's no way she's not going to assume we're in cahoots."

I raise a brow. "Did you really just use the word 'cahoots'?"

He rolls his eyes. "Focus, Tee. She knows you've never been quiet about your singlehood. You took my side in the divorce and even acted as a character witness for me in the first custody trial. If we don't act like we are cuckoo for cocoa puffs over each other, it will draw suspicion. Hell, for all I know, she might hire a P.I. and interview the neighbors." His jaw clenches with remembered anger. "And you know how much that pack of hyenas likes to gossip. She's seen me in love; she knows how I act when I'm married." His eyes search mine. "It's got to look real or—."

I nod, understanding. "I get it. Don't worry, I won't let you down."

He shakes his head, his Adam's apple bobbing with a swallow. "It could get messy, Tee. If we need to call this off, I can still figure something else out. It was easy to plan it all when we were away, but now it's—."

"Go time?" I finish and he nods. "I know. Like I said, I've got you." And I hope with all I'm worth that I'm telling the truth. I reach up to grip his jaw, letting my thumb brush his cheek. Anyone who passes by might see a sweet, affectionate couple, but in reality, I simply want to reassure him with my touch. "I promise, Joel; I'm good. Whatever you need, I'm there."

He drops his forehead to mine and it should feel forced or like this really is all pretend, but I can't deny how nice the connection is. "You know I can't ever thank you enough for this, right?"

I huff a laugh and let my eyes fall closed. "I haven't even done anything yet."

He lets out a small, amused puff of air and pulls back just before pressing a kiss to my forehead and looking into my eyes. "Still, you've already gone way above and beyond by simply offering. Following through will probably be enough to grant you sainthood."

I roll my eyes and turn, running my hand down the inside of his arm to lace our fingers together so we can walk out hand-in-hand. "How do you know it's not all an elaborate ruse so that Jethro can have unfettered access to your pool?"

"Ah, I see; the long con. I bet you're not even filthy rich, are you?"

I elbow him good-naturedly. He grins and I'm relieved to see the anxiety written in his features seems to have dissipated in the last few seconds. "No, just moderately wealthy," I reply, and he chuckles.

Knowing the plan needed to change, I send Joel to pick up Jethro while I go home and pack some clothes to take next door for the next few days. Joel offers to pick up supper and I don't even argue because lord knows I have no desire to cook after we've been cooped up in the cabin for the last few days pretending to have all the sex.

Of course, in truth, there's been none, and once I'm alone in my car, my mind begins to turn over with images of Joel dressed for Jonas's wedding, for our elopement, doing shirtless workouts, the sounds he made that first morning, and what he said on the porch. Especially that last one.

A week ago, I would just make a pit stop at the bar near the house to find someone to spend a few hours with. I can't do that anymore. But like I told Joel, I'm a big girl and can take care of myself.

Planning to do exactly that, I bolt from my car and into my house and have just reached my bedroom door when my phone rings. I debate letting it go to voicemail even before I know who it is. But seeing my father's name on the screen makes me pause as a pang of longing for my parents hits me in the chest.

I immediately forgo plans of opening my nightstand drawer to work out some of my frustrations as I swipe the screen. "Dad? Hey." I put the phone on speaker and set it on my dresser as I pull out my big suitcase and open it up on my bed, planning to fill it up.

"Teagan. I see you're set to collect the inheritance Tootsie left you. Awful convenient you were able to find someone to marry so quickly."

Frowning, I'm unsure how to even process the accusation in my father's tone. Even if he's not wrong, he sounds so hateful and not at all like the man who told me he was proud of me for wanting to become a teacher and guidance counselor. I stop pulling clothes off the hangers to focus on the conversation.

"How did you find out I got married?"

"Oh, so you don't deny it? Henrietta Wallace happened to be in Gatlinburg over Memorial Day and saw you walk out of a wedding chapel wearing a wedding dress. You were with a man and there was a photographer and you were both wearing rings. Seriously, Teagan, *Gatlinburg*? What, Vegas too classy for you?

"What were you thinking? That you'd make an easy buck and live the high life while your mother and I struggle to make ends meet? You and I both know Tootsie was planning to leave her assets to your mother and me. We talked about it for years. I still don't know how you got her to leave you everything."

The venom in my father's tone stuns me. I've heard of wills and estates turning people jealous, spiteful, and hateful, but this is all new for me as far as my parents are concerned.

"Is this even a real marriage? Or did you pay some guy who wants a quick buck to pretend? Do I actually get to meet my new *son-in-law*, or will he conveniently be away on business anytime your mother and I visit?"

Hurt and angry at the way my father is speaking to me, I can't help but spit out, "You act like you and Mom actually visit me, Dad. Last I checked, I've made the trip to Tallahassee every month for the past ten years. Well, the past ten years minus the two months since Tootsie died.

"And for your information, you have met my husband. When you helped me move in after college. Joel, my next-door neighbor?"

"I thought he was married. What did you do, break up his marriage? Teagan, your mother and I didn't raise you to be some home wrecker."

I scoff. "Give me a little credit, Dad. Jesus, you act like I'm some fallen woman. No, Joel and his wife divorced a year ago. And it wasn't because of me, in case I need to be clear about that. We've been hanging out. He went with me to Jonas's wedding, we realized we have feelings for one another, one thing led to another, and we got married. It's called romance; look it up."

"Teagan, don't be naïve. I think we both know if you and that neighbor of yours have become a little friendly and you let spill about Tootsie's estate, he's probably thinking you'd be an easy mark."

Bitterness rising in my chest, I blow out a deep breath. "Oh, so now I'm naïve? Nice, Dad. I figured you'd be happy for me. All you and Mom talked about for years was me settling down. I've done that and you're still not happy."

"Oh, please. Your mother and I gave up any hope of that happening when you got your diagnosis. And let's face it, with all that running around you've done for years, that's a turnoff for a lot of men. So, what man is going to willingly choose a woman who can't bear his children when she's got the kind of reputation you do? A man is only as good as his legacy. He's after a payday, Teagan. And you know when—not if—he leaves you in a few months, he'll be entitled to half of your assets."

Tears burn my eyes with my father's words. "So, let me get this straight," I say, my voice choked with rage and sadness. I clear my throat and blow out a breath. "I'm naïve and a whore and because I'm sterile, no one could ever want me. Thanks, Dad. Nice to know what you really think of me after all these years." I square my shoulders as bile rises up my throat. "I'll see all of Tootsie's money burned in a pile in the middle of Times Square before you ever get a dime of it." I disconnect the call and drop my phone to sob into my hands.

A few seconds later, arms encircle me and a scent I now recognize as Joel fills my nostrils. Shame at the possibility that he heard all my father's vitriol floods my chest and I pull away, not wanting him to see me like this.

I mop my face as I try to stop crying. Joel is kneeling in front of me, his expression sympathetic as he takes my hands in his. "I'm not afraid of your emotional shrapnel, either, Tee."

"You sure about that?" I quip and sniffle, tears still rolling down my face. "You're not super into *feelings*, remember?"

He nods. "For myself, yeah. But for my friends," he swipes my tears off my cheek with his thumb, "and especially for my wife, I'm good at being supportive. And everything your dad said was a pile of shit."

My lip quivers as another choked sob works its way up my throat. I just hang my head and cry even harder than before, knowing Joel heard everything. He scoops me up, sitting on the bed with me in his lap as I cling to him the same way he did me on the porch of the cabin. For what seems like hours, I mourn the probable loss of my relationship with my parents. Although the circumstances are completely different, I can't help but feel like in this, Joel and I can empathize with each other.

He just holds me until I'm cried out as he rubs my back. Thankfully, he doesn't tell me everything will be okay. Sometime later, I've moved on to hiccuping while he's still holds me. I should pull away, because him holding me feels a lot nicer than I want to admit to myself.

When I finally make myself release him, he swipes away a few remaining tears, offering me a small smile. "You'd be so proud of me; the first thing I did when I got home was turn Jethro loose and didn't even yell at him when he ran to jump into the pool." I snort a watery laugh and Joel tucks a stray hair behind my ear. "Probably a stupid question, but do you feel better?"

"No. And yes, it's a totally stupid question."

He laughs. "Noted. And I take it you're not packed? I've got Chinese over at the house. Want to come eat? After, we can come back and I'll help you gather some things to take over, okay?"

I stand. "Sure."

Nodding, he rises, picking up my phone to hand it to me before taking my hand in his. He tugs me out of my bedroom, through the yard, and over to his house.

CHAPTER TWELVE

JOEL

It was an entirely accidental eavesdrop. I'd knocked on the door and when I found it unlocked after Teagan didn't answer, I let myself in. I thought she might need help packing. Of course, then I heard everything her father said, and I was frozen in rage and shock until she hung up on him. When she began to cry, there was no way I could let her be alone after that.

It's a mild evening, so while Jethro continues to wear himself out in the pool, we eat our lo mein and broccoli beef on the deck with bottles of water. Teagan is quiet, and mostly pushes her food around her plate, looking heartsick. I'm sure it's not too far from the truth, with everything her father said.

"I wish you hadn't heard all that stuff my dad said," she says after she finally just pushes her entire plate away.

"It just let me know I need to make sure we don't send them a Christmas card this year."

She lets out a soft laugh. "Nice. I guess we don't have to worry about traveling to see any family this year, huh? Since we're both currently having some...difficulties with our parents?"

"You have such a way with words, Tee," I reply with an eye roll. "*Difficulties* might be the most euphemistic way to put what's currently going on with our fathers."

She nods and I watch as Jethro climbs the pool stairs, shakes off, and comes to lie under the table. Within seconds, he's snoring. "I'm guessing he sleeps pretty good after a swim?"

"Usually. You didn't get any hateful calls right after we got back to town, did you? Any neighbors I need to give the stink-eye?"

I shake my head. "Knock on wood, but it seems we're in the clear for now. I talked to Gus on my way back from the kennel and told him I had something to tell him when he got home."

"And he didn't ask you to go ahead and tell him on the phone?"

I huff a laugh. "You know he did. But I said it was something I needed to tell him in person."

"You think he'll be okay with things?"

"I hope so. We'll see. I'll probably tell him on the flight back, since Brooke's too pregnant to fly and, on principle, I don't want my father flying down with him."

"Understandable," she agrees. "Have you spoken with your lawyer since Saturday?"

"No. I was planning on calling her tomorrow to tell her we got married."

"What do you think will happen after that?"

"With the custody hearing?" She nods and I shrug. "We'll have to wait on a date to be set and go from there. Hopefully, it will happen before the end of summer, but I doubt it. And until the hearing, the current custody agreement stands."

"So will Gus go to Brooke's anymore this summer?"

"There aren't any plans for that currently, but she can submit a request through the lawyers if she wants him to visit her. Or she can come here like she's done until recently. I guess

I know why she hasn't come to see him for the past few months."

"You think she wanted to shock you with the pregnancy or something?" Teagan asks with a furrowed brow. "You think it was malicious? Or did you know she was pregnant before we dropped Gus off?"

I blow out a breath and push my plate away, my appetite gone. "No, I didn't know. Of course, unless it's some sort or emergency, I only communicate with Brooke via text or email—something with some sort of proof—or through the lawyers. And I sure as shit don't talk to my father anymore."

She holds up her bottle of water. "Here, here."

"If I was going to guess, Brooke will want Gus to come visit after she has the baby, but I have no clue when she's due. If it's after school's already started, I could see him going for a weekend or something, but I'm not letting her pull him out of school."

"Why do you think she's trying to get custody of him now, a year later?"

I sigh and shrug. "Truthfully, I hope it's that she misses him and thinks he'd have a better life with her and my father."

She lifts a brow. "I think we both know that's not the case. You are an amazing father and Gus adores you."

"Unfortunately, Gus's feelings don't have a lot to do with it right now. In a few years, he can decide who he wants to live with and the courts will take his opinion into account. Right now, it's all up to the judge."

"Well, we'll do everything in our now considerable power to ensure Gus is where he belongs. What I don't get is, why doesn't Brooke just move back to Florida and y'all share custody? Or, for that matter, was there a reason—you know, other than the fact you were pissed and hurt and betrayed—that you didn't follow her to Tennessee?"

I roll my shoulders as I clench my jaw. I figure Teagan has pretty much seen me at my worst at this point, so what the hell? "Because *she* left. She *chose* to move. She had a perfectly fine job here. I honestly believe she thought I'd chase her if she ran. That I loved our family so much that if she threatened to leave, I'd run after her. But after I found out about her and my dad and she—." I swallow against the pain of the memory as my cheeks heat with embarrassment. "I wasn't going to chase her. I'm not over it, but I don't love her anymore. I can't."

"I'm not sure all of that is something you get over. It didn't even happen to me and I'm not over it."

"Thanks for the solidarity," I say with a sad chuckle.

"We're a team now, right?"

"Looks that way," I agree.

She's about to open her mouth when a sound wafts our direction that has both our eyes widening as we share a resigned sigh. Teagan groans, "Oh, God. I'm not sure I can handle her today."

"Yoo-hoo, Joel." The grating voice of the nosiest busybody in our entire neighborhood filters around the side of the house. Teagan buries her face in her hands, and my heart skips when I see her ring.

"Take off your ring," I hurriedly whisper.

"What?"

"Your fucking ring," I hiss. "Take it off. If Ellen finds out, it'll be back to Brooke before she even leaves the yard. I don't want her finding out before Gus." I tug mine and it gets hung up on my knuckle, but finally pops free and I stick it in my pocket.

In a panic, she attempts to yank it off and her eyes go even wider. "Fuck. It's stuck. I swell when I fly and we ate fucking Chinese food."

I grab her wrist to tug on the ring, and she grunts in pain, pulling it away. She shoves her hand under the table just as Ellen comes to stand at the pool gate. She's a tall, slender woman who always gives me the distinct impression of what a human praying mantis might look like. She's white and in her mid-forties, with a severe bob and is currently dressed in a green T-shirt dress. It gives me even stronger mantis vibes.

"Ellen, what can I do for you?" I ask, trying to keep my tone polite. "Teagan and I were just enjoying some supper."

Her eyes travel from me to Teagan and back and she smiles, but I don't trust Ellen as far as I can throw her; never have. Especially because she and Brooke were thick as thieves for nearly ten years. "I just wanted to check on you. You know, since Gus's with his momma. Didn't want you wasting away." Her brow lifts as if she's figured out some big conspiracy. "But I can see you're just fine."

"Yeah, he is," Teagan says with a friendly smile. "Of course, we both miss Gus like crazy, but he'll be home before you know it, so we'll try to survive."

As if to agree with Teagan, Jethro harrumphs from under the table, and I nearly want to smile. But then a small, metallic ping rises from the deck as Teagan's ring bounces, lands on Jethro, and slides to the ground, where it spins like a coin. I cover it with my foot and stick my head under the table as if to see what made the sound and stealthily pluck the ring from under my shoe. "Huh. Looks like a screw fell out of this table. I really should fix that."

Ellen narrows her eyes and examines Teagan and me again. I offer her my fakest, warmest smile. "Well, if you'll excuse us, we're going to finish our supper. Thanks for checking on us."

"Sure. Glad to see you're not overwrought with Gus being gone."

"Like I said," Teagan pipes up, "he'll be home before we

can really miss him; just a couple more weeks. I'm sure we'll find something to keep us occupied until then."

"Well, you holler if you need anything before he gets back, okay?"

"Thanks, Ellen. Have a good evening," I call after her as she turns.

In a lowered voice that only I can hear, Teagan spits out, "Fly off on your broom, you nosy bitch. Make sure you keep the neighborhood informed." She extends her hand to me and I drop her ring into it and take some strange sort of pleasure watching her slide it back onto her finger. "Quick thinking about the rings. Of course, Brooke—and the entire neighborhood—will now assume we're sleeping together."

I shrug. "Probably won't help quell that rumor when you're spending the night here."

She laughs. "Nope." I fish my ring out of my pocket and put it on and Teagan tilts her head, her expression curious. "Can I ask you something?"

"Sure," I reply, lifting my bottle to my lips.

She seems surprised that I've actually agreed and blinks. "Okay. Just out of curiosity, did Brooke ever accuse you of cheating before you found out about her and Clive? I remember back in college, when Jonas was engaged, his fiancée accused him of cheating when it was actually her."

Taking another long drink of my water, I swallow to stall, not really wanting to answer her question, but then Teagan nods. "I kinda figured as much. With me, right?"

I blow out a breath. "Yeah."

"How long before you found out about her was she throwing out accusations?"

I try to think back. "A few months. She said—. It doesn't matter what she said."

"I guess not, but if I was going to speculate, it was something along the lines of because I'll sleep with just about anyone, I'd have no issues also wanting to sleep with someone's husband, right?"

I wince because that's almost verbatim what Brooke said and Teagan shrugs. "It's fine. Definitely not the first time I've been slut shamed. But honestly, before today, it's only ever come from other women, believe it or not. My dad is the first man who's ever done it."

"I'm sorry you've had to deal with that."

She splays her hands, shrugging as if to say, *it is what it is*. "It doesn't bother me. I hate the double standard of it, since men rarely ever get called out for promiscuity, but I'm not ashamed of who I am or what—or who—I've done," she says with a smirk and then neutralizes her features again. "I can attest that, to my knowledge, I've never slept with anyone who was in a relationship. I'd say ninety percent of the time, I verify before anything goes down. Cheating is a hard limit for me."

"Me, too," I agree with a humorless chuckle. "Even after I found out about her and my dad, I went out to a bar and thought about wanting to even the score or whatever, but I couldn't do it. Even though she'd broken our vows, I couldn't bring myself to stoop to her level. I'm not a cheater, even when I essentially have the green light to do it."

"That's because you're a good man, Joel. And what they did isn't a reflection on you. I know you can never truly know what goes on behind closed doors, but I'd like to think I've had a front-row seat to most of your marriage. It was clear to anyone with half a brain cell that you were so in love with Brooke and you were in love with your family."

I pinch the bridge of my nose and shake my head, no longer wanting to discuss how much or how hard I loved Brooke or our family. "I think I'm feelinged out for tonight."

Teagan huffs a laugh. "Sure. I know it was a lot of *feelings* for you today."

After cleaning up our supper mess, we leave Jethro snoozing on the deck and make our way back over to Teagan's house so she can pack some things for my house. It takes about an hour for her to gather her clothes and toiletries and for me to pack up the perishables from the kitchen so they can be used.

Once we're finally back next door, Jethro curls up in his bed and she sets out his food and water bowls. I drop the groceries in the kitchen as she takes her suitcase to the office off my bedroom. And then, we both collapse onto the sofa, exhausted. For a few minutes, neither of us says anything and I lean my head back and shut my eyes.

Knowing if I stay like this for long, I'll likely fall asleep, I sit up. I open my mouth and turn to tell Teagan I'll help her put sheets on the pullout, but she's already asleep. And because she's slept on a sofa for nearly the past week, I rise to go make her bed myself.

As soon as it's ready, I return to the living room and scoop her up into my arms. She stirs, but lays her head on my shoulder and easily drifts back off as I carry her down the hall. I walk through my room and intentionally avoid looking at my bed. I ferry her to the pullout, which is about twenty feet from my bed, and I'm *definitely* not thinking about laying her down on it simply so I can lie beside her and curl my body against hers.

But I don't do that. I gently place her on her bed and pull off her shoes before draping the covers over her petite frame. Before I can do something silly and quite possibly dangerous for me, like watch her sleep or brush her hair off her face to press a kiss to her cheek or imagine her waking up and tugging me down to her and—.

Quickly backing out of the small room, I quietly shut the door that separates the office from my bedroom. After a few deep breaths, my eyes fall on my suitcase and once I have everything unpacked, I haul my dirty clothes to the laundry room and toss everything in. The socks with Teagan's face on them catch my eye and I can't help but smile as I dump in the detergent and start the machine.

I was in such an awful place when she gave those to me. The divorce had been final for about six months. Because it was Christmas and Gus was spending Christmas Day with Brooke and her family across town, I was alone. I contemplated getting drunk, but knew Gus would be home later in the day and I didn't want him to see me like that.

Watching him leave in a car with Brooke and my dad was almost too much to bear, and I was really struggling. I was just reaching for the photo album from when Gus was a baby when there was a knock on the back door. Because Teagan has only ever used the back door to enter the house, even when Brooke and I were married, I knew it had to be her.

Her perpetual cheerfulness wasn't something I felt like I could stomach, but during the divorce, she'd been the only person to offer me support and stand up for me. So regardless of my desire to just tell her to go the fuck away and leave me alone, I opened the door.

At the time, her hair had been this dark red and cut to her shoulders. In the rich green sweater dress she wore, she looked festive and pretty, but I don't think I even said anything to her.

As has always been her custom, though, Teagan Roth has never needed anyone to fill the silence. She's pretty good at it all on her own. She'd stopped giving me sympathetic smiles weeks earlier and, for the most part, had simply returned to treating me like the grumpy neighbor whose kid she was fond of.

She'd held out a cookie tin and a small gift bag. I eyed them like they might bite me. She'd simply rolled her eyes and shoved the items into my arms. I think I made some sort of grunting noise or something and she'd lifted an eyebrow. "Oh, wow, so you've gone past grump and moved into Neanderthal territory. I mean, you do have the shaggy hair and beard, so it could probably work for you."

I still didn't say anything, and she'd sighed. "You know, it's bad form to not at least open a gift so you can adequately express appreciation for said gift." Her smile had grown, and she pumped her eyebrows. "Come on, you know how much money we make, so I have to really like you to actually buy you a gift. And trust me, these weren't cheap."

Wanting to just be alone with my anger and grief, I figured if I complied, she'd get out faster, so I tossed the cookie tin on the counter and, exasperated, I yanked out whatever was in the gift bag. What came out was the gaudiest pair of bright yellow socks, and they had Teagan's smiling face all over them.

"What the hell are these?" I didn't ask it to be rude, I don't think; it was simple shock.

She'd grinned like a fool. "Well, I figure you might need a leg up." She nudged me. "Or, I just wanted to help you put one foot in front of the other." Letting out a soft laugh, her eyes sparkled with glee. "Or, my favorite, I wanted to help you totally nail some killer fashion."

When I simply stared at her, she scoffed. "Come on, man; I worked on those foot puns for hours." Sobering, she'd shrugged. "I'm sure today is super shitty for you. And I know it's just a pair of socks, but I wanted to let you know I was thinking of you. Merry Christmas, Joel."

After a quick nod and a small smile, she'd pivoted to walk out the door.

Now, when I think about the socks, I'll probably always associate them with seeing Teagan in that amazing dress at our elopement and the way her face lit up when I showed her I was wearing the eyesores.

I think I like that memory better.

CHAPTER THIRTEEN

TEAGAN

A little over a week later, I'm clearing out the remainder of the food in my kitchen and packing up the rest of the items I plan to move over to Joel's house. The movers—because people in their thirties are lying to themselves if they think they can bribe friends to move their shit with beer and pizza anymore—will be by later today to pack everything into a storage pod to keep my things safe while I rent out my house.

I could probably charge more rent if the house was furnished, but the idea of strangers using all my stuff gives me a bit of the ick, so I'll happily take the hit to keep my things mine.

As I'm boxing up the last of the canned soups and jars of peanut butter and jelly, my doorbell rings. Hopping down from the counter and dusting my hands off on my cutoffs, I head toward the door, unsure who it might be. Looking through the peephole, I can't help but smile when I see Jonas and Callahan on my porch.

I yank open the door and throw myself at my best friend, who immediately sweeps me up in a big hug and grunts. "Hey, Teag. Missed you, too."

Stepping back, I usher them in and after giving Callahan a quick embrace, I ask, "What are y'all doing in town? Did I know you were coming and forgot? It's been a busy couple of weeks, so I totally could've."

Jonas shakes his head and looks around, his expression morphing into curiosity. "No, we were headed over to the beach for the weekend and thought we'd stop by for a minute." Gesturing around the space where boxes are stacked and paintings are leaning against the wall instead of hanging on them, he frowns. "You moving? When did this happen? Where are you moving?"

As if on cue, Joel sweeps in the side door, Jethro in tow. "I swear, if you tell me you have more canned soup, we're just going to toss it. It's unnatural for one person to eat that much soup and we don't have room for it in the—." He stops short and smiles. "Jonas, Callahan. Hey."

He strides over to offer them both warm handshakes, and as everyone says hello, Callahan's eyes dart between Joel and me. She doesn't say anything, just raises a fair brow in question. At least until Jethro jumps up, planting his front paws on my chest and I absentmindedly scratch him behind the ear. Joel does, too, and then her eyes widen in shock.

Grabbing both of our left hands, she shrieks "What are these? Did y'all get married? Holy shit! Tell me everything."

All the color drains from Jonas's face and his mouth falls open. "What?" His eyes search mine. "You got *married*?"

I huff a laugh, heat rising to my cheeks as Joel and I share a look. "Surprise," I mutter.

"Oh, my God," Callahan says excitedly. "I knew there was more than just 'he's my cute neighbor' going on." She looks to her husband as if for confirmation. "Didn't I tell you they were going to hookup?"

Jonas, still looking a bit bewildered, seems to have trouble processing. "Married?"

I nod. "Yeah." I spare a glance at Joel. "But we haven't told Gus yet, so if y'all could wait to post anything on social media until after we do, that'd be great. We don't want Gus's mom to find out before he does."

Callahan nods solemnly. "Of course." She smiles broadly again. "Wow, this is such a wonderful turn of events. Congratulations."

"Thanks," Joel says warmly.

I'm still eyeing Jonas, who looks like a bomb has been dropped on him, and I suddenly feel guilty for not already telling my best friend this news. I glance at Callahan and, seeming to read my thoughts, she gives me a small nod. "Joel, why don't you and I take Jethro out for a bit? From what Teagan has told us, he's pretty obsessed with your pool, right?"

Joel's gaze slides to me, and I nod. He drops his forehead to my temple and whispers in my ear, "If you feel the need to embellish about my abilities in bed, you have my full support. You know, to sell things and all that."

I snort a soft laugh, even as heat climbs up my neck, and he chuckles, pressing an affectionate kiss to the side of my head. He shoots Jonas a smile before heading out into the yard, Callahan and Jethro following close behind. The kiss should've felt weird, but it only felt sweet, and I attempt to ignore the warmth that spreads through my chest at the simple gesture.

Jonas's eyes follow Joel out, but it's not until he's completely out of sight that he gives me his attention. I offer him a curious frown. "Why are you freaking out?"

"You mean, other than the fact that you, Miss Never-Gonna-Settle-Down, settled down? After one weekend with the guy? Are you okay? Did you experience some sort of head trauma I'm not aware of?"

I roll my eyes. "Jeez, nice to know I have your support."

My best friend sobers. "For real, are you okay? There's not some sort of blackmail plot and he's holding you hostage, right?"

"Jonas, be serious. Have you ever known me to something I don't want to do?"

"No, and that's the thing. This isn't something you'd ever do. You've said so, I don't know, only about a million times since college. 'I don't want marriage. I don't want kids.' Was that not your mantra forever?"

I fold my arms across my chest. "Things change. Aren't you going to at least ask me if I'm happy? Shouldn't you, as my best friend, be more concerned about that than anything?"

"Are you happy?"

I can't help the smile that pulls at the corners of my mouth. "I am. And yes, it was sudden, but I've known Joel almost as long as I've known you. He's a good man and a wonderful dad, and his son is amazing."

"But you always said you didn't want to be a mom."

I look down at my feet and sigh. "That's not exactly the truth."

"What's that supposed to mean?"

Looking back up at him, I swallow. "People tend to react differently when you say that you don't want kids versus when you say you can't have kids."

He frowns. "What?"

"I *can't* have kids, Jonas. I'm sterile because I was born without a uterus." He blinks in shock and I press forward. "I always assumed no one would ever truly want me without my ability to bear children. I understand that's a bit irrational, but it's always something I've dealt with. Joel doesn't want more kids because he already has the best kid ever."

"You never said anything. I'm so sorry."

I sigh. "I didn't want your pity. I don't want anyone's pity when it's no one's fault. It's just something I was born with."

"Does he know?"

I nod. "Yeah. And like I said, he doesn't want any more kids, so it's all good. I'm sorry I didn't tell you and I'm sorry you had to find out I got married like this. I should've told you; you're my best friend. And I understand why you're shocked, but it wasn't exactly a big party for me that last time you and I hooked up, and you burst into tears because you didn't tell me about Callahan before we had sex. It was liable to give me a complex, you know."

He gives me a sheepish smile. "I know. I'm sorry. So, he's a good guy, though? You're happy?"

"He is. We've got shit to work out with his ex-wife, and I'm definitely not looking forward to that because she's a real piece of work, but I'm not afraid of her. And yes, I'm happy. Being married is easier than I anticipated."

Jonas nods. "Yeah. Combining lives isn't as scary as I thought it'd be, either. So I take it you moved in next door?"

I shrug. "His house has the pool, and Jethro's kinda attached to it. Plus, Gus has been through enough upheaval with his mom getting remarried and about to have a baby, so we wanted to give him as much stability as possible. I'm going to rent my house out."

My best friend closes the distance between us and pulls me in for a hug. "I'm sorry for my reaction. If you're happy, I'm happy."

"Thanks. Let's go check on the spouses."

He huffs a laugh and steps back and we make our way over to the side door. "Man, that's weird. We're *married*, Teag."

"Fucking surreal, right?"

He snorts. "Definitely."

As we walk across the yard to Joel's house, he and Callahan are laughing like old friends while Jethro splashes in the pool. They're having beers and when he sees me coming, Joel smiles. As I get closer, he tugs me toward him. I pluck his beer his hand, bringing it to my mouth for a long drink. Snaking his hand around my waist to settle on my hip, he asks, his voice hushed, "Did you make me look good?"

I nod, and take another sip of his beer before he pulls it out of my hand to have a drink. I smile up at him, keeping my voice low enough that only he can hear me. "I made sure to sing the praises of your ten-inch dick and your ability to make me come so hard I pass out."

He chokes on his drink, liquid spewing from his mouth, and I burst out laughing as he mops his face. "Jesus, Tee," he croaks, his cheeks beet red above his beard. He narrows his eyes, his stare turning wicked as he yanks me to him, rubbing his beer-soaked beard all over my cheeks and neck. I let out a high-pitched squeal that makes him laugh as I try to extricate myself from his grip.

He just pulls me tighter against him. His puffs of breath play over my skin, making my heart rate ratchet up as my body seems to mold itself to his. Awareness of how strong and solid he is and how nice his arms feel wrapped around me registers somewhere that is definitely not my brain and tendrils of warmth spread down my body.

I stop trying to fight him, and simply wrap my arms around his waist, splaying my hands over his lower back. I'm unable to hold back a contented sigh, even though I probably should. His movements slow, and things can probably only be classified as nuzzling at that point. I should pull back, but I don't, and neither does he until he brushes a soft kiss under my ear, making my breath hitch.

He smiles against the side of my neck and whispers, "How did you know my dick is ten inches? I thought that was a well-kept secret. Did you find my special ruler?"

I laugh despite the very real heat that floods my lower abdomen and the visual my brain wants to conjure. After he gives me a final squeeze, he lets me go. When I turn, Callahan is trying to hold back her grin. "Babe, I think we've taken up enough of Teagan and Joel's time. I'm sure they have a lot more interesting things to do than entertain us."

Jonas says nothing, seemingly so caught off guard by my exchange with Joel, that it's not until his wife lightly elbows him in the ribs that he blinks. "Right, Darlin'. Yeah, thank you guys for letting us monopolize your time for a little while. Callie's right; we should go."

Jonas's gaze slides to Joel's and the men seem to have some sort of non-verbal conversation before he smiles and gives my husband a nod. The men exchange a handshake before my best friend pulls me in for a hug. "Happy looks good on you. And at least wait until we're in the car before you get each other naked, okay?"

I snort a laugh and give him a tight squeeze. "No promises." God knows that idea isn't totally abhorrent in the least.

Callahan and I hug briefly and all of this should feel strange considering my past with Jonas and them being married, but it's not. "Congrats, Teagan. I'm so happy for you. And I swear, if you don't rip that man's clothes off as soon as we leave, you will be doing yourself a great disservice. Damn, girl."

I blush as she steps back to say goodbye to Joel. As the couple depart through the pool gate, walking back over to my driveway hand-in-hand.

Still trying to calm my racing heart, I glance at Joel. "I guess I need to finish packing."

He clears his throat and blows out a breath. "Right. Packing." He whistles for Jethro, who immediately exits the pool and shakes off, following us over to my yard and curling up under the picnic table on my patio as we head inside.

Once the movers come and go, I stand in my empty house and sigh. "Is it weird?" Joel asks, coming to stand beside me.

"Isn't that kinda our everyday anymore?"

He chuckles. "Yeah, I suppose it is. Was the house empty when you moved in? I can't remember."

I shake my head. "No, Tootsie left it furnished when she moved to San Diego. I've traded pieces of furniture and stuff since I moved in, but I've never seen it empty. It seems a lot bigger without stuff."

"Most places do. Are you sure you're okay with renting it out?" The question comes out gentle, like he's worried I'm going to have some sort of emotional response to seeing my house like this.

I shake my head, walking over to shut off the kitchen light. "No. I'm good. Plus, it's not like I'm not right next door."

"When does the property management company come to do their thing?"

"They'll open it up for rental applications tomorrow. They've already listed it. They came to take pictures while it still had furniture and have already had a lot of calls about it. They seemed to think it would rent pretty quickly, too. This is a decent neighborhood in a good school district. It's got three bedrooms, so they said it'll probably be a good draw for a small family with kids. Maybe Gus will have someone to play with."

As I start to head back next door after locking up, Joel takes my hand in his. Surprised, I look down at our intertwined fingers, but I can't make myself pull away. He calls for Jethro as he fishes a leash from his back pocket to hook the dog up and, without another word, tugs me down the sidewalk.

Okay, I guess we're going on an evening stroll. As a couple. This is new.

I can't say I hate it.

CHAPTER FOURTEEN

JOEL

I can't say what inspired me to suddenly want to take a walk with Teagan and Jethro; it just seemed like a good idea. It most definitely doesn't have anything to do with what happened by the pool while Jonas and Callahan were visiting. It has nothing at all to do with the way Teagan smelled after packing all day and then getting covered in beer combined with that scent that's just her. It's like this citrusy scent mixed with something tart—green apples, maybe? Whatever it is, on her, it's *good*. It has nothing to do with the way she wrapped her arms around me and seemed to melt against me or the fact that I kissed her neck or the way her breath hitched when I did it.

I sound entirely convincing, I'm sure.

It's not until we've walked to the end of the neighborhood and are nearly back to the house that I realize she's asked me a question and I haven't heard it. "What? I'm sorry, I was spaced out."

She huffs a laugh. "I said that I think Jonas was pretty convinced of everything."

"It seemed that way." I glance at her. "Was he upset about things?"

She considers. "I think upset is too strong. Taken aback, maybe. He did ask if you were blackmailing me or something."

I laugh. "I should be flattered that he thinks I'm that devious."

"He just kept saying that for years, I'd been adamant about not wanting to get married and now, what, I've suddenly decided to settle down?"

"What did you tell him?"

She shrugs. "I mean, I couldn't tell him *everything*, so I told him about the no-kids thing and how I thought no one would want me if I couldn't have kids. I said I knew it wasn't rational, but it was something I'd dealt with for years, but I didn't feel that way anymore. And then he just asked me if I was happy."

It's probably stupid to hope that she actually feels that way, but I still find myself wanting her words to be true. But I don't say anything and just nod as we turn into the driveway of my house. Although, I guess technically, it's hers now, too.

It definitely takes some doing, but we find places for all of Teagan's cans of soups, and after we get done breaking down the boxes we've used, I start prepping supper while Teagan goes to take a shower.

While I'm sauteing onions and breaking down some Italian sausage for spaghetti sauce, my phone rings with a call from Gus. Smiling, I swipe my thumb over the screen to answer. "Hey, buddy."

"Hey, Dad. What's up?"

"Not much, just making supper. How are things up there?"

"Good," he says excitedly. "I got to go with Mom to the

doctor today and see the baby on the ultrasound thing. Did you know baby's heartbeats are super fast?"

My grip tightens on the wooden spoon I'm using to stir the food, and I let out a slow breath. "I did know that, actually."

"It was pretty cool."

"I'm sure," I agree, not wanting to ask questions, but also not wanting to discourage him from talking about whatever he wants to.

"You're still coming to fly back to Florida with me, right?"

I clear my throat. "Yep. Three more days. I've missed you, buddy. Pretty sure Jethro's missed you, too."

"Did Miss Tee ask you if he could swim in the pool? I told her you'd probably be okay with it if she just asked."

I can't help but smile. "Yeah. He's been in there almost every day. I think he uses the pool more than you do."

Teagan comes around the corner, humming some song I can't place. She dressed in leggings and an oversized T-shirt, her hair up in a towel. Her face is bare, and I'd be lying if I said I don't like the look of her so at home here. I probably like it too much.

"Dad, did you hear me?"

I blink to awareness as Teagan takes the spoon from my hand. "Go clean up," she whispers. "I'll finish up."

"Yeah, bud, I'm here. I'm sorry, what?"

"I asked if you and Miss Tee watched the ballgame the other night. Did you see the play at home plate?"

Shooting Teagan a smile, I head back toward the bedroom to shower. "Yeah, it was great. I'm guessing you watched it, too?"

"Yeah, Gramps and I did. He said you made a play like that in high school."

I swallow against the bitterness in my throat at the thought that my father is apparently pretending all of this is completely normal. So he's just content to still talk about me like we're anything to each other anymore?

"I did," I confirm. "Not sure I could do it again, though."

"I don't know; you're still pretty good, Dad." I hear something in the background, and he answers in the affirmative to whoever it is. "Sorry, I have to go eat."

"Alright. See you in a few days. Love you, buddy."

"Love you, Dad. Tell Miss Tee and Jethro I said hi."

"I will," I promise. The call disconnects and I blow out a breath and start the shower. After dragging off my T-shirt and shorts to drop into the hamper, I take a moment to clean up my beard. I'm just about to ditch my boxer briefs to climb under the spray when my phone buzzes with a text. Glancing at the screen, I see it's from Gus, so I open it, all the breath whooshing out of my lungs.

The text isn't a text at all, it's a photo. It's an ultrasound with the caption: *My baby sister, Lily.*

Tears burn my eyes as my hands start to shake, and I don't even register that I've punched the mirror until the sting radiates through my fist. But I don't care. I just keep hitting the glass until a hand on my arm makes me pause as Teagan screams my name.

"Joel, what the hell?" I simply collapse onto the floor, my ass hitting the tile with a thud. The next moment, she's on her knees in front of me, taking my face in her hands. "Hey, what happened? Are you okay?"

The fear and worry in her voice is finally what breaks me out of my trance. I blink, reaching to squeeze her wrists to reassure her, but I grunt with the pain in my hand.

She sighs, gingerly taking my hand in her much smaller one to examine my knuckles. "You're cut up, but I don't think there are any shards in your hand. And I don't think it's broken."

Opening a drawer, she pulls out a washcloth and a bottle of

rubbing alcohol and proceeds to dab my knuckles with the dampened cloth and I hiss with the sting. "You know, they make these nifty things called punching bags if you need to take your anger out on something. Want to talk about it?"

I shake my head and she nods. "Okay." After a few final dabs, she looks over her work. "I'll put some ointment on them after you get out of the shower. Supper should be done by then, too. We'll go get a new mirror tomorrow."

She begins to rise, but I reach for her with my uninjured hand, needing something good in this moment. Teagan is good. God, she's so *good*. She's so much better than I deserve right now with how bitter and angry I am most of the time.

I don't care. Right now, I want to feel something other than bad. I run my hand up her arm, over her shoulder, and up the side of her neck, her breath hitching when I slide it to the back of her neck. When I tug her toward me, she comes willingly, shifting to straddle my lap as she drapes her arms around my shoulders. She leans in, and it's not until her mouth is centimeters from mine that my brain switches on and I pull back, horrified with myself. She deserves better than to be used to make myself feel better in a low moment. She's better than that.

Teagan's brow furrows, confusion blatant in her face, and I shake my head. "I'm sorry, I don't—."

She puts a finger to my lips and searches my eyes, her expression soft and knowing. "It's okay; you don't have to explain." Pulling her hand away, she presses a soft kiss to my lips as she rises. "I'm going to go finish supper. Take your time, alright?" After shooting me a small smile, she pivots, leaving the bathroom.

I stand under the spray until the hot water runs out and even after it turns frigid, I don't move. Eventually, the cold water doesn't even feel cold, so I figure that's probably a bad sign and I shut off the water and hurriedly dry off.

When I emerge from the bedroom dressed in comfy sweats and a T-shirt, Teagan is already sitting at the kitchen table, food at the ready. She offers me a warm smile, pouring me a glass of wine as I drop into my chair. "Thank you," I mutter.

"You're welcome. How was your talk with Gus earlier?" she asks, dishing some pasta and sauce onto her plate.

"Fine," I answer, not wanting to dwell on it and remember reading his text after. I add food to my plate and mechanically shovel it into my mouth and chew, feeling like shit for letting my anger and bitterness get the best of me. I'm feeling extra shitty for almost taking advantage of Teagan. *That* feels unforgivable.

"Good. So, I was thinking, with Gus coming home, we should make his favorite foods and watch a ballgame, hopefully get back to our normal, you know?" I nod and sip my wine, but don't taste it. "Or we can go over to the beach. I haven't been in a few months and I'm sure it would be crowded, but Gus loves the beach, so that might be fun."

I push away my plate, my appetite nearly nonexistent. Teagan's eyes drop to my uneaten food and her mouth draws down in a frown. "Was there something wrong with the sauce? I made it the same way I always do."

"No, I'm just not hungry. I'm sure it's great, Tee."

"Okay. On the bright side, we're in the home stretch. Gus will be back home soon; I'm sure that has to be comforting."

I close my eyes and sigh, pent-up rage, frustration, and helplessness simmering in my chest. "Can you not be so damn cheerful for once? Please? Sometimes, there is no bright side;

no silver lining. Sometimes, things are just shit and there's fuck all you can do about it."

I stand and ball my hands into fists, ignoring the pain that shoots through the knuckles on my right hand. "There is nothing that your perky, hopeful attitude can fix this time, Teagan. I don't want your optimism today. Today, I just want to be angry."

Teagan stands and rolls her shoulders. "Yeah, because being angry has gotten you so far this year, Joel. Does it make you feel better to rail at the sky? Does it feel good to take whatever happened earlier out on me when I don't even know what the fuck set you off? Ooh, the big, scary grump is scary and big.

"You can be as angry as you want, but it won't fix anything. You can break as many mirrors as you want and I'll patch up your hands and replace the broken glass. But if you think that you pushing down all this bitterness and resentment isn't going to someday blow up in your face and all that emotional shrapnel isn't going to land on Gus, you're delusional. I'm a big girl; I can handle it. I'm not afraid of all this, and I'm not afraid of you."

She closes the distance between us and I stiffen, but she doesn't stop reaching for my face to grip my jaw with both hands to force me to look at her. Her eyes are serious and searching and I really don't want her to see me like this, but I guess it's too late for that. "You are trying so hard to keep it together for your kid and pretend like everything is perfect. All these bitter feelings are going to fester and eventually, you won't be able to keep it from coming out in your everyday life and Gus will be the one who suffers.

I start to close my eyes, but she gives me a gentle shake. "You have to talk to someone; even if it's not me. Although, if you wanted to talk to me, you know I'm happy to listen. I want to be there for you, but you cannot keep pushing all this down.

You're going to give yourself a stroke or heart attack, and I need you around. I've gotten kinda used to your surly ass, and I'd miss you if you weren't here."

She lets me go and steps back, returning to her seat to resume eating her food. Resigned, I drop back into my chair, draining my wine. I clear my throat, my chest still aching. "Gus went with Brooke to an OB appointment and got to see the ultrasound. He sent me a picture." Teagan doesn't respond, just takes my hand across the table. "It's a girl and they're naming her Lily." I swallow around the giant lump in my throat. "That's my grandmother's name—my dad's mom's name—and it was always the name we'd picked out for a girl. I'm shocked I'm even shocked by this shit anymore. I just wasn't expecting that; I should've been."

I lift my eyes to hers, hoping she sees how remorseful I am. "I know you were trying to take care of me and I—." My cheeks heat with shame as I drag in a breath. When I speak again, my voice is thick with emotion. "I'm so sorry, Teagan. If we had done anything in that moment, it would have been for the wrong reasons and you're better than that." Tears burn my eyes. "I just wanted to not feel bad for a second and wasn't thinking. There's no excuse for my actions and I swear, I'll never do that to you again. That's not who I am. I'm so, so sorry."

CHAPTER FIFTEEN

TEAGAN

Tears roll down my cheeks seeing the pain and guilt in Joel's expression. Personally, I never felt like he did anything wrong—hell, we didn't even kiss. But he's obviously distraught over the mere thought that he was even considering taking advantage of me.

My heart breaks for this man whose life is nothing like he imagined it would be. And truth be told, I would have been happy to have sex with him if it would make him feel better. People have sex for all kinds of reasons, right? And I'm sure I could probably seduce Joel, but it's obvious he's not built for casual; he said so himself.

Is marriage casual, though?

Mentally shaking the thought away, I focus on the man in front of me. He's still in so much pain from the betrayal of his father and wife, I have no clue how long it will take for him to come out of this. I mean, if he ever can. I know some people live with this sort of betrayal for the rest of their lives.

But I won't be one of those things he's torn up over; not when he did nothing wrong. Giving his hand a squeeze, I shake my head. "You don't owe me any kind of apology; you didn't do anything wrong. Even if we had done anything, I don't think it would've been wrong."

His eyes close as if he's still in disbelief that he even entertained the idea of using sex with me to feel better. If he only knew how many times that's the only reason I went out on a given night. But this isn't about me. It's about Joel. And apparently Joel needs more than words right now.

Releasing his hand, I rise from the table, coming around to sit in his lap, straddling him. Shock flashes through his eyes as I grip his shoulders. "What are you doing?" he asks, his voice still laced with his earlier emotions, but I don't miss how his hands automatically come to rest on my hips.

"Well, I thought I'd start with kissing you and then maybe find out if you actually do have a ten-inch dick," I reply with a slow smile.

Color rises to his cheeks as he swallows thickly. "Teagan, we—."

I shake my head. "Don't you dare say we can't. Doesn't that ring you put on my finger mean we can?" I lean in and run my nose up his jaw, his beard tickling my cheek. Joel inhales a slow breath and I can practically feel his heart pounding through his ribs and into my chest. I can't resist pressing a kiss to the sensitive spot under his ear and his breath catches, his grip on my hips tightening. "You deserve something that's just for you, and I can give that to you. How long has it been since you got to got to bury what I'm sure is an exceptionally impressive cock deep in a hot, wet, tight—."

"Teagan." My name comes out almost like some sort of warning and I'd be lying if I said a thrill didn't shoot through me at hearing him say my name.

I lean back to look at him, my smile smug at the sight of his pupils blown wide and his chest heaving. "Yes, dear?"

His nostrils flare; with what emotion, I couldn't say, but the look in his eyes is barely contained hunger. "It's not right."

I blink. "Excuse me? How much more *right* can we be? We're both consenting adults. We're fucking *married*, Joel. I'm missing the *not right* part."

He shakes his head. "I'm not going to use you like that. Even the thought of it makes me sick."

I lift a brow. "So, you imagine that if we had sex, it would only be good for you?"

His brow furrows. "What? No, of course not."

I can't help but smile. "That's what I thought."

He levels me with a gaze. "That's not the point."

"Is the point that you don't find me attractive, so it would be a chore for you to enjoy sex with me?"

Joel rolls his eyes and scoffs. "You and I both know that's not the case."

I rake my top teeth over my bottom lip until it pops free and his eyes track the movement. "Oh, so you've thought about what it might be like?" He swallows and I let my eyes roam over his features, warmth spreading through my chest at the thought of how good this man is. "I know I've never really done any sort of actual relationship and you've never done casual. Although, to be fair, marriage is inherently an actual relationship and not casual, right?"

"Yeah, but—."

"But, what? You thought about wanting to lose yourself in sex earlier and now you're feeling guilty about it? I'm here to tell you right now, even if I said I can give you what you need, that doesn't mean that I don't know how to take what I want. Consensually, of course."

I take his face in my hands again to search his eyes, hoping he hears how sincere I am. "I don't want to pressure you. I can see you're struggling with what you want to do and what you think is right, and I respect that.

"I know I don't have the greatest—okay, any—track record to prove myself in this, but I'm in this, Joel. I like you as a person and a man and a father. I enjoy living with you and I know there are a lot of things ahead that we can't predict, but this isn't casual for me.

"I'm sure that sounds silly to possibly refer to a marriage as casual or whatever, but until now, you know that's all I've been accustomed to. But I like what we have and I enjoy being married to you.

"And if the reason you don't want to do anything is because you don't like me—you know, as a woman or a person or like a husband should like a wife—then I can respect that, too, because I know you don't sleep with people you're not in a *real* relationship with."

I bite my bottom lip as my heart starts to pound. "And I don't know that I've ever been in love or anything like that, but you are someone who, if I ever did fall in love someday, it'd be with you. You are smart and funny—when you're not a grump-ass—and handsome. You are a good man. I care about you and I care about your son.

"I promised I would never hurt him and so, by extension, that means I wouldn't be able to hurt you, either. Because to hurt you would be to hurt him and I'd never want to do that."

After a last look into his eyes, I give him a soft smile and rise from his lap, gathering up the supper dishes to ferry to the kitchen. After pulling a storage container from the cabinet, I pack up the leftovers and stash them in the fridge.

I always assumed that if I ever got into an actual relation-ship, it would be a daily struggle to avoid boredom and tedium. But honestly, right now, my life is kinda boring, and it's pretty damn nice. And I didn't plan on spilling all the "I'm all in" stuff, but it wasn't a lie and I don't regret telling him.

Humming the chorus to a Sam Cooke song, I rinse the dishes and load the dishwasher, doing my best to not look over my shoulder to see if Joel is still at the table. I want to give him space, and fully understanding that he really may not want to engage in a physical relationship with me, I simply focus on the task at hand.

As I'm washing my hands after wiping down the stove, I pause when the song I'm humming begins to play for real. "Bring it on Home to Me" streams from the bluetooth speaker on the countertop and when I glance over at it, Joel is leaning against the edge of the counter. "You knew what song it was?" I ask, shutting off the water and drying my hands.

He huffs a laugh. "You favor oldies music in the kitchen—mostly Ray Charle, Otis Redding, or Sam Cooke and maybe a little Patsy Cline if you're in a rare sort or mood." He considers. "But I think I've only heard you hum her stuff once or twice."

He folds his arms and crosses one ankle over the other, relaxing against the counter. "When you're in the shower, it's 2000s pop. When you're in the car and traffic is bad, it's emo punk shit that tries to be grunge but will never be grunge."

I huff a laugh and his lips pull up at the corner. "You are the most infuriatingly hopeful optimist I've ever met in my entire life. You push me to talk about my feelings and shit and dammit, I always feel better after I talk to you.

"You know I'm broken, angry, and bitter. Still, you've offered me more kindness and friendship than I could ever hope to repay." He snorts a laugh. "You gave me fucking *socks* with your face on them and made foot and leg puns simply because I was alone at Christmas and you wanted to cheer me up." His smile falls. "You are the only person who's stood by me during this entire shitty ordeal. You are amazing with my son and he adores you." He glances over at Jethro where he snores in the corner. "And your dog's not so bad, either."

Fidgeting his wedding ring, he drops his gaze to it and I'm unsure how to read his expression. "Honestly, I never thought I'd get married again. And if it weren't for the possibility of being able to fight for my son, I probably would've never even entertained your proposition.

"Most days, I'm still so angry and hurt over how people who were supposed to love me unconditionally broke my heart. I don't understand it and I don't know if I ever will. Truthfully, I think there's a part of me that will always be broken now. Any goodness that's left in me is all reserved for Gus, because he's all I have."

Trying not to take his statement as anything other than him speaking his truth, I wrap my arms around myself and try to focus on Joel and what he's trying to say.

"Or, I thought he was all I had." He raises his beautiful eyes to mine and the look in them is open and honest. You could nearly knock me over with a feather since a majority of the time, his gaze is guarded because he holds himself back so much. Right now, I'm dying to know what he wants to be honest about.

"But since Brooke and I separated, you have become my family, Teagan. You have offered me friendship, compassion, and a smile when all I wanted to do was blow up the world. You've been there for my kid and you've been there for me, even when I wanted to hate you for it.

"You've never once badgered me to talk and process my shit even though, most of the time, I suspect you'd like to do exactly that." I shrug, splaying my hands to let him know he's not wrong.

He lets out a slow breath as he pushes off the counter. My heart kicks over as he walks toward me, his eyes not leaving mine, and by the time he's in front of me, my chest is heaving. Planting his hands on the sink on either side of my hips, he bends until we're eye level. I swallow against the ball of nerves that's lodged itself in my throat.

"You asked me if I've thought about what it would be like between us." He closes his eyes and blows out a breath, as if recalling a memory before bringing his gaze back to mine. "Teagan, I've imagined you naked nearly every day since my divorce was final and even more often since that first morning at the cabin and you wore that thing that could hardly be classified as a nightgown. I've imagined fucking you against every surface of any room we're in since the first time we kissed."

My breath hitches, and he gives me a slow smile. "Why do you think I made you go on a walk with me earlier? I was afraid if we came home right after the incident on the pool deck and us packing, I'd have a hard time not wanting to paw you like some wild animal."

His hand comes up to cradle my face, and his expression softens. "The idea that I would ever use you as some sort of outlet for my frustration or anger or whatever is never something I would be okay with. You are not someone I could share myself with like that and it mean nothing.

"You tell me you're all in and that terrifies me, Tee. Because I'm not sure if I can survive my heart getting broken again. Truthfully, I'm not sure there's much left. But if we went all in, I would end up falling for you." I let out a slow breath and his throat bobs with a swallow. "But I'm willing to try. For you, I want to try."

"Really?" I ask, my voice breathy with apprehension and anticipation.

Still cradling my jaw, he says nothing, but simply lowers his mouth to mine. My breath catches in surprise, but I waste no time kissing him back. Where our wedding kiss was sweet and a bit tentative, this one is hungry and frantic. Joel *takes* when he kisses; my sense, my reason, my logic, my breath.

Gripping his hips, I yank him flush against me and run my hands up his shirt, needing to feel his skin under my fingers. He's solid and warm and *mine*. The thought of having someone to call mine and being overjoyed about it is this entirely new and heady thing, and I can't bite back a moan as Joel grinds himself against me.

He slides his hand around to the back of my neck, threading his fingers into the hair at the base of my skull. He tilts my head back as he kisses, nips, and licks his way down my jaw and neck. A groan works its way up his throat and the sound reverberates over my skin, goosebumps scattering down my arms and torso.

"God, Joel." I tug up the hem of his shirt. "Off," I command, and he takes half a second to rip his shirt over his head before returning his mouth to mine. Finally having more of his body to touch and memorize under my fingertips, I trail my hands down his chest and around to his back, the muscles flexing under his skin, reminding me exactly how strong and solid he is.

As if to show me exactly how strong he is, he runs his hands around to my ass, gripping firmly. After a brief second to give it a possessive squeeze, he lifts me easily off the floor, and I inhale sharply in surprise. Instinct has me wrapping my legs around his waist as he continues kissing me while he carefully carries me to the bedroom. When we enter the room, he slams the door with his foot before ferrying me the rest of the way to the bed, his mouth never leaving mine.

He pivots when we reach the mattress to sit, allowing me to straddle his lap. Forced to pull back simply so I can breathe, I examine his face. And even though I can already feel how hard he is and, Jesus, how good this kissing is, I still want to make sure this is something he wants. "This is really what you want? I don't want you to have any regrets, Joel. I know we still have everything with the custody hearing and it could still get messy. We can keep things the way they've been if it's easier for you."

He shakes his head, his expression resolute. "I want you, Tee. I want us. I shouldn't want you to want me. I should want you to run far away from my shit, but I don't want that. I want you for myself; all to myself."

I nod, slowly dragging my shirt over my head. His eyes fall to the thin lace bralette I wear under it, his chest heaving. "Well, you've got me all to yourself right now. What are you gonna do about it?"

He leans in, and kissing a path up my jaw, his breath ghosting over my skin, making my breaths come short. "I have some ideas."

A soft chuckle falls from my mouth as I thread my fingers through his hair and arch my back as he kisses his way down my neck and chest. "And what sorts of ideas would those be?"

He skims his fingers up the outsides of my thighs, gripping my hips to yank me more fully against him. I gasp with the sudden sensation of his dick exactly where I need it, unable to resist rocking my pelvis. He groans, his grip tightening even harder. His beard tickles my chest as he continues to kiss his way down my sternum. "Ones where I make you come so hard you pass out."

I can't help but smile as I pull his face back to mine. "Try me," I say, covering his mouth with my own.

CHAPTER SIXTEEN

JOEL

It's a marathon, not a sprint. It's a marathon, not a sprint. A fucking marathon, Joel.

I have to remind myself or I will break my celibacy in about thirty seconds like some kind of chump. And while I would enjoy those thirty seconds, there's no way I want that to be my first experience with Teagan.

I know what it cost her to say the things she did. Despite us only being married for a little over two weeks, I know my wife. She's my best friend. And knowing her history with men and knowing she's never wanted a relationship, but wants one with me? How can I do anything but jump at the opportunity?

I'm sure it has to do with our increased proximity and the fact that we've had to do some pretending with the PDA as of late. We're both wound tight and I'm sure I could come from a stiff breeze right about now. I don't know what—if any—sort of dry spell she's had, but having seen her not going out much at all since her aunt died and knowing for a fact she hasn't brought anyone home during that time, I'd say she's on edge, too.

Whatever the reason is, I'm happy to be exactly where I am at this moment. To feel her mouth on mine, her hands on my body, her weight in my lap, and *Jesus Christ*, the feel of her ass in my grip. God knows I could come just with her grinding on me, the delicious heat of her radiating through her leggings and my sweats, but again, I refuse to be a chump.

Wrapping my arms around her, I pick her up, flipping our positions on the bed. She lets out a small squeak of surprise, and I can't help but smile. If I thought the weight of her in my lap was great, feeling her beneath me with her knees bracketing my hips is even better. Being able to grind myself against her and listen to the small gasps that fall from her lips is fucking heaven. What will it be like when I actually get inside her?

My hand nearly shakes as I skim my fingertips up her waist. I imagined how soft her skin would feel and how it would be to have her like this, but the reality is more than I could've ever dreamed. She huffs a breath, flinching when I touch a spot just below her ribs, and I raise up to look at her.

"Sorry; tickles," she explains, her breathing labored. I take a moment to appreciate how flushed she is, how big her pupils are, and how swollen her lips are from our kissing.

"Fuck, you're beautiful."

Smiling, her blush deepens, and she bites her bottom lip as if she's suddenly shy. "Thank you."

Bringing my hand up to splay over the left side of her chest, I enjoy the way her heart thunders under my palm. "Your heart is beautiful, too, you know. I know, for whatever reason, you think you've never been cut out for a relationship, but I'm here to tell you, you're great at it."

She breathes a soft laugh, and I raise my hand to her face to cradle her jaw. I look into her eyes as I brush my thumb over her bottom lip, her mouth falling open on an exhale. "How you ever thought someone wouldn't want you for things that don't matter, I'll never know. I understand that what I'm about to say might sound like lip service, but I swear it's not. Your ability or lack thereof to bear children would've never entered my mind if I pursued a relationship with you. Even if I hadn't seen you with my son and knew how amazing you are with him, I would've wanted you. Because you are enough, all on your own." She blinks rapidly, her eyes growing wet, and I give her a soft smile. "But the fact that I get to be the one to prove to you how good you are at this relationship thing and reap the rewards? I'm sure as hell not gonna complain about it."

I trail my hand down her throat before dragging my fingertips down her chest and over the fabric of the lace bra thing she currently wears. "The fact that I get you all to myself? That I get your mind and your heart and this gorgeous body all to myself? Pinch me, because I'm pretty sure I'm dreaming."

She huffs a laugh and I yelp when, a second later, she pinches the skin above the waistband of my sweatpants. "I guess you're not dreaming?"

I snatch her hand away and pin it to the mattress. "It's a figure of speech, Tee. Damn."

She grins, opening her palm to intertwine our fingers as she lets out a slow breath. "And I think you're not the grump you try to be all the time. Although, if I'm the one who gets to see you be a not-grump when no one else does anymore, I'll take it."

I shrug. "I think I'll still struggle not to be an angry asshole."

Teagan brings her free hand up to my face to grip my jaw. "You are allowed to be angry. You're allowed to be hurt and bitter. But you're not broken. I know you think you are, but the fact you're still the you that you were before with Gus tells me you're not. You're so good with him, and I know you're trying to make sure he's not touched by anything that's happened. It is so very admirable, but it's also okay if he sees you hurting. Because shouldn't he know that you're only human? I'm sure you're his hero, but you're not superhuman, and you trying to pretend to be is going to blow up in your face."

I let my forehead fall to her chest and try to breathe as her words wash over me. She runs her fingers through my hair and drops a kiss on the top of my head.

It's not until sometime later, as I'm waking up, that I realize we've fallen asleep. It's almost laughable. I fucking fell asleep when I have a gorgeous and willing woman in my bed after eighteen months with just myself? What the hell is wrong with me?

My thoughts are interrupted by a knock at the front door, followed by Jethro's bark. That must've been what woke me in the first place. A glance at my watch says it's after nine, so I'm at a loss for who'd show up this late. And for the record, if you're over thirty-five and mostly introverted, nine might as well be midnight.

The banging grows more persistent and, leaving Teagan snoozing, I pad down the hall. I pick my shirt up from the kitchen floor, and tugging it over my head, shoo Jethro away from the door so I can peek out through the glass at the top.

I frown, because I don't recognize the woman on my porch, but after commanding Jethro to go lie down—which he does immediately—I open the door. "Yes? Can I help you?"

The woman is in her sixties and petite, with short, dark-blonde hair and blue eyes. It's the eyes that give away who this is. Other than that and the height, there's not much of my wife in this woman who I know must be her mother. At least, until those familiar eyes take me in and her posture and expression morph into one of appraising curiosity, and I see Teagan's personality.

"I'll give my daughter this; she's got good taste. I'm Teresa Roth, Teagan's mother. May I come in?"

I open the door more fully and usher her in. "Yes, ma'am." Extending my hand to shake hers, I offer what I hope is a reassuring smile. "Joel Briggs. Nice to meet you."

She accepts the handshake, and for a small woman, her grip is firmer than I would've imagined. Jethro whines from his bed and Teresa glances at him. She makes a kissing noise, and he bolts to her side, excitedly wagging his tail as the woman affectionately scratches him behind the ear.

"Can I get you something to drink? Water or coffee or anything?"

She stands up straighter, smoothing her hands down the summery tunic she wears over a pair of capri-length leggings. "Red wine if you have it."

I nod. "Yes, ma'am." As I pick up the bottle Teagan and I opened for supper to pour her a glass, I watch as she lifts a framed photo of Gus to examine it. Currently, it sits next to a photo from Teagan's and my elopement. You know, for the public image. Although, I guess not anymore. I nearly smile at the thought.

"This is your son?"

I bring her the glass of wine and she accepts it with her free hand. "Yes. That's Gus."

"And Teagan's met him?"

I huff a laugh. "Yes, ma'am. They're very close."

She returns the photo to its original spot and gives a cursory glance to the one of our wedding. "And how does he feel about the two of you getting married?"

"I'll let you know after we tell him."

Teresa blinks in surprise, but doesn't say anything.

Standing a bit straighter, her eyes drift around the living room. My home isn't some showplace. It's lived in with comfortable leather furniture, scuffed wood floors, dinged walls, baskets of Lego, and board games stacked on a shelf. It's all character that reminds me that Gus lives here. I wouldn't have it any other way.

"So he's not here? He doesn't live with you?"

"Actually, he does. He's been visiting his mother for a few weeks. He'll be back this weekend."

"From my understanding, you've been divorced about a year. Is that correct?"

I nod. "Yes, ma'am. But my ex-wife and I were separated for six months prior to that as well."

She takes a longer sip of her wine. "And may I ask how long you and Teagan have been carrying on?"

Her tone is accusatory, and I square my shoulders. "If you're implying that Teagan and I were in any sort of romantic relationship at any time during my marriage, I'm more than happy to correct your assumption. There was definite infidelity, but it wasn't on my part. We didn't get together until we went to a wedding together."

Her brow tics up at the mention of infidelity, and she nods. "And can you tell me, where is my daughter?"

"In bed."

Her brow furrows, but she nods. "I assume you also know about the falling out between Teagan and her father?"

I fold my arms, unable to stop my jaw from clenching at the memory of the things he said to her. "I actually overheard their last conversation," I reply, my tone chilly.

Seemingly unaffected by my curtness, she takes another sip of her wine. "I see. Well, we all say things we don't mean some-times, and my husband is no exception to that."

"I'm sure if he hadn't meant at least a bit of what he said, he would've already reached out to Teagan to make amends. Last I checked, he hasn't. If he would like to come here himself and apologize to her, it would probably go a long way in working toward those amends. Instead, you're here. I'm assuming it's with in the hopes she'll cave to what your husband said about the money he feels the two of you are entitled to."

Color rises in her cheeks. "It's not as if she needs all of it anyway. You're her husband. Don't you want her to have a good relationship with her parents? Surely you can talk some sense into her about this. To let something this trivial get between us is absurd."

I can't help but wonder if Teagan's parents have always been this manipulative. If that's the case, I say good riddance to bad rubbish and all that. However, this is her mother, so I try my best not to be an outright asshole.

Nodding, I shove my hands in the pockets of my sweatpants. "You're right about one thing; I'm her husband, not her keeper. I have not and will not tell her how and when to spend the money and assets her aunt left her or any other money that's legally hers. So, no, I won't be 'talking sense' into her when she's got plenty to begin with. Seeing as how my ex-wife cheated on me with my father, I'm not sure I'm the right person to encourage someone to maintain relationships with their parents."

Her mouth opens and closes, her shock clear in her expression, and I continue. "You're also right about this entire thing being absurd. It's entirely absurd that you and your husband would let something she didn't even ask for come between you. If anything, I'd assume you'd be overjoyed for her. As parents, don't we want better for our children than what we ourselves had? Don't we want them to not struggle and claw for everything good that comes their way?"

She rolls her shoulders, leveling me with a gaze. "We raised our daughter to show us respect. You respect your parents by helping them when they need it."

"With all due respect, ma'am, respect is earned. And from what I can see, you and your husband aren't being respectful to Teagan, so why should you expect the same from her? Your daughter is not some flighty, immature, spendthrift. If her aunt left her everything she did, I have to assume she had her reasons."

"And what are your reasons?" she asks, her tone again accusatory.

I frown. "My reasons? My reasons for what?"

Teagan's mother downs the remainder of her wine, setting the glass on the table next to Gus's photo. "Your reasons for marrying my daughter." Her eyes drag down my frame. "I mean, I see what she gets out of this. You're handsome, your son is adorable, you have a nice home, and you're obviously intelligent."

Shifting her weight from one foot to the other, she splays her hands. "What do you get out of this? Revenge on your ex-wife by marrying your pretty, younger, next-door neighbor? Having someone to help raise your son without having to worry about providing for additional children? Having someone always willing to share your bed? Living next door, I'd imagine you were privy to the revolving door of people coming and going from her house. Or, is it all about some big payday for you? You thought—."

"That's enough." I'm so beyond livid, the words come out barely above a low growl and it's a wonder she even hears it. It's only when the pain radiates through my hand that I realize I've even balled them into fists in my pockets. I take a couple of deep breaths as I pull my hands out and flex them.

"As the mother of my wife, I will be as respectful as I

possibly can, simply because I care for her. Why Teagan and I got married is no one's business but our own." I take a step forward and she swallows. "You will not speak about my wife as if she's anything other than the amazing, kind, selfless, beautiful, compassionate woman she is. She is the best person I know and if *this*," I gesture up and down Teresa's body, "is what she comes from, it's a wonder she even turned out any kind of decent."

"Mom?" I whip my head toward the hall, where Teagan stands, her face a mask of confusion and pain. My heart sinks knowing she probably heard at least a bit of our conversation. Her eyes don't leave Teresa, who takes another step back. "Is that really what you and Dad think about me? That no one would want to marry me just for me? They would need some sort of ulterior motive to stomach my body count or the fact that I can't have kids?"

I take a step toward her, but she cuts her eyes at me, so I freeze. She closes the distance between her mother and herself. "How much, Mom?"

Teresa frowns. "What?"

Teagan's throat bobs with a swallow and her eyes harden, even as unshed tears shimmer on her lashes. "How much do you and Dad feel like you're *owed*? How much of Tootsie's estate would've made y'all happy?"

Her mother's cheeks turn pink as she takes yet another step back. "We just want our fair share, Teagan; we're not trying to be unreasonable." Teresa drops her eyes to the floor. "We're struggling, honey."

Teagan folds her arms, seemingly unmoved by her mother's admission. "Yeah, because Dad can't stop buying scratchers, you have fifteen credit cards, and cars and a house that are all too expensive. Because you two don't know how to manage the money you have. Because you've made terrible financial decisions. Hell, maybe Tootsie knew you would act like this. She always was a good judge of character."

She huffs a bitter laugh. "I'm guessing if you and Dad had gotten all of Tootsie's estate, you probably would've already spent half of it. Lord knows the money I gave you every month was gone almost before I left the driveway.

"So, what? I cut y'all off after you were so hateful to me for no damn reason after Tootsie's will reading, and now you're desperate? Having trouble keeping the lights on since you don't have me to bail you out every month? I meant what I told Dad the last time I spoke with him. I'd rather see all of Tootsie's money burned in a fire than for you all to see a dime. Now, get out of my house."

Teresa's nostrils flare. "You'll be hearing from our lawyer. We were promised that estate and we'll have it."

Teagan walks over to the door and opens it. "Good luck finding one who will work for IOUs. Goodbye, Mother."

CHAPTER SEVENTEEN

TEAGAN

No sooner has my mother stepped out of the house do I slam the door and lock it, blowing out a breath. In spite of the fact I once again want to crawl under the covers and cry for the things my parents have said, I feign annoyed indifference, rolling my eyes as I turn to face Joel. "I swear, the hits just keep on coming. I don't know about you, but I'm worn out after this day."

Closing the distance between us, I snake my arms around his waist, giving him a wicked grin. "Although, I'm not too worn out to let you finish what you started earlier."

Joel takes my face in his hands as searches my eyes, his expression concerned. "I think I'd rather know how you're feeling."

I shake my head, pushing away the urge to spill my guts over things that I can't change. "And I'd rather you get me naked."

"Teagan, seriously."

Heaving a frustrated sigh, I take a step back. "I don't want to talk about it. What good will it do?"

He splays his hands. "You're the one who always wants to talk about feelings. I'm just trying to return the favor."

I plant my hands on my hips. "Well, for once, I don't want to talk. I'd think you'd recognize the signs." I rip my shirt over my head and hurriedly shuck my leggings. Joel's breath hitches as his eyes, widened in surprise, drop to my underwear.

As I step forward again, his gaze returns to mine. "I'd really, *really* like it if you help me forget about anything but how good you make me feel." I run my fingers down his arm until I get to his hand and, lifting it, I press a kiss to his palm before placing it on my breast.

His tongue darts out to wet his lips as he brings his other hand to settle on my hip to tug me closer. "You want to forget?"

I nod. "About everything except this moment and your hands on my body."

The hand on my breast shifts as his thumb brushes my nipple. I huff a ragged exhale, and he smiles. "And you talk about my scandalous noises."

I trail my hands up his arms to loop around his neck, rising on my toes until our mouths nearly touch. "I'd very much like to hear your noises; scandalous or otherwise."

He lowers his mouth to mine, and whatever leash he's had on his control finally snaps. His kiss is greedy and claiming and I am *here* for it. My heart races as searing heat surges to my lower abdomen, my nipples stiffen to tight peaks, and God, I really hope we finish what we started last time. He shuffles me toward the bedroom as I'm shoving at his sweatpants and tugging up his shirt. He pulls his mouth from mine just long enough to ditch the offending articles of clothing.

The backs of my legs hit the mattress and Joel guides me to sit on the bed, his mouth trailing down my jaw, neck, and chest. When I try to pull him back with me, he shakes his head, wrapping his fingers around the outsides of my knees to yank me flush with the edge of the bed.

He kneels between my spread thighs, continues to kiss his way down my chest and over my breasts, and I gasp when he swirls his tongue over the nipple through the lace. Between the wet heat of his mouth and the delicious friction, I can't stop the moan that works its way up my throat.

I'd love nothing more in this moment than to press my thighs together, but he's in the way. I'm already so close with just him stimulating my nipples, and I curl my hands into the covers, letting my head fall back. "Fuck, Joel," I breathe, and he groans, the vibration causing me to whimper with need.

He yanks down the front of my bralette until both my breasts pop free, and he makes an appreciative noise in the back of his throat as he shakes his head. "Damn. Fucking perfect." He lowers his head again to trail kisses down my sternum, turning his head at intervals to lick, suck, and nip at my breasts and nipples.

When he pulls his mouth off my right nipple with a soft *pop*, my hips buck, and I cry out with the pleasure. I can't resist reaching between my legs to relieve the ache that's settled in, but just as I slip my hand into my panties, Joel snatches my hand away.

"Please," I plead, my chest heaving with my rapid breaths. I'm *this* close and just need a nudge.

He grins up at me as he kisses his way down my stomach, guiding my hand to his hair. "You want something to do with you hand? I can help you with that."

Threading my fingers more fully into his dark locks, I recline onto my other elbow, closing my eyes as his tongue skims under the waistband of my panties. I expect him to drag them off my hips, but he doesn't. He simply presses kisses over the lace as his thumbs brush small circles over my inner thighs.

I can feel his breath, warm and gentle, through the fabric, and I'm nearly trembling with need.

"Have you thought about this, Teagan? What it might be like when I lick this pretty pussy for the first time."

I raise my head to look at him as my chest heaves. "Yeah."

He hooks his fingertips in the waistband of my panties and smiles. "Was I any good?"

I huff a laugh. "In my fantasy? Hell yeah, you were."

Nodding, he tugs my underwear off my hips and down my legs before dropping them to the floor. He kisses his way back up my left leg before hooking it over his shoulder. "Let's see if reality is better, shall we?" he asks, pumping his eyebrows, a wicked grin pulling at the corners of his mouth.

I'm about to laugh again, but it dies in my throat as he licks a lazy line up my pussy to my clit and I close my eyes on a moan. I rock my hips, grinding against his face, tightening my grip on his hair when he sucks my clit into his mouth. Joel's fingertips dig into my thighs as he groans against my heated flesh.

Yeah, this is *so* much better than anything I could've conjured in my fantasies. In my imagination, I couldn't feel his hair between my fingers, his grip on my thighs, or his beard rasping against the most sensitive parts of myself. I also couldn't imagine the way it would feel to hear him groan while giving me pleasure.

My breathing has turned into stilted pants punctuated by "fuck", "don't stop", "just like that", "oh, God", and "Joel". My man takes direction well, because he keeps going, not changing a thing. When electric pleasure shoots through my entire lower body, I cry out, my legs trembling as my back bows off the bed.

Even as I try to breathe, I sit up, pulling his mouth to mine as I wrap my legs around his torso. He grips my hips to scoot me up the bed so he can join me. Meanwhile, I'm dipping my hand into his boxer briefs, needing to feel him. He doesn't stop me, thank God, but he huffs into our kiss when I wrap my fingers around him to give his dick a lazy stroke. I'm thinking maybe he wasn't exaggerating much about the ten-inch thing.

Aren't I a lucky girl?

"Fuck," he groans.

I can't help but smile. "Did you think about this, Joel?"

He drags in a breath. "Too fucking much."

"And has it been better than your imagination?" I ask with a soft chuckle.

He yanks my hand away to shove down his underwear, heaving a relieved sigh when his cock pops free. He settles between my thighs, but seems to consider something, and rises to his knees. "Fuck."

I frown and, sitting up to reach for his face. "What is it?"

"Do we need condoms? I mean, I know you can't get pregnant, but—."

I shake my head. "No, I'm clean and haven't been with anyone since the last time I was tested."

He relaxes. "Me, too."

Giving him a small smile, I lift a brow. "Any other possible roadblocks we need to address?"

"Not a one."

I lie down, pulling him with me. "Then please, for the love of all things holy, come fuck your wife."

Grinning, he lowers his mouth nearly to mine. "Happily." He kisses me deeply before slamming into me, and we both moan. A beat later, I'm forced to break my mouth from his simply to breathe. He doesn't move for several seconds as he rests his forehead against mine. "Fuck. Definitely better than my imagination."

I snort a laugh, threading my fingers through his hair. "Right?" As I rock my hips, we begin to move together, and I let my hands trail down over his body to memorize every ridge and plain. He seems to have similar ideas with his fingertips skimming the length of my arms and sides, my breasts, hips, and ass. He's particularly fond of my ass.

For a long time, our movements are languid and easy, with sweet kisses, playful touches, soft laughter, and smiles, and my heart squeezes unfamiliarly. I can't recall sex ever being like this before. Because while it's more pleasurable than I can recall in recent memory, it's also fun and not at all what I would've expected from Joel; aka, Mister Broody McGrump. But even more than pleasurable or fun, it's also sweet and there's this emotional connection that I don't think I've ever experienced before.

Is that possible? That despite having had countless amounts of sex—even with Jonas—and feeling nothing other than the enjoyable experience of satisfying a physical need, I actually do feel something deeper than physical with Joel? I suppose if it were going to be with anyone, who better than my husband, right?

The thought makes warmth bloom in my chest and I can't help but smile as I reach up to touch his face. His movements never falter, but he brings his gaze to mine, turning his face to press a kiss to my palm. He drags in a lungful of air, his exhale sounding like a contented laugh. "You can't look at me like that or I'm gonna bust my nut."

I huff a laugh as I rock my pelvis harder. "Like what?" I ask with a moan, and he groans through gritted teeth.

"Fuck, Tee."

Keeping my eyes on him, I roll my hips, gasping as my clit rubs against his pubic bone. "Like what? Like I like the way my husband fucks me? Sorry, I can't look any other way."

His jaw clenches, and beads of sweat pops on his brow. I

reach between us to work my clit, watching his face as I get closer and closer to my second orgasm.

His chest heaves, and he drags his top teeth over his bottom lip as his eyes fall to where our bodies are joined and my fingers are buried. "Jesus, that's a sight. You gonna come around my cock? Fuck. Now, Teagan. Shit," he rasps, his brow furrowed in concentration.

Hearing him so lost in his pleasure, my name on his lips, is actually what triggers my release and my eyes close on a sigh, my breaths coming in ragged puffs.

With a final buck of his hips, he tenses, his body shuddering, a low grunt falling from his mouth as his forehead falls to mine. For several seconds, I pepper his face with soft kisses until he pulls out with a groan, dropping to the bed beside me. He wastes no time tugging me into his arms as he heaves a relaxed sigh.

I raise up to look at him, and he rolls onto his back. I fold my arms under my chin as I lay on his chest. "Now see, wasn't that better than talking about shitty shit?"

He laughs, pressing a kiss to my forehead. "Marginally." Sweeping some stray hairs off my forehead to tuck them behind my ear, he searches my eyes, his expression growing sober. "How long have you been giving your parents money?"

I heave a much less relaxed sigh, closing my eyes for a beat. "Since I got my first full-time job."

"So, college, I'm guessing?"

I nod. "Yeah. When they originally started asking for it, they said it was because I was still living at home, but working, I should contribute to household expenses. When I moved here, they'd say they were a little short for the light bill or water bill or groceries. And I'd feel guilty because they're my parents and I didn't want them to struggle.

"As I got older, I realized what was really going on, so I'd only gave them store or restaurant gift cards or I would tell them I'd call to pay their utility bill myself. I refused to give them cash, but I'm sure they probably figured a way around the gift card thing.

"When Tootsie died, they almost seemed giddy. Tootsie was several years older than my mom and never married or had kids. She was also wicked smart; I'm talking genius-level. She actually ended up inventing some stuff and sold her designs and patents for a lot of money. I never knew exactly how much, but I'm guessing my parents had some sort of idea.

"I really thought she'd leave everything to my parents. In the back of my mind, I was concerned about what that kind of money would do to their gambling and shopping addictions. She must've been worried about it, too. Part of me wishes she'd left them at least a little something just so it wouldn't have caused such a rift, but what can I do?"

He gives me a sad smile. "I think you've done exactly what you're supposed to. From what it sounds like, your parents have emotionally manipulated you for most of your life. It takes real courage to break free from that kind of abuse. I hate they felt like they could say that kind of stuff about you."

I shrug. "Like you said earlier, I'm shocked I'm still shocked by them. I shouldn't be. Thank you for standing up for me. It meant a lot."

He nods, a small, sincere smile pulling at the corners of his mouth. "Of course. You're my wife; my family. I've got your back." He rolls me onto my back, slotting his knee between my thighs. As he leans in to kiss my neck, he skims his hand down my chest. "I'm happy to have your front, too."

I huff a laugh, pulling his face to mine. "Amen to that."

CHAPTER EIGHTEEN

JOEL

When I wake up, I'm curled around a sassy brunette who is still snoozing peacefully. We're both still naked, and I can't resist wrapping my arm around her to pull her more firmly against me, burying my nose in her hair. As I breathe in her shampoo and a scent that's wholly her, I can't help but marvel at all that's happened in the last twenty-four hours. It was a roller coaster to be sure, but the way the day ended? Pure bliss.

Judging by the way Teagan is shifting her hips against me, I'm hopeful for more *bliss* in the next few minutes. I nuzzle against her neck and press a kiss under her ear as she makes a sleepy, contented sound that has me smiling. "Morning." She grunts. "You're really not a morning person, are you?" I say with a chuckle.

She grunts again as she shifts her hips, her ass sliding deliciously over my dick. I nip at her neck. "You keep that up and you're going to be very awake in a minute."

Breathing a drowsy laugh, she snakes her hand back to skim her fingertips over my hip and down my leg. "And what a terrible wake up that would be." Her voice sounds gravelly from sleep, and it's sexy as hell.

She rolls toward me, tangling her legs with mine, and brushes a kiss across my chest, her hand trailing down my stomach. She's just grazed my belly button when my phone dings three times in quick succession.

I ignore it, opting to take my wife's face in my hands, but just before my lips meet hers, it rings. She sighs. "You better get it. It might be Gus."

Groaning, I give her a quick peck before rolling over to pick up the offending device, my annoyance rising even more when I see Brooke's name on the screen. Wanting to continue to ignore it, but knowing it could be an actual emergency, I reluctantly swipe the screen and clear my throat.

"Hello?"

"Joel?"

I pinch the bridge of my nose. "You called me, Brooke, so yes, it's me. What can I do for you?"

"Clive is flying to Florida with Gus. They should land in about an hour."

I blink, sitting up straighter. "Excuse me?"

"I started having some symptoms of preterm labor, so they want me on bedrest and Gus doesn't need to see that. It's only a couple of days and I figured it would save you a trip. A thank you would be nice, you know."

I blow out a breath in an attempt to control my rage. "I would've come up to get him. I didn't want him flying down with my father; I thought I made that clear. You didn't even give me the option, Brooke. A head's up that my kid was going to be on a plane would've been nice."

Teagan nudges me and mouths, *chill*. Again, I take a deep breath.

Brooke scoffs. "Jesus, Joel, it's not like he's with a stranger. He—."

"Trust me," I spit out. "I know exactly who he's with. Don't worry, I'll be at the airport. Which terminal?"

"United. Seriously, I don't know why this is such a big deal."

"It's a big deal because he's my kid, Brooke. As the custodial parent, I'm supposed to be informed of travel plans prior to the actual travel."

"We'll see how much longer that is, won't we? I hope Selena's ready to get her ass kicked. Just be at the airport. Or, don't; it doesn't matter to me. Of course, we both know that for Gus, you'll always show up; even when you don't for other people."

"What the hell is that supposed to mean?"

"Nothing. Goodbye, Joel."

The call disconnects and as I typically am whenever I get done talking to Brooke, I'm nearly shaking with rage. I toss the phone onto the nightstand and rub my eyes with the heels of my hands.

A few seconds later, a weight settles into my lap as hands grip my jaw. "Hey. Wanna talk about it?"

I sigh, dropping my hands to Teagan's waist, letting my forehead fall against hers. "I have to get ready to go."

"Gus is coming home today?"

I nod. "Brooke is having some complications or something. My father is flying him home."

"That's good he'll be home; regardless of the circumstances. I know your default is grump-ass, but maybe for Gus, we can try a little optimism? Your kid is coming home today. After over two weeks of only seeing him through a phone screen, you'll get to hug him and ruffle his hair."

"I also get to tell him we got married. I was looking forward to having the entire plane ride to Knoxville to plan what I wanted to say. Now I have, like, forty-five minutes."

"Just tell him that Jethro said he was tired of having to sneak into the pool. He demanded to be allowed permanent access, but he's an old-fashioned kind of dog, so things would need to be legal before he could move in. You had no choice but to marry his mom."

Despite how frustrated I am about my plans being shot to hell, I huff a laugh as I pull back to look at Teagan. "I'm sure that's exactly the explanation that will work."

She gives me a soft smile, pushing my hair off my forehead. "Well, whatever you tell him will be right. You're his dad; his favorite person. It'll be fine."

"For starters, I think you're his favorite person, Tee. I just don't want to fuck up my kid," I admit. "I know we did this for him, but I can't tell him why, and I hate the thought of lying to him."

She nods. "I know. But on the bright side," she leans in to kiss a line down my neck and dear God, I now wish I had time to indulge the ache settling into my balls, "at least, when you tell him we're married, it's not all a sham anymore." She rolls her hips against me, making me groan. "I don't know about you, but I sort of like being married to you."

"You do?" I ask, digging my fingertips into her hips, my words coming out in a pained huff. Okay, maybe I do have a little time.

She rises a few inches, gripping my cock to guide it past her entrance with a moan. "Hell yes, I do." Shifting her hips side-to-side, getting comfortable, she presses a kiss to my lips. I can't help but deepen it; morning breath be damned.

Teagan smiles into our kiss as she rocks her pelvis, finding her rhythm, and I buck my hips, making her gasp. I trail my mouth down her jaw to nip at her earlobe. "Show me how much," I command. "Ride my cock like it's yours."

She moans, and I fuck up into her harder as she pulses around me, her tits bouncing with every thrust. "Fuck, Joel. Shit. Don't stop." Her nails dig into my shoulders, and the sting is just enough to help stave off my climax.

I thread my fingers through her hair, dragging her mouth to mine while I grip her hip hard enough that I'm not sure it won't bruise. "I'm not gonna stop, Tee. Fuck, you feel good. Come for me. I want to feel it."

She whimpers, her own need building, before reaching between us to work her clit, her mouth falling open with a raspy sigh a moment later. As she clamps down around me, I can't hold my own release at bay. I grunt through gritted teeth as I buck my hips a final time, electric pleasure shooting up my spine.

Teagan laughs into the side of my neck a beat later. "Sorry, I just thought you might be in a better mood if you got out of your head for a minute."

I shake my head as I lean in to give her a deep kiss. "Never apologize for wanting to get me off." I give her ass a playful slap as I hurriedly climb from the bed, knowing I'm going to have to rush.

Teagan didn't offer to accompany me and I didn't ask her to come along since she knew I wanted this time with Gus to tell him about our marriage. As I stand at the gate, waiting for my son, I again try to think of the best way to broach the subject with him. Working my wedding ring off my finger to drop into my pocket, a thought occurs to me and I pull out my phone.

> Joel: I'm going to take Gus to lunch to tell him and make sure he doesn't have any questions or wants to talk before we come home. Want me to bring you some food?

Less than a minute later, my phone vibrates in my hand.

> Teagan: I'm good. Take your time. If you need more time after, I can make myself scarce for a while. Just let me know. Good luck. XOXO.

I shoot back a thumbs-up emoji and blow out a deep breath. Just as I'm shoving my phone back in my pocket, I see a familiar flash of dark hair, focusing on the miniature version of myself barreling right toward me. "Dad!" Gus yells, running into my outstretched arms.

I pull him in for a tight hug, feeling like I can finally breathe again. "Oh my gosh, kid, I've missed you. Good flight?"

He nods as we separate. "It was fine. Did Mom call you?"

"Yeah." My eyes snag on my father as he steps up a few feet behind Gus. I don't address him or even look at him fully, but I still say, "Tell your grandfather goodbye, okay?" Because even though I no longer care to have any sort of relationship or connection with my father, my son loves him. So, for him, I will try to muster an ounce of civility.

"Oh, Gramps said he needed to talk to you."

I shake my head. "I'm sure he can tell me later. We need to go; remember me telling you I had something to tell you?"

He blinks. "Yeah, but he said it's important." Gesturing to a bench a few feet away, he takes a step toward it. "I can wait over there. I promise not to talk to any strangers and I won't go anywhere."

I don't react, even though inside, I'm fuming. Knowing my father has gotten Gus involved in wanting to speak with me, I'd love nothing more than to punch him in the nose. Darting a glance at my dad, I return my attention to my son. "Okay. I'll be just a minute. And yes, don't move; don't talk to strangers."

Gus rolls his eyes. "I'm not four, Dad. I can follow basic instructions."

Despite myself, I smile. "Good." Taking a few steps in my father's direction, but turning my body so I can keep Gus easily in my peripheral vision, I fold my arms and lower my voice. "What do you want? And don't ever get my kid to be your messenger again."

"I tried to talk Brooke out of the custody suit; I want you to know that."

I blow out a breath as I pinch the bridge of my nose. "Are you expecting some sort of 'thank you' or something? Although, I guess that didn't stop you from hiring a fancy lawyer for her, did it? Guess you have to do stuff like that for your *wife*, huh, Dad?"

His jaw clenches, but he doesn't react otherwise. I huff a disgusted laugh. "What, nothing to say about that? It's bad enough you had to humiliate me in front of my entire neighborhood and most of my colleagues. How's Gus supposed to explain this as he gets older? Not only did you have an affair with your fucking daughter-in-law, but you *married* her? You're having a baby with her?"

He heaves a put-upon sigh, as though he's regretting even speaking with me. *Good.* "You can't help who you love, Joel."

I take a step closer, bile rising up my throat. "She wasn't yours to fucking love. You also don't steal your son's wife or pretend that any of this is normal. Y'all want to fight me for custody? Bring it on. But for the record, you're dead to me."

Turning away, my father's next words have me pivoting as I barely quell the urge to knock him the fuck out. "What did you say?"

He lowers his voice again when I get closer. "I said you're

going to lose. You and I both know you can't afford a lengthy trial. Brooke just wants more uninterrupted time with Gus. With the baby coming, she wants Gus to have a relationship with his sister." He swallows. "She's your sister, too."

I ball my hands into fists as I roll my shoulders. "Like I said, bring it on. I'm not afraid of Brooke or whatever lawyer you've hired. And if she really wanted more time with him, she wouldn't have moved over five hundred miles away to begin with." I look into his eyes and hope he sees the unbridled hate in mine. "I can't have a baby sister because both my parents are dead."

Turning toward Gus, I give him a smile. "Ready, bud?"

He glances between my father and me as he rises from the bench. "Yeah. One second." He jogs over to give my dad a quick hug before returning to my side. "Can we go get some lunch?"

I ruffle his hair. "My thoughts exactly."

<hr>

After picking up a drive-thru burger, fries, and shakes, I make a detour to a park so I can talk to him before we go home. Sitting at a picnic table in the shade, we each dig into our meals. "Mom's going let me pick out the middle name for the baby."

Not wanting to talk about the baby, but understanding why my son would, I nod. "Oh, yeah?"

He smiles. "Wanna hear it?"

"I want to hear anything you want to tell me, bud." At least, in this, I'm being honest. I love talking to my kid.

"Teagan."

I nearly choke on my burger, my eyes going wide. "What?"

He shrugs. "She's, like, the coolest person ever, and her name is unique."

Swallowing my bite, I clear my throat. "I'm glad to hear you like Teagan, but I'll be surprised if your mom actually uses that for a name."

He frowns. "Why not? It goes with Lily, right?"

"I'm sure, but Teagan and your mom aren't really friends anymore, so she may not want to use that name. Usually, when you name your kids and you choose the name of someone you actually know, it's because you want to honor them. I don't think that applies in this situation."

He takes a drink of his milkshake, considering my answer. "Are you going to be mad at Mom and Gramps forever?"

My son's question takes me by surprise. "Probably," I admit. "But I did really have to tell you something." No way I want to stay on the subject of Brooke and my dad any longer, so abrupt subject change it is, I guess. Wiping my hands on my thighs, trying to dispel my nerves, I blow out a breath. "You still think Teagan is the coolest person ever?"

He grins and nods emphatically. "Yeah."

"Well, what if I told you I also thought she was the coolest person ever?"

His brow furrows. "Then you would be correct."

I can't help but chuckle. "Yes. The thing is, I think she's a lot more than cool. I think she's pretty great." He eyes me with curiosity, popping a couple of fries into his mouth.

Just fucking spit it out already, man.

"In fact, I think she's so great, that I married her and asked her—and Jethro—to move in with us."

His eyes go wide as he stops chewing. "You and Miss Tee got married? Like Mom and Gramps? Are you going to have a baby?"

I choke on my drink, milkshake spewing from my mouth as I cough. Mopping my beard, I shake my head. "No, we're not having a baby. We're not going to have any kids; it'll just be you.

And it's a little different than your mom and grandfather. But we got married. It wasn't something we planned on, but after I dropped you off with your mom, I was kinda bummed and Teagan asked me if I wanted to go to a wedding with her."

"Like, as her date?"

"Yeah," I agree. "But we spent some time together and realized we really like each other. She loves you and you seem pretty fond of Jethro, so at least this way, he doesn't have to sneak into the pool anymore. He can get in whenever he wants."

Gus chews a bite of his burger, nodding as he absorbs my words. After a beat, a huge smile crosses his face as he says, almost as if to himself, "It worked."

Confused, I frown. "What worked?"

He blinks as though he hadn't meant to say it out loud. Color creeps into his face as he looks anywhere but at me. "Nothing."

My dad antenna immediately goes up, and I narrow my eyes. "Augustus, is there something you want to tell me?"

My use of his whole name makes him sober and drop his burger onto its wrapper. I so rarely pull it out that it still has quite the effect on him when I do. "You're married? Like, legit married? You can't take it back?"

I huff a laugh. "No, not without a lot of legal trouble. But I don't want to take it back. Can you tell me what worked?"

Guilt flashes through his eyes. He drops his gaze to the table, suddenly looking a lot younger. "Jethro didn't escape from the yard. I let him out and acted like he did."

Unsure what that has to do with me marrying Teagan, I simply wait to see if he elaborates. He still doesn't look at me as he fidgets with his burger wrapper. "You were so sad and mad all the time after Mom moved out. The only time you weren't was when we would hang out with Miss Tee. I thought if you spent more time with her, you might not be so sad. You always seemed to be in a better mood after she left. I also thought you might think she was pretty, because you'd always watch her walk home and you'd get this goofy grin on your face."

He shrugs. "I figured if you and Miss Tee started going out, you might smile more and maybe stop being so mad at Mom and Gramps."

I almost want to laugh at the thought that Gus was trying to play matchmaker in his own way. Although, knowing how bad a job I did trying to hide my sadness and anger from him makes me feel like shit. Even so, I also don't want him to have false hope that I'll ever be able to have any sort of relationship with my father or Brooke ever again.

"Yeah, I guess it did work. And I was really sad and mad when your mom moved out. I'm still sad and angry sometimes and I'm sorry you've had to see that. I don't know if I'll ever not be mad at your mom and Gramps again. I'm sorry I can't tell you that I'll be able to get over things. When you're older, you might be able to understand all this stuff a little more. And just because I am happy with Teagan doesn't mean that I'm not still mad and sad about what happened with your mom."

"You're really mad at Mom and Gramps because they kissed, right? And you're not supposed to kiss people when you're married to other people?"

I nod, thankful he's boiled things down to their simplest parts. "Yeah. Just because Gramps wasn't married when he and your mom kissed doesn't make it okay, because I was married to her."

"So, it's like you getting a birthday gift that you really like and someone comes and takes it before you're done with it?"

"Sort of," I confirm.

"But Mom and Gramps got married, so it's okay now?"

I blow out a breath. "I think they think it makes things

okay; that's not really for me to say since I don't know their minds or hearts. But it's never okay to take something that isn't yours. Whether that's someone's money or their wife. You see, when you get married, you make these things called vows. Marriage vows say that you will only kiss the person you're married to. You make the promise in front of other people so they know you mean it. When you make those vows, it's like locking it inside your heart. But when the vow gets broken, a lot of times, your heart does, too."

"You had a broken heart?" he asks somberly.

I nod. "Yeah, I did. Because I made vows to your mom and she made vows to me. Also, when you're a parent, you're supposed to put your kids first. Your mom broke our vows and your grandfather didn't put me first when he kissed your mom."

He considers my words. "So, when you make vows to someone else, does it help fix your heart?"

I sigh. "I'm not fixed, if that's what you're asking. My heart is still a little broken. It's like when you break a plate and try to glue it back together. It still works and you can use it with new foods and stuff, but it might be a little more fragile."

He frowns. "But you and Miss Tee made vows, right? Promises?"

I nod, smiling. "Yeah, we promised that we'd be there for each other and spend our lives together."

"And you kiss Miss Tee?"

Laughing, I nod again. "Yeah. I like kissing her." That feels like the understatement of the year.

"Good. And Jethro likes living with us?"

"Are you kidding? He loves it. Want to go home and see him?"

CHAPTER NINETEEN

TEAGAN

Jethro whines from his spot on the couch as I continue to pace, chewing my thumbnail. I know Gus's plane landed over an hour ago, but despite checking my phone several times, there's no update to how things went. When the barks, tail wagging, I stop in my tracks. As he jumps off the sofa, running to the interior garage door, I finally hear what he must've already: two truck doors slamming.

I try not to feel nervous, even though I'm about to come out of my skin. I've showered and dressed in a casual T-shirt dress, and braided my hair back in the hopes of making a good impression. It's so strange; the feeling of insecurity when it comes to Gus. It's not that I'm worried he won't like me anymore; the kid's my buddy. I only worry that him learning of Joel's and my sudden nuptials will somehow change something between all of us.

The door swings open, Gus's eyes lighting up when he sees Jethro. The boy and dog greet each other affectionately and I hope it's a good sign that my stepson doesn't seem surprised Jethro is in the house.

Joel nudges him, saying something I can't hear, but then Gus's head snaps up, his eyes locking with mine, a big smile creasing his face. It's not until that second I actually relax. After a final scratch behind Jethro's ear, the boy jogs over.

"I swear, I think you've grown a foot. They got some kind of special food up there in Dollywood?"

He smiles. "Nah, you've just shrunk."

I snort a laugh as I ruffle his hair, and he examines me. "So, what am I supposed to call you now?"

Frowning in surprise, I glance at Joel, but he shrugs. "Tee or Teagan, same as always. You know me, I'll answer to anything. Nothing's changed, bud."

"Except you and Jethro live here now, right? And you and Dad kiss?"

I nod. "Well, yeah. I guess those things did change. But the important stuff hasn't. We'll still watch ballgames and order pizza and at least now, Jethro won't have to escape the yard to get to the pool. All he has to do is walk out the back door."

Gus's eyes widen slightly, and he swallows. "I'm going to go unpack. We're watching the game tonight, right?"

Confused by his expression, I nod. "Yeah, sure." As he passes me to go to his room, I pat his shoulder. "Welcome home, Gus. We missed you."

He tosses me a grin as he walks into his bedroom, Jethro padding behind him. Turning to face my husband, I jerk my thumb over my shoulder. "What was with his face when I talked about Jethro? Did I miss something?"

Joel settles his hands on my hips, tugging me toward the laundry room, out of earshot of Gus. When we get there, he presses me against the wall next to the door. It doesn't escape my notice that we are also out of sight, but would be easily able to hear Gus's bedroom door open.

I trail my hands up his arms to loop around his shoulders.

He leans in to kiss me as though it's been way longer than two hours since he left the house. Moments later, when he finally pulls back, both of us short of breath, I huff a laugh. "Well, that was a nice hello."

He grins. "What can I say; I missed my wife."

"Is your dad still among the living? Or did you not see him?"

He sighs, his eyes falling closed for a beat. "Yeah, I saw him. Yes, he's still alive. Physically, anyway. I told him he was dead to me, so emotionally, he's gone."

I bring my hand up to grip his jaw. "I'm sorry. Other than that, was everything okay, though? With telling Gus, I mean. He seemed kinda cool with it, but I just wanted to make sure he wasn't putting on some sort of front."

"Turns out," Joel says, an amused smile pulling on the corners of his mouth, "Jethro wasn't actually escaping the yard."

I frown. "What?"

"Gus was an accomplice. He was letting Jethro out of the yard so you'd have to come over to get him. You know, since you and I would always talk when you came over." His eyes soften. "He said he thought I was always in a better mood after you left and if we spent more time together, I might not be so sad or angry after everything that happened. When I told him, he got this look on his face like he couldn't believe his luck. He was just like, 'Huh. It worked.' So, looks like he masterminded this whole thing."

He considers what he just said. "Well, actually, his goal was for us to date, but I'm guessing this is even better."

My mouth falls open in delighted shock. "That little sneak. Looks like he gets all the gifts for Christmas this year, since I already have everything I want." I pump my eyebrows suggestively, my smile taking over my entire face.

Joel snorts a laugh. "Jesus, that was cheesy. Adorable, but cheesy."

I give him a saucy shrug. "Yeah, but you kinda like me, so it's okay."

His eyes darken with hunger as his smile turns decidedly more wicked. He plants his hands on the wall on either side of my hips as he leans in. "I do like you. I like you naked, clothed, and everything in between. I like you on my fingers, tongue, and cock. I like you in my bed, and I suspect I'd like you pretty much anywhere else." He bends to brush a kiss down the side of my neck and my breath hitches. I grip his waist to pull him closer. "I like it when you make that little sound, and I fucking love it when you say my name."

Heat pooling low in my belly, I tug up the hem of his shirt to begin working the fastenings of his jeans. As I slip my hand into his underwear to wrap my fingers around his length, giving him a lazy stroke, Joel groans into the side of my neck. "Fuck, Tee."

I let out a soft, sultry laugh, adding pressure to the head as I come back down his shaft. He hisses, rocking into my grip. "I like it when you say my name, too. And damn, I love the way you feel." Going up on my toes to nip at his bottom lip, he chases my mouth with his own, gripping the back of my neck to kiss me properly.

With his free hand, he gathers up the fabric of my dress, running his fingers up the inside of my thigh as he nudges my knees wider with one of his own. "Open up for me, sweetheart; I want to feel how wet you are for me." I widen my stance, and he smiles, sweeping a knuckle up the outside of my panties to brush against my clit. I huff a ragged breath as he increases pressure, making me pant. "That's it."

Momentarily distracted by his hand, I've stopped moving mine, and resume fisting his cock. He clenches his jaw as he drags in a breath. Needing more friction to get closer, I roll my hips, grinding myself against his hand.

I let my head fall back, closing my eyes to simply *feel*. Then suddenly, I feel nothing. Well, nothing except the absence of Joel's hand or body as he jerks away. I pop my eyes open to see him hurriedly fastening his jeans. It's only then that I hear the footsteps and I sigh.

Cockblocked by a ten-year-old.

Definitely not something I thought I'd ever have to deal with. Even so, I can't be mad about it as I follow Joel out of the laundry room after ensuring my dress is correct.

He tugs me to his side, whispering in my ear as Gus passes us on the way to the laundry room with his dirty clothes. "Welcome to parenthood. You get your kicks when you can and get foiled by tiny people who have no idea more often than you'd imagine."

I huff a laugh. "I think we'll survive."

He scoffs, but it's with a grin. "You might, but I think you're forgetting that I was celibate for over eighteen months. My body's been starved and I'm allowed to feast again. And God knows I'm still hungry."

Giving him a playful shove, I roll my eyes as I'm unable to keep the smile off my face.

Because of a rain delay, our plans to watch a baseball game get derailed. So after a supper of takeout pizza and brownies I'd made while I was stressing about how things would be when Gus got home, we all decide to take a walk. Gus has Jethro on his leash, walking a few feet ahead as Joel and I walk hand-in-hand, same as we did last night.

Occasionally, Joel will pull me to him for a quick kiss or to whisper something dirty in my ear, and I'm not sure I've stopped blushing or smiling since we left the house.

"Hey, Dad?"

Joel looks ahead to Gus, who doesn't turn around as he continues to walk. "Yeah, bud?"

"Will I get to go see Mom after the baby's born?"

"Probably. It'll depend on when she has the baby. You may only get to go up for a weekend or something, but we'll make sure you get up there, okay?"

"Mom said she might be moving back to Florida."

Joel and I exchange a glance. "Yeah? Where to?"

He shrugs, patting Jethro's head when we get to the stop sign, ready to make the return trip home. "I'm not sure. She just said after the baby was born, so probably sometime after next month."

A look at Joel tells me he'd love to say something uncharitable, but true to his nature where Gus is concerned, he simply lets out a slow breath as he chooses different words than what originally came to mind. "I'm sure you'll be happy to have her closer again."

As we lie in bed later, I roll to face Joel, who's currently reading. Propping myself on my elbow, I simply watch him for a moment. I'm not surprised, exactly, that he reads in bed. He's a smart guy, and I always assumed he had more hobbies than simply watching sports and working on his truck.

If I ever did imagine him reading, I would've said John Grisham, Stephen King, Michael Crichton, or some sports-related biography. I would've never expected him to read Carl Sagan. Casually reading about astrophysics isn't at all what I pictured. Knowing he might be a closet brainiac? Well damn, that's downright sexy.

I don't interrupt his reading because, duh, that's rude. I simply wait for him to get finished and when he slides a weathered Derek Jeter baseball card into the book to mark his spot, I can't help but smile. He lays the book on his nightstand and lies down, mirroring my position. "What's that face about?"

"You read astrophysics and use a baseball card as a bookmark? It's interesting is all. Carl Sagan, really?"

He shrugs. "I think it's good to stretch my brain. Plus, Sagan is super quotable."

I lift a brow as I walk my fingers up his bare chest. "Oh? What's your favorite quote?"

Lifting my hand from his chest, he brings it to his mouth to press kisses to my fingertips before moving to my palm. "Well, he's got one about extinction being the rule and survival being the exception. I like that one." His lips trail up to the inside of my wrist and he nips at the sensitive skin, making my breath hitch.

A small smile pulls at the corners of his mouth as he brings his eyes to mine. "He also said something like—and this is a total paraphrase, so I'll probably butcher it—'because we're such small creatures, the vastness is only bearable through love'. I'm pretty sure he was referring to the universe, but I think it's applicable to life, too. Life is vast while we live it and without love, is there even a point to the whole damn thing?"

"So, you're also a philosopher? Who knew my husband was such a renaissance man?"

His smile turns cocky. "Hey, I'm more than a pretty face, I'll have you know."

I nod, running my hand up his jaw to slide around to the back of his neck. "But, oh, what a pretty face it is. And knowing how big your brain is, too? I might as well swoon."

He chuckles as he leans in to press his lips to mine, shifting on the bed until he's between my legs. I bring my knees up to bracket his hips as, he sighs into our kiss. He doesn't seek to deepen it and nor does he seem to be initiating sex. Honestly, I'm content to simply feel him close to me like this.

Discovering that I have actual feelings for Joel was like finding a hidden room in an old castle. It's not something you expected and the journey to figure out where the room leads is definitely exciting. I sure am enjoying this journey.

He pulls back to peer down at me, his expression relaxed, and I rest my hands on his jaw. "Are you happy Gus's home?" He nods, but he doesn't smile like I expect him to, and a beat later, his expression morphs to one of concern. "What's this face about?" I ask with a frown of my own.

He huffs a breath through his nose. "Brooke doesn't do something for no reason."

"Elaborate," I encourage.

He drops back to his side of the bed, scratching his beard in thought. "Gus said she's moving back to Florida. I can only think of a few possible reasons she'd do that."

"And those are?"

Looking across the room, but not really focusing on any particular point, he counts off the reasons on his fingers as he continues to brainstorm. "One, Brooke is going to quit working after the baby comes, so she doesn't need to be in Tennessee anymore. Two, she's gotten a new job down here. Three, Dad doesn't want to stay in Tennessee and misses the ocean." His jaw clenches and he swallows. "Four, her lawyer said she needed to move before the hearing so she can appear to be a team player. She'll spin it as if I'll be able to see Gus all the time if she gets custody, when in reality, she'll move as soon as the gavel drops if it goes in her favor."

"She's only human, you know. She's not some devious

mastermind. Maybe she does finally want to be closer to Gus. You know she's not my favorite person, but I'm willing to give her the benefit of the doubt when it comes to Gus. Maybe she wants him and the new baby to be able to bond and have a good relationship. Sort of hard to do when they're over five hundred miles apart."

He huffs a laugh, pressing a kiss to my forehead. "While I love and appreciate your optimism, I will continue to be my grumpy, cynical self where Brooke is concerned. Besides, I think you underestimate how devious she is. Let's hope that side of her doesn't factor in, but I'm not holding my breath."

CHAPTER TWENTY

JOEL

Fucking hell, I hate being right sometimes.

As I stand out on the back deck with my cup of coffee, tossing Jethro's tennis ball into the pool for him to fetch, I watch in equal parts horror and rage as a moving truck, followed closely by a very familiar black minivan, pull in next door. My conversation six weeks ago with Teagan about not underestimating Brooke comes flooding back as I watch my ex-wife exit her vehicle.

Honestly, I'm shocked she's even been cleared to travel yet. She just gave birth a week ago, for crying out loud. Is she seriously going to direct movers and setup house this soon after delivery? As if in answer to my thoughts, she straps a tiny pink bundle to her chest and begins doing exactly that as furniture is pulled from the back of the truck.

"This is a joke, right?"

Teagan's question, spoken only loud enough for me to hear, snaps me out of my thoughts. I sip my coffee, rolling my shoulders before tossing Jethro's ball once more. "Looks pretty real to me."

She blows out a breath and sips her own coffee, tugging me out of sight of the interruption to what's left of my sanity. "Okay, I know you said she was devious, but really? My house? Next fucking door?" she asks through gritted teeth. "How did she even find out my house was available for rent? It's not like I had a sign up. Besides, the rental company had people interested in it before it was even listed and had a tenant lined up two days after it was opened up."

A shrill, grating sound has me choking on my coffee as Teagan's eyes go wide. "You have got to be fucking kidding me." She peers around the side of the house before balling her hands into fists. "Fucking nosy, busybody bitch."

I don't even have to look to see that Ellen and Brooke are embracing like long-lost sisters. "I guess we know how she found out. Nice of Ellen to keep Brooke apprised of all the neighborhood goings on." Unable to stomach hearing the sounds of the two obviously gleeful women, I pull Teagan back into the house as I call for Jethro, who obediently climbs out of the pool and shakes off.

While we grab towels to tag team drying the dog, my wife shakes her head. "This will be fine. If anything, it's a good thing."

I pause reaching for one of Jethro's paws. "I'm sorry, how exactly is my ex-wife, my father, and their baby moving in next door a good thing? You know I love your optimism, but I'm not seeing the upside here, Tee."

"She signed a lease. It's for a year. So, barring anything major, she's here for at least the next year. Even if she wins sole custody, Gus will be right next door. Or course, I don't think she will, but I'm just tossing out ideas."

"I'm going to be patiently waiting for the other shoe to drop, thanks."

As he's mostly dry, Teagan shoos the dog away and we

stand to hang the towels on hooks in the laundry room. After refilling both our coffees, she wraps her arms around my waist. "What shoe? Nothing has changed since the last hearing except you've both remarried and she's had a baby and moved next door. If anything, it just makes her look flighty moving so much in a short period of time. And not that they can take into account the fact that she married her ex-husband's father, but it's just tacky."

I open my mouth to tell her she might be surprised exactly what the courts consider, but she goes up on her toes and presses her lips to mine. "No more talking," she commands, her mouth still smooshed to mine. "Gus is at camp and we have an hour before he's back. Come make love to your wife where she doesn't have to be quiet."

Despite how annoyed I am, I smile as I pull back. "Not quiet, huh?" I shuffle her back toward the bedroom. "How not quiet can you be?"

"Why don't you come and see?"

"Oh, I plan on coming," I quip, quickly bending to pull her over my shoulder into a fireman's carry. She squeals, and I give her ass a playful slap as I ferry her to our room.

It strikes me that in spite of knowing Brooke will now be living next door, I'm happier than I've been in a long time. It shouldn't feel as though all the shit that happened in the last couple of years happened to someone else.

In truth, nothing much has changed except I finally spilled all my shit to Teagan and she's helped me shoulder my grief and anger. She's seen me broken, and has only ever offered me compassion, kindness, and acceptance. She doesn't expect me to be in a good mood all the time and just rolls with my grumpy ass.

Oh, and I'm having sex again. Lots and lots of fantastic sex with a beautiful woman who also happens to my best friend. It's a pretty sweet life I've got here, not gonna lie.

The kid and dog are pretty good perks, too.

As I toss Teagan onto the bed, she giggles. I tug my shirt over my head before planting my knees between her legs, bracing my weight on one arm while I cradle her jaw with my free hand. She's currently still in her nightgown, the fabric riding high on her thighs. *Damn*, I could sink my teeth into her supple flesh.

I let my gaze wander over her features that, during the past ten years, I've memorized, and now get to see every day. I get to wake up to see this face and fall asleep with her kiss lingering on my lips. I am one lucky bastard.

"God, you're something, you know that?"

She blushes, skimming her hands up my ribs. "And what am I?"

Bending to brush soft kisses across her lips, cheeks, jaw, and down her neck, I can't help but smile when her breath hitches like it always does. She tilts her head to allow me better access and I take full advantage of being able to kiss, lick, nip the swath of skin.

"For starters," I supply as I drag the tip of my nose along her jaw, "you are a passible driver and your cooking's not terrible."

She snorts a laugh, and I trail my hand down her chest to cup her breast through her nightgown, a huffed exhale leaving her mouth when my thumb brushes her nipple.

"For another thing, you're not a morning person, and lord help anyone who gets between you and your coffee, but you'd give a total stranger the shirt off your back."

Her eyes flash with mischief as she shimmies her night-gown up and over her head before tossing it to the floor. "I don't need a shirt right now anyway."

I can't bite back the noise of appreciation that works its way up my throat at seeing her in only a pair of panties. "It's not incredibly difficult to look at you." She chuckles, brushing my hair off my forehead, and I can't stop looking into her eyes. "Your morning breath could use some work, though."

She gives me a playful jab to the ribs, and I snatch her hand, pinning it to the bed. As I shift to lower myself until I'm pressed against her, there's no way she can miss how hard I am. Rocking her hips, she doesn't break her gaze from mine, even as her mouth falls open on a soft moan.

"You are smart, funny, and eternally sunshiny, even if you have lots of reasons not to be. You are a great partner, stepmom, and dog mom." Her expression softens, and she bites her bottom lip. "You are a good friend and an amazing wife." Blinking rapidly, she lets out a slow breath and I still don't take my eyes from hers. "You are the best friend I've ever had and I'm thankful I get to share my life with you."

I drop my forehead to hers and breathe her in. She runs her hands up my arms, over my shoulders, and up the side of my neck to thread into my hair. "You think you're not cut out for love, but that's exactly what you were made for, Tee. All you've done since we met was love me, exactly as I am, even when it was just as a friend. Because when you love someone, you're selfless with them."

Pulling back to look at her, I don't miss the wetness on her lashes. "You've been so incredibly selfless with me. You've offered me friendship, a shoulder to cry on, and an opportunity to fight for my kid while asking for nothing in return. You gave up your house and your lifestyle and you've fit yourself into a life you probably never would've asked for.

"And God, if I wasn't already in love with you," I close my eyes for a beat as I swallow against the lump in my throat, "seeing how you love my kid would've been enough to push me over the edge. Seeing how much you were willing to sacrifice for him? Jesus, how could I not love you?"

"Joel," she says, her voice thick with emotion.

I shake my head. "I don't expect you to say it back, and honestly, I don't think this was ever how I would've planned to tell you I love you for the first time. But I realized that despite the shit with Brooke and all the stuff coming down the way and all my feelings about that, I'm happy. I'm happier than I can remember being in a long time. I know it's because you've helped me piece my heart back together.

"I was so angry and pushing all that hurt and bitterness down. If we hadn't been at the cabin with no one but each other for company and nothing to do, I'm not sure I would've actually spilled all of it. But finally letting some of it out, I think it helped. That was because of you. I wouldn't trade any of it, though, because I am happy. I have you and Gus and that's all I need."

Tears roll down the side of her face into her hairline as she pulls my mouth to hers. She rolls her hips, and I can't bite back a groan as she grinds against me. I relish the feel of her skin under my fingers, the smell and taste of coffee on her, the sounds she makes when I slip my hand into her panties to search out her clit.

She breaks her mouth from mine, gasping for breath. "Joel, oh God. Please," she whines and I yank my hand out and practically rip her underwear down her legs. I retake my position, and still bracing my weight on one arm, look down at her as I slide two fingers inside her, crooking the digits against her g-spot, making her cry out.

"That what you wanted, sweetheart?" Giving me a jerky nod, she attempts to pull my face down to hers, but I shake my head. "No, I want to watch you get off. I love to see you come. Can you do that for me?"

Her head falls back on a long moan as I circle her clit with my thumb. I enjoy watching the flush that travels down her face and chest, along with the way the tendons in her neck go taut the closer she gets to her orgasm. "Fuck, Joel. Don't stop. S-so close."

I can feel it, too. Her pussy pulses around my fingers and I can almost countdown to when she lets go with a ragged sigh, her chest heaving as I withdraw my hand. "Jesus, I could watch that all day."

Teagan huffs a laugh as she leans up to capture my mouth with hers for a quick kiss. "Dare you to do it again."

Chuckling, I shove down my shorts and boxer briefs, kicking them off before settling between her legs. I hook one of her knees over my elbow, dropping my gaze to watch my cock sink home. Fuck, that's a sight I don't ever want to forget; or the sound she makes every time I enter her. It's a breathy moan that makes my blood heat and my dick throb.

I'd be lying if I said that Teagan wasn't the best sex of my life. Not that I have a ton of experience or anything since I can count on one hand the number of women I've slept with, but it's just different with her than it's ever been with anyone else. Some might say it's only because it's new, but I don't remember it ever being this fun and explosive with others.

I've always considered myself to be a normal man with a typical sex drive. Honestly, though, I feel like I'm ready to go at just a word or glance from Teagan. And her body is always ready with the least bit of coaxing. I'm sure as hell not going to complain about it.

God knows I'm not complaining right now. Right now, I'm in fucking paradise. Watching her tits bounce with each of my deep thrusts and feel her nails dig into my shoulders as her breathing turns into stilted pants. Seeing her eyes light up when I dirty talk her and give her praise. Feeling how pliant and yielding her body is under my hands. Hearing her beg for more as she pleads for me not to stop. Listening to my name on her lips as she comes, clenching down so tight around me, I can't do anything but follow her over into my own release with a low grunt, entirely spent but still wanting her. I'm not sure I'll ever stop wanting her.

When I collapse beside her on the bed, she rolls, settling on my chest, her arms folded under her chin, her breathing labored. "You know, I kinda like this whole married sex thing."

I huff a laugh as I fold one arm behind my head so I can prop my head up and see her better. "Yeah? What do you like about it?"

She inches up my chest to press a kiss to my lips. "I like how I no longer have to endure some fuckboy's incessant chatter about his fantasy football league simply for the possibility of mediocre sex."

I nod, understanding how that sort of lifestyle could get old, even if it could be exciting for a while. I'm sure at some point, everyone gets to the point where they need more mental stimulation to fully enjoy an interaction. "So, would you say all the sex you've had prior to now was mediocre? I mean, not that I don't find that idea flattering, but surely some of it was decent."

Teagan chuckles. "Yeah, some of it was actually great. And when that was the case, I'd usually try to at least keep them on the roster for future hookups."

"So, like Jonas?"

"Would it be weird to talk about him?" she asks.

I shake my head as brush a stray hair off her forehead. "No. Besides, my ex-wife is married to my father and they now live next door. With their baby. I hardly think us talking about your best friend who was your steady hookup for a decade registers as weird for us."

She shrugs, a thoughtful frown pulling down the corners of

her mouth before her gaze returns to mine. When it does, it's serious as her eyes search mine. "I never felt anything with anyone. I mean, yeah, it was good a lot of times, but it was only physical. I never felt more than just the physical with them. I thought there must be something wrong with me."

I frown in dismay at what she'd think about herself. "There's nothing wrong with you."

She nods, her expression warming. "Oh, I know. Because I feel things with you." Color rises to her cheeks, and she gives me a sexy smile. "And more than just your massive dick."

I can't help but laugh. "Thanks."

Teagan sobers. "I'm serious, Joel; I have real feelings for you. It's scary for me, but I know how vulnerable you've been with me and I'm sure that's difficult for you. I can't tell you I love you yet; I wish I could. I have feelings that are a lot more than 'like', but I don't think I'm quite there yet."

Knowing she has feelings beyond friendship and the physical connection we share is huge for her, and I take her face in my hands. "I didn't say it because I expected you to say it back. That's not something I'd ever want because I don't want you to say things you don't mean. But someday, if you ever do feel like you're ready to say it back, I will be honored because I'll know you mean it. Until then, I'm just happy to be exactly where I am."

She smiles, giving me another kiss before lifting my wrist to check my watch as she sighs. "Gus will be home in twenty minutes. Guess we should probably not look like we just crawled out of bed when he gets back, right?"

I snake my hand down her back to give her butt a possessive squeeze. "But I like it when you look like you just crawled out of bed. It reminds me of what we just did."

She chuckles, amused, and nods. "Be that as it may, I need

a shower. He's going to be starving when he gets home. Why don't you go whip up some waffles?"

"Waffles, huh?" She rolls to leave the bed, but I yank her back against me, nuzzling her neck. "What if I'd rather join my smokin' hot wife in the shower and we can order pizza?"

She gasps when I nip under her ear. "You're insatiable. But I could do pizza if you're going to keep that up," she says as I massage and knead her breast, plucking her nipple between my fingers.

"We'd have to hurry."

She laughs. "You started this, so I think you're the one who needs to remember that."

"I was reminding myself," I supply, and she laughs again.

CHAPTER TWENTY-ONE

TEAGAN

Despite the upheaval Brooke's presence next door brings to Joel and me, Gus seems genuinely happy that both his parents are in such close proximity. He's even taken to splitting his time pretty evenly between our house and his mother and grandfather's.

One evening, a few weeks after Brooke moves in, Joel and I are alone and discussing school starting next week, so I change the subject. "Why can't you just do joint custody? You know Brooke's not my favorite person, and not that I want Gus gone more than he already has been these past few weeks, but is that something you've ever tried?"

He sets down the pen he's using to make notes about his upcoming class list and sighs. "I offered Brooke joint custody, but when she moved, it wasn't an option. It was the middle of the school year and the judge agreed that to pull him out wouldn't be ideal. I'd be happy to do half-and-half, and I talked to Selena last week to see about approaching Brooke's lawyer with the option, since she's now so close again."

"And," I prompt.

His eyes lose focus for a moment. "She not only wants full custody, she wants me to only get every other holiday and two weeks during the summer."

My stomach drops. "What? That's not reasonable in any sense of the word."

Shrugging, he lifts his beer bottle to take a long pull. "No, but like I said, I don't know who Brooke is anymore."

"And what did Selena say about all that?" I ask, suddenly feeling helpless.

"She said she probably wouldn't get anything that drastic, but worse things have happened. If Brooke is granted full custody and moves out of state, it might very well be my reality until Gus is old enough to decide for himself. Truthfully, I don't want to keep dragging him through all this. Right now, he's not really part of anything, and I feel like we've tried to keep him out of the fights, but there's still the fallout that affects him. I want him to not have all this trauma he needs to unpack when he's older. If I felt like Brooke and I could come to some reasonable solution, I'd be happy to go that route. She's not being very reasonable right now.

"Selena and I went over the witness list her lawyers sent over. I don't even recognize some of the names, but they must be some character witnesses for her or something."

"Am I on your list?"

He shakes his head. "No, you testified at the last hearing, so they already have your previous statements on record. I mean, I guess they could subpoena you, but I don't see why. The fifth amendment keeps you from having to testify against me and I'm unsure why they'd bring you in to begin with. Nothing you say could help them."

I nod. "Have they set a date?"

"No, but Selena thinks it'll be before Christmas. We'll probably get about thirty days' notice and the lawyers will be required to present discovery by then. At that point, it's pretty much letting Selena do her research while we wait for the day." He gives me a tentative smile. "I hope you'll be with me."

I take his hand across the table, lifting it to press a kiss to his palm. "Of course I will."

At Gus's request, we've agreed to all get together at the house for a birthday cookout the weekend after Labor Day. Honestly, it's probably his attempt to foster some sort of mending of fences between his parents. It's most likely a pipe dream anymore, but you have to give the kid credit for trying, right?

We all paste smiles on our faces, but the animosity is palpable between the two couples. I'm sure it has nothing to do with us having a court date for the week of Halloween. At this point, I feel like I'm constantly trying to keep the tension to a low boil when we're all forced to interact. I try to be civil, and continually remind Joel to be as well. The last thing we need is for him to have some sort of emotional outburst with witnesses that can be used against him in the custody trial.

Gus and his friends are still swimming, and we bring out the cake so he can blow out the candles, only to see that I've forgotten the cake knife. Joel offers to run back in, but I wave him off, darting into the kitchen to retrieve it. After grabbing the utensil, I turn, freezing when I see Brooke standing in the kitchen. Gesturing to the bathroom, she gives me a stiff nod, but doesn't move any closer to the hallway.

Unsure what to do or what she's waiting on, I return her nod. She glances around, her gaze landing on the console table with our wedding photos, as well as some we've taken in the last few months. I still don't move, but set the knife on the counter lest it appear to be some sort of threat.

"Awful convenient y'all got married the same weekend he was informed of me taking him to court," she says, her tone flippant as if she's figured out some big plot.

I splay my hands before leaning against the counter. "What can I say? We got caught up. Can't say you really factored into things." Truthfully, it's not a lie. We did it for Gus; it had nothing to do with Brooke.

Her jaw clenches. "So caught up you had time to buy a dress and book a fancy chapel?"

"Anything worth doing is worth doing right, wouldn't you say? This is the only time I plan on getting married, so it stands to reason I'd want to look my best." I can't help but smile as my eyes drop to the photo. "I think we look pretty good. Besides, we were a little busy for a couple of days before that."

Also not a lie, since we were planning everything. Although, the smug smile I give her makes it seem like we were busy doing a lot more than simply *planning*. I have no objections to her jumping to that conclusion.

Her nostrils flare as her eyes flash with something close to outrage. "You know, I always knew you had a thing for him. I bet you threw a party when we separated. You bided your time until it was appropriate and then you pounced."

"Not that I owe you any sort of explanation about Joel's and my relationship, since you gave up any rights to him the moment you were unfaithful. To which, I have to say, keeping it in the family? Classy, Brooke. But to ease your mind, I never cheered for the demise of your marriage and I sure as hell never had any designs on Joel prior to the weekend we spent together; let alone while you were married. I think we both know you're projecting, since you obviously had your sights on Clive for a while."

Color rises in her cheeks. "You know nothing."

I level her with a gaze. "I'd say that goes both ways here.

Don't pretend to know anything about my relationship with Joel, and I won't assume what things must be like between you and Clive."

"Just so *you* know, if I have my way, you'll never see Gus again after all this is over. No way in hell I want my son anywhere near someone like you."

I roll my shoulders. "Considering I'm married to Joel and he's done nothing but be the best kind of father there is, I'm not sure your threat holds a lot of weight. And I love your son. I have never and will never attempt to take your place because I know you're doing what you think is right for him and I admire that. I only want to be there to support him and support Joel. I know Joel wants nothing but what's best for Gus; same as you."

Her eyes drag down my body with contempt. "I think we know exactly what Joel wants, and it's going to bite him in the ass."

"You know, I've never understood what you have against me. We used to be friends, Brooke. And no, I've never been secretive about my sex life, and I'm assuming that's what your current snarl is about. I've had a lot of sex with a lot of different people and I'm not ashamed of that fact.

"I've also watched you and Joel raise Gus and you're both amazing parents. He's a lucky kid. If your issue with me is that I stood by my *friend* when his wife and father broke his heart and he had no one else, I make no apologies for that, either. You may assume that because I very much enjoyed my status as a single woman that I lack morals. I can promise you that's not the case. Infidelity isn't something I've ever been okay with.

"I was your friend, too, Brooke. Had Joel been the one to stray, it would've been you who had my support. But we both know that's not something he would've ever done. I don't pretend to understand why you and Clive did what you did.

All I know is, you hurt the best man I've ever known and I will stand beside him, no matter what."

Her nostrils flare again as she squares her shoulders. "You think he'd say the same about you? That he'll stand beside you no matter what? If it came down to you or Gus, who do you think he'd choose?"

I sigh, tired of this conversation. "Gus is the most important thing in Joel's life. I don't even have to ask myself that question; Gus will always come first for him. His love isn't a competition and I have no desire to treat it like it is."

An earlier conversation with Joel flashes in my mind. *I honestly believe she thought I'd chase her if she ran. That I loved our family so much that if she threatened to leave, I'd run after her.*

My mouth falls open in disbelief as I examine her face in wonder. "Oh, my God. That's what all this is about."

She huffs in annoyance. "What are you on about?"

I'm about to speak when the back door opens, the sound of a baby whining streaming in our direction as Clive steps into the room. I clamp it closed, and he looks from Brooke to me and back, confused, as he bounces a visibly fussy Lily. "Everything okay, ladies?"

I nod, picking up the knife. "Yep. I'll see y'all outside." Stepping past the couple, I go outside, my head spinning with the realization that Brooke is most likely still in love with Joel. Is it possible that every bit of her behavior is because she's jealous of *Gus*, as well Joel's devotion to him?

"Hey, what's this face about?" Joel asks, planting a kiss on my bare shoulder as we lie in bed later.

I blink, still considering the ramifications of everything if

I'm correct in my assumption that Brooke has done everything in an attempt to try to garner attention from Joel. Any behavior analyst will tell you that negative attention is still attention, and at this point, she wants any sort of attention she can get from him. I'm not ready to voice all of that to Joel until I give it some more consideration, so I relax my expression. "What face?"

He lifts a brow. "It's gone now, but you looked awful deep in thought for someone who threw their first party as a married woman and stepmom; and a party with Brooke, to boot."

I shrug. "Just tired, I guess. It was a busy day and the sun always takes it out of me. Gus seemed to have a good time, though."

Joel smiles. "I think so. I think he enjoyed having everyone there and I'm glad we were all able to be civil. Is it wrong to hope we can try to have more gatherings like this in the future? You know, if they're for something Gus-related. I'm not seeing us having any fancy dinner parties and inviting Brooke and my dad or anything like that."

"So I guess no big block parties, either?"

He rolls his shoulders, his jaw clenching, and I immediately regret the question. "No. No block parties, Tee."

"Sorry. I shouldn't have brought that up."

Absentmindedly scratching his beard, he sighs. "It's okay," he says with a sad sort of smile. He leans over to press a kiss to my temple before dropping his forehead to the same spot where his lips just were. "You know, most of the time anymore, it seems like all that happened to someone else."

I pull back. "Sometimes, it doesn't though."

He shakes his head. "No, sometimes it's really, *really* real." Letting his head fall back against his pillow, he looks at some undetermined spot on the ceiling. "I've never been able to suss out how long before that they were together. I know it was after Mom died, or at the very least, when she'd slipped into the coma there at the end. I was walking back from the nurses' station and I must've been in just the right spot because I saw them. They were standing next to my mother's bed. Dad had his arm around Brooke, and her head was on his shoulder. The next second, she looked up at him and he kissed her forehead.

"I honestly didn't think anything of it at first because it could've been almost paternal. I mean, Brooke had known my parents for almost twenty years, and she was close to my parents; both of them. My mom loved her so much. She'd wanted a daughter so badly, but I guess they couldn't have more kids after me; I never asked."

I nod. "I remember your mother at some parties in the past. She adored Brooke."

He nods, too, but he doesn't look at me as he's still lost in his own thoughts. "After Mom died, I didn't think anything about Brooke going over to check on my dad. We'd all go, and I'd go and she went. That's what family does, right? I never thought to question their relationship because he's my dad; I never thought I had to.

"He wouldn't talk to me, but he seemed like he was coping better within a couple of months, so I assumed he was talking to Brooke. I'm sure now they were doing a lot more than just talking," he says flatly.

"I invited Dad to the block party because I thought it might help him get back to normal or at least get him out of the house, you know? But overhearing them talking about needing to tell me and then hearing them kiss wasn't exactly what I had in mind. I probably could've handled all that a bit better. I'm sure me flying off the handle at the party wasn't a good look for me."

I take his hand in mine. "You are allowed to express your emotions and your pain. The fact that they were sneaking around at a party at *your* house just shows how far gone they were. You didn't deserve to be embarrassed like that. I saw how devastated you were. I knew how much you loved her; loved them both. I could almost see your heart break in real time."

He blinks against the wetness pooling in his lashes. "I think she wanted me to fight for her, but I couldn't even consider that as an option. All I could think was that she'd destroyed our family. She'd broken my heart and would possibly take away my son. I'd seen other messy divorces and custody trials with some of Gus's friends' parents. I honestly think she thought I'd beg her to stay. And I did; for Gus. I asked her not to move because he deserved to have both his parents around.

"She'd said, 'What about what I deserve? Don't I deserve happiness?'" He snorts in disgust. "I asked her if she wasn't happy now that she'd broken our home? I said, 'What, fucking my dad wasn't enough? Did you want me to just pretend it didn't happen and take you back and us be a family again?' She actually had the nerve to say yes, that if I ever loved her, I'd be able to forgive her. That I would choose to forgive her."

Swallowing thickly, he swipes his thumb over his lashes. "I said that Gus was my priority. That I couldn't forgive her and pretend and still be any kind of man that I could be proud of. I said she would always be Gus's mother and for that reason alone and knowing that he was created out of love, I would never speak ill of her in front of him. I would never be hateful where she was concerned. I would never stop her from seeing him or try to influence what kind of relationship they have.

"I truly believe my father loves her and he loves Gus and Lily. I think he loves me. I think he was a broken man who made a terrible mistake and I want to say it was that way for her, too. In a perfect world, I want to believe it was a mistake borne of their shared grief for the loss of my mother.

"And maybe that's my fault. I've never been good at being vulnerable with my emotions. My dad is open and honest and has never had an issue sharing his feelings. Brooke is the same way. I'm sure they never actually meant for it to happen and I don't think it was some malicious plot to intentionally hurt me. But I can't forgive it."

He closes his eyes as his face pinches in pain. "I miss my dad so much. I miss being able to call him to talk about baseball and work and even ask his opinion about random, everyday shit. I feel like I didn't even get to process my mom's death fully because all that happened so soon after.

"I don't want to be bitter. I don't want Gus to see me be bitter. I want to be the bigger man. I'm not the bigger man. I'm so fucking angry and heartbroken. Still. It's like this oppressive weight on my chest. And I'm glad we can all be civil for Gus, but I know it will never, no matter what, be anything like it was before."

He turns his head to look at me, his eyes full of anguish. "I'm sorry that this is all that's left of me, Tee. I wish I could be more of who I was before for you, because you deserve someone who's not pieced back together with superglue."

I roll to face him, my heart aching for this man who I...love. Admitting it to myself is like finally being able to breathe. I *love* Joel. For the man he was and is and will be in the future. Shaking my head, I shift until I'm straddling him, bracing one arm beside his head while gripping his face with my other hand. "I don't need who you were before. I love you exactly as you are, for exactly who you are. Because who you are loves me. I have to believe we are exactly who we're supposed to be for each other. And who I am loves who you are, Joel Briggs; pieces and all."

He lets out a slow breath as I drop my forehead to his. Joel's hands come to rest on my hips and, like he always does, he gives them a gentle squeeze. Just a slight tightening of his grip as though to remind himself that I'm real.

"I can't tell you how to reconcile with your dad. I think we both know I'm the least qualified individual to give that sort of advice. But I am your family and I'm here for you however you need me to be.

"Regardless of what happens in a few weeks, I'm right there with you. If Brooke somehow wins and takes Gus away, we will follow her. He's your son and you should always be where he is. We'll do whatever we have to do to ensure that you're part of his life as much as you possibly can be."

Joel tilts his chin until our mouths meet, and it's a tender, slow kiss. It doesn't last very long, just enough to make me want him more, but he seems content to simply hold me. I'm more than okay with that, too.

CHAPTER TWENTY-TWO

TEAGAN

Looking around the courtroom as we wait for the custody hearing to begin, I can't help but think about my parents and how everything worked out. Much to my their dismay, their attempt to tie up Tootsie's estate in probate court fell flat, as there was no evidence to support their claim that she promised anything to them. I'd be lying if I said I didn't miss my parents, because I do. I only wish things were different so we could have a relationship. Although, I suppose that's not meant to be right now.

Joel and his lawyer, Selena Sato, sit in front of me at a large wooden table in the Duval County Courthouse. She's around Joel's age, and slim. Average height with warm, medium-brown skin, short, wavy black hair, she wears a killer light-gray pencil skirt and black silk blouse. My husband, despite how much he hates dressing up, looks handsome and put together in a solid black suit.

Thankfully, Gus is at school with plans to go home with a friend after in the event court runs later than when he gets out. And while I'm only here for moral support, I'm as nervous as a long-tailed cat in a room full of rocking chairs and I'm sweating like a sinner in church. Hopefully, the navy blue shift dress I've chosen doesn't show the sweat stains.

A quick glance to my left tells me that Brooke is looking polished as well in a black pencil skirt, a thin, light pink sweater, and black pumps. Her hair is styled in a chic chignon and she wears minimal makeup, along with a set of pearls. Clive sits behind her looking like an older and grayer Joel in an expensive navy pinstripe suit.

Brooke's lawyer, Tolliver Givens, who wears a shrewd expression, is a white man in his late fifties. He's average height and stocky, with short dark-blonde hair and horn-rimmed glasses. Dressed in an immaculately tailored charcoal gray suit and highly polished loafers, he looks like he's ready to go for the jugular. Selena described him as "exceptional". I believe it.

Even from where I sit, I can see Clive steal glances at his son. I can't help but wonder how he must feel about all this. As a father and grandfather, how can he justify the things he's done? Was it some sort of momentary lapse that's morphed into too many decisions to take back? Does he feel remorse for the destruction of not only his relationship with his son, but his son's marriage as well? I'm not sure I understand his stance in this at all.

As Lily isn't in attendance, I can only surmise they've gotten a sitter for the day. *Probably Ellen*, an uncharitable part of my brain says. Of course, I wouldn't trust that woman with my dog, let alone a human child. I'd worry some of her toxicity would leach into the baby. I bet—.

"All rise for the honorable Judge Amanda Demille."

The small group in attendance rise and a matronly Black woman in black robes with a dark red, chin-length bob strides to the bench. She takes a seat, sliding a pair of reading glasses onto her face. "You may be seated," she remarks, not looking in our direction. Reaching for a document, she scans it before lifting her gaze. "We are here today to determine legal and physical custody of minor child Augustus Clive Briggs. Is that correct?"

"Yes, Your Honor," both lawyers answer.

She nods, turning her attention to Brooke's lawyer. "Counselor, your client wishes to seek sole legal and physical custody?"

"That is correct, Your Honor. My client feels the past year being separated from her son has been detrimental to her mental and emotional wellbeing and she seeks to rectify this situation."

The judge nods as she examines the document in front of her once more. "Your client also alleges that the minor child's current living situation—that is to say, with his father—is no longer acceptable. Is that correct?"

"Yes, Your Honor," Givens answers.

"On what grounds, Counselor?"

"Your Honor, my client feels her son is no longer safe living with his father."

My heart lurches. Joel blinks, his chest heaving, but he doesn't react beyond that. Selena told us they are allowed to allege whatever they want, but unless they can prove what they say, it doesn't mean anything. I spare a covert glance at Clive, whose posture is tense, his spine rigid, his jaw clenching, as he looks down at his hands. He doesn't like the accusations being leveled at his son. He probably doesn't believe these claims any more than we do. What does it say about him that he'll let Brooke make them, though?

Judge Demille nods, absorbing the lawyer's statement before she shifts her gaze in Selena's direction. "I believe you also have a countersuit in this case?"

Selena nods. "Yes, Your Honor. My client wishes to amend

the original custody agreement that's already in place to adjust for Mrs. Brooke Briggs's relocation to Florida. Originally, my client sought full custody because Mrs. Briggs had moved to Tennessee. He would prefer to seek fifty-fifty joint legal and physical custody between himself and Mrs. Briggs. He believes it would be in the best interest of their child to have equal access to both his parents. He also wishes to keep the current agreement on child support in place. That is to say, there currently is none, and he wishes it to remain thus."

The judge nods again, seeming to consider Selena's statement before directing a question to Givens. "Does your client wish to entertain the idea of a fifty-fifty custody agreement?"

"No, Your Honor," he answers immediately. "Again, my client no longer feels her son is safe in Mr. Briggs's home. She still wishes to seek sole legal and physical custody."

"Can you provide evidence to support your claim, Counselor? According to my records, Mr. Briggs has, up to this point and according to this court's records, been an exemplary father." She glances down at a document. "According to the files I have on hand, Mr. Briggs has been to every required parenting class, has no recorded instances of misconduct, has ensured his son has maintained all required dental and medical wellness visits, has complied with every request for Mrs. Briggs to have access to her son, and by all accounts is a stand-up guy. Do you wish to allege that Mr. Briggs is somehow negligent in the care of his son?"

"Your Honor," Givens begins, "my client's issue is not with her ex-husband. You see, he recently remarried and my client feels her son is not safe in the custody of Mr. Briggs's wife."

All the warmth leaches from my face. *Me? I'm unsafe?* I'm unable to catch my breath for a moment, and when I look at Joel, his expression is stony. Selena places her hand on his arm, as if to restrain him.

"So, let me make sure I understand. Your client is alleging that her son is not safe in the care of his stepmother? Do I have that right? And because of this, Mrs. Briggs wishes to seek sole legal and physical custody?"

"Yes, Your Honor," Brooke's lawyer says, his tone matter-of-fact.

The judge's expression remains neutral. Meanwhile, I'm about to come out of my skin. I have no clue what sort of behavior Brooke and her lawyer consider "unsafe". Considering I've been around Gus his entire life and we're close, I don't know how that might play. I've never been accused of any misconduct at work or had any complaints lodged by parents. Hell, I've never even had a speeding ticket. I'm at a total loss as to what evidence they can have to support any kind of claim against me.

Joel looks over his shoulder to give me a quick supportive nod, and I try to keep my face free of emotion.

"Alright. Miss Sato, I'm assuming your client wishes to rebut these allegations?"

"Of course, Your Honor," Selena supplies. "My client's wife has been in Gus's life since the day he was born. Until just today, Mrs. Briggs has never wished to bring forth any allegations of misconduct against her."

Judge Demille turns her attention to Brooke's table. "Mr. Givens, do you have proof of any wrongdoing or misconduct by," she drops her eyes to a sheet of paper, "Teagan Roth?"

Givens nods. "Your Honor, we have witness testimony to support our claim that Mrs. Briggs's son would be best served by having no contact with his stepmother. For his safety and wellbeing."

Bile rises up my throat at the thought that I could be the reason Joel loses this case. Even if I know I've never done anything wrong where Gus is concerned, it's terrifying that they're going to speak about me as though I'm not even here.

The Judge glances down again. "I don't believe Teagan Roth is listed as a witness for either side today."

"Your Honor," Selena says, "Miss Roth was a character witness in the previous trial on behalf of my client."

"I see. Well, if there was going to be testimony regarding her, I would've preferred she be on this list in the event she needed to be examined." She levels an annoyed look at Brooke's table before bringing her gaze back to center. "Is Miss Roth in attendance?"

I raise a tentative hand, and she nods. "Miss Roth, you will need to step out until the testimony can be heard, and if your personal testimony is required, you'll be summoned." She turns to the bailiff at her side. "Please escort Miss Roth out to the hall where she will remain until such time as this court requires her testimony."

Joel reaches back to give my hand a quick squeeze and, with a racing heart, I stand to follow the officer out to the hall. He gestures to a bench along the wall before stepping over to where another officer is standing; I'm assuming to relay the message from the judge.

I can't help but fidget, and because we weren't allowed to bring our phones into the building, I jiggle my leg in an attempt to dispel my nervous energy. A sound to my left draws my attention, and a man in his mid-to-late twenties who looks vaguely familiar, sits on a bench identical to mine. He has olive skin and black hair, although I can't see his eyes, so I have no clue what color they are. He looks to be well above six feet tall, even sitting, and he's wearing a nicely tailored black suit.

He glances my way, offering me a smirk, and I'm struck with the feeling that I've met this man before but have no clue where or when. "Hey, Teagan."

The officer clears his throat. "No talking to other witnesses."

This must be one of Brooke's witnesses.

There's honestly no telling who this guy is, but he appears to be the only witness here, so hopefully that's a good sign.

I don't wear watches; never have. But I've never wanted to be wearing a watch more in my life than I do at this moment. I have no clue how long I sit, literally twiddling my thumbs. It feels like hours, but is probably only about twenty minutes. Even so, I'm as antsy as a meth addict in withdrawal.

The door to the courtroom opens suddenly, and the bailiff steps out. "Bryant Halpert," he calls, and the vaguely familiar man stands. All the breath leaves my body. Finally realizing why he looks familiar, I can't help but close my eyes against the sudden pain in my chest.

I very well may have just cost Joel his son.

CHAPTER TWENTY-THREE

JOEL

A man I don't recognize steps into the courtroom. He's in his late twenties and at least six-four and stocky, with a confident gait and smirk to match. I recognize his name from the list Brooke's lawyer provided, but I don't know this kid from Adam, so I have no clue what's in store. Not after everything that's transpired up to this point.

Caught completely off guard would be a good way of putting it when talking about how I'm feeling right about now. The idea that Teagan is anything less than a saint with Gus is laughable. But as Brooke's lawyer made claims against Tee on the grounds of her past promiscuity—which Selena objected to on the grounds of relevance and was sustained—I wanted to throttle my ex-wife. She also claimed that Teagan's and my marriage wasn't "real"; also objected to by Selena and sustained. She even went so far as to suggest that I married Teagan for money. That one did make my heart lurch, but considering none of Teagan's accounts save the one we've been using to pay my legal fees have my name on them, that was also objected to by Selena and sustained.

But now with this guy she's brought in, I have no clue what to expect. He takes the stand and, after he's sworn in, drops onto the seat, his posture relaxed. Brooke's lawyer, Tolliver Givens, rises, coming to stand midway between their table and the witness stand. "Can you state your name, age, and occupation for the court, please?"

He nods. "My name is Bryant Ennis Halpert. I am twenty-seven years old and I'm a graduate student at the University of Georgia."

Givens nods. "Mr. Halpert—may I call you Bryant?"

"Sure."

"Thank you. Okay, Bryant. Can you tell me why you're here today?"

One of his brows tics up. "I was subpoenaed by your office."

"In regards to the Briggs custody trial?"

"Objection," Selena calls. "Leading the witness."

"Sustained."

"I'll rephrase," Givens offers. "Why were you subpoenaed, Bryant?"

"The paperwork stated I would be a witness on behalf of Brooke Briggs," he answers.

"Thank you. You stated you're currently studying at the University of Georgia, is that right?"

"Yes."

"Is that where you're from?"

"No," Halpert answers.

"Where are you from, Bryant?"

"Tallahassee, Florida."

"Have you lived there your whole life?"

"Until college, yes."

The lawyer shifts his weight from one foot to the other

before adjusting his glasses. "Bryant, do you know my client, Brooke Briggs?"

His brow furrows, and he shakes his head. "No."

"Do you know her ex-husband, Joel Briggs?"

"No."

"Have you ever met their son, Gus?"

"No."

"So, before today, you had never seen my client or her ex-husband, and you've never seen their son?"

"Objection, Your Honor. Asked and answered," Selena remarks.

Judge Demille nods. "Get somewhere relevant, Mr. Givens."

"Your Honor, I'm only establishing that Mr. Halpert has no connection to either party or their son. I promise my point will be made shortly."

"See that it is," the judge orders.

Brooke's lawyer nods. "Yes, Your Honor. Bryant, have you ever met Mr. Briggs's wife, Teagan Roth?"

Halpert nods, a small smile pulling at the corners of his mouth. "On several occasions."

"Where did you initially meet Miss Roth?"

"At a bar in Tallahassee."

"Can you recall what were you doing the first time you met Miss Roth?"

He considers the question, searching his memory for a beat. "I believe I was playing darts with some friends."

"What were the circumstances of your meeting?"

"She bumped into me, spilling my drink, and offered to buy me another one."

"Did she buy you a drink, Bryant?"

"Yes."

"Can you tell us what happened after that?"

"I went home with her," he answers matter-of-factly.

"Did you have sex with Miss Roth?"

My jaw clenches, and I wait for Selena to object on the grounds that whether Teagan slept with this punk has no bearing on her ability to care for my son. But she doesn't object.

"Yes," Bryant says.

"Were either of you drunk or under the influence of drugs?"

"No."

"Did you and Miss Roth meet on any other occasions to engage in sex?"

"Yes."

Givens nods. "On how many more occasions would you say that you and Miss Roth had sex?"

"On and off for a few weeks."

"Where would you meet with her?"

Selena stands. "Objection, Your Honor. Relevance?"

"Sustained. Mr. Givens, please make your point."

"Yes, Your Honor." He once again shifts his weight from one foot to the other before squaring his shoulders. "Bryant, how long ago did you engage in a sexual relationship with Teagan Roth?"

"Ten years ago."

I blink, and even Selena seems taken aback by his answer. Givens nods. "And how old were you at the time you and Miss Roth first engaged in sexual activity?"

"Seventeen."

All the breath leaves my body as my mind reels with what I've just heard. It takes me a minute to realize Selena's written something down on a legal pad and slid it my direction.

Fucking 17?! You better hope she has a rational explanation, or you are <u>FUCKED</u>.

I don't write anything in response, and my stomach churns with acid.

"No further questions, Your Honor," Brooke's lawyer responds to the bombshell.

Judge Demille nods. "Miss Sato, cross?"

"Yes, Your Honor." She clears her throat as she stands, tugging on the cuff of her blouse as she strides to the spot Givens just vacated. "So, Bryant—may I call you Bryant?"

"Sure."

"Thank you. Bryant, you claim that you and Miss Roth met at a bar in Tallahassee ten years ago. Is that correct?"

"Yes."

"And you were seventeen?"

"Objection, asked and answered," Givens says, and the judge nods.

Selena holds up her hands in a placating gesture. "Yes, Your Honor; just ensuring I'm correct about my facts."

"Yes," Bryant replies.

My lawyer nods, considering. "Why were you in a bar at seventeen?"

The witness gives a slight shrug. "Just wanted to hang out with my friends; throw some darts."

"How did you gain access to the bar where you met Miss Roth?"

"I had a fake ID"

"I see. You claim that Miss Roth bumped into you, spilling your drink, and offered to buy you a new one. What were you drinking before Miss Roth bumped into you?"

"I believe it was ginger ale."

"Just so I'm clear, at seventeen, you had an illegal—fake—ID, which you used to gain access to a bar where, legally, you had no right to be. Am I correct in that statement?"

"Yes," he admits.

"Alright. When Miss Roth offered to buy you a drink, what drink did you request?"

"Budweiser, I believe."

Selena furrows her brow. "So, prior to Miss Roth buying your drink, you were drinking ginger ale. Why switch to beer?"

Again, he gives a small shrug. "I wasn't buying."

Nodding, my lawyer tilts her head in curiosity. "When you ordered your beer, were you asked to show your ID?"

"Yes."

"Did Miss Roth see you show your fake ID to the bartender?"

"Yes, I believe so," he answers.

"Approximately how long after the beer that Miss Roth purchased for you and you showed ID for, did you leave with her?"

He thinks for a moment. "About an hour, I guess."

"And during that hour, did you and Miss Roth chat?"

"Sure."

"What about?"

Halpert's brow furrows. "I'm not sure I remember; that was a decade ago."

"But you remember it was Miss Roth with whom you had a sexual relationship? You just said it was a decade ago. A lot can change in a decade; memory fades. How can you be sure it was Miss Roth?"

The witness's brow tics up. "You never forget your first."

Selena frowns. "Your first what, Bryant?"

"The first time you have sex," he supplies.

"Alright. So, after about an hour of conversation, where did you and Miss Roth go?"

"To her apartment."

"Did you drive?"

He shakes his head. "I didn't have my driver's license yet."

"Did you ride with her?"

Bryant nods. "Yes."

"Did she ever question why you didn't have a car?"

"I told her it was in the shop and I'd caught a ride to the bar with a buddy."

"So you lied?" Selena inquires.

"Not really. I rode to the bar with a friend who had a car," he counters.

"But Miss Roth had reason to believe you could drive, correct?"

"I guess so. I'm not her, so I can't say exactly what she believed."

"At any time before you and Miss Roth went to her apartment to engage in sex, did you tell her your actual age?"

"No."

Relief floods me. Even knowing there had to be a good explanation, it's still nice to have it confirmed that Teagan didn't know the kid's age when they slept together.

Selena frowns at Bryant's answer. "Why not? If you all were having a good time, why would you not reveal how old you were?"

Bryant looks uncertain about the question. "It never came up."

"But you knew how old you were, correct?"

"Well, yeah."

"Did you know how old Miss Roth was?"

"She said she was in college, so I assumed she was over eighteen. She seemed to know a lot of people in the bar, so I figured she was a regular."

"So, even knowing she was well above eighteen and you weren't at least eighteen, you didn't tell her?"

"No," he answers, his voice flat.

"Why not?"

"Like I said, it never came up."

"Is the reason you didn't bring it up because you knew if she found out your actual age, she wouldn't have left with you or engaged in sex with you?"

"I don't know; she was pretty into things. She came on to me."

Selena nods, and I force myself to take some slow breaths. My lawyer asks, "Earlier, you stated that for a few weeks following your initial meeting, you were engaged in an on-and-off sexual relationship with Miss Roth, is that correct?"

"Yes."

"What caused the relationship to end?"

Color rises to his cheeks. "I dropped my wallet as I was getting dressed to leave her place and my driver's license—my real one—fell out. She picked it up and confronted me."

"So, Miss Roth ended it?"

"Yes."

"So, as soon as she found out your actual age, she ended the relationship?"

"Yes," Bryant replies.

Selena's quiet for a beat before asking, "Did you ever report your relationship with Miss Roth to the authorities?"

"No," he admits.

"Why not? What happened between the two of you wasn't legal. You weren't a consenting adult. Do you not feel as though what Miss Roth did was wrong?"

Bryant swallows before letting out a slow breath, his expression full of regret. "I never should've been in that bar; I was seventeen. And no, I wasn't an adult, but I knew exactly what I was doing. I was a stupid kid who made a stupid mistake. As soon as Teagan found out the truth, she made the right choice. If I had it to do over again, I wouldn't have put her at risk like that; her freedom, her future. So no, she didn't do anything wrong; I did. I never reported it because I didn't—and still don't—want her to get in trouble."

"No further questions, Your Honor."

The judge releases Halpert as Selena retakes her seat. I lean over. "How bad is it?"

"It's not great, but it could've been a hell of a lot worse," she admits. "Do you want Teagan to testify?"

I blow out a breath. "Will it be worse if she does or doesn't?"

"Could go either way."

I pinch the bridge of my nose as the judge asks, "Miss Sato, do you have any witnesses you'd like to call?"

Selena glances at me, and I nod, knowing Teagan will be honest, no matter what happens. And although I'd love five minutes with my wife to talk about this with her, I know it's not allowed. "Your Honor, I call Teagan Roth to the stand."

Givens shoots to his feet. "Objection, Your Honor. Miss Roth is not on the approved list of witnesses."

Selena stands. "Your Honor, Mr. Givens's client's entire argument hinges on the fitness of Miss Roth as a caretaker for the minor child. The last witness just made claims about her. Does she not get an opportunity to substantiate or refute the claims made about her?"

The judge peers over her reading glasses at the lawyers. "Mr. Givens, I think we both know that had Miss Sato and her client been informed of your intention to raise questions about the fitness of Miss Roth as it relates to being a caretaker of the child in question, she would have been on the list. I'm inclined to believe that your intent was to catch Miss Sato and her client off guard by not being forthright. Miss Roth will be allowed to testify.

"Miss Sato, as Miss Roth has testified previously on behalf of Mr. Briggs, only content relevant to the testimony of the previous witness and the events described are admissible."

"Yes, Your Honor," Selena agrees, and I don't miss the look of pure rage on Brooke's face. I don't even bother looking at my father.

A moment later, Teagan is escorted into the courtroom and, despite how nervous I know she must be, she holds her head high as she makes her way to the witness stand. She is sworn in and takes a seat, perching on the edge of the chair.

Selena walks to the middle of the room, offering her a warm smile. "Miss Roth, can you please state your name, age, and occupation for the court?"

She clears her throat. "My name is Teagan Hannah Roth. I'm thirty-one and I'm a guidance counselor for Duval County Schools."

"Thank you, Teagan. Can you tell me your relationship with my client?"

She glances at me, and I give her what I hope is a reassuring smile. "Joel is my husband."

"Right. Does the name Bryant Halpert mean anything to you?"

Teagan's throat rolls with a swallow. "Yes."

"Where did you meet Mr. Halpert?"

"At a bar in Tallahassee."

My lawyer nods. "Do you recall when you met him?"

"About ten years ago."

"What were the circumstances of your meeting?"

She thinks for a beat. "I was returning from the bathroom and bumped into him. I believe I spilled his drink and offered to buy him a new one."

"Did he accept your offer?"

"Yes," she replies.

"Do you recall what drink he ordered?"

"It was a beer, I think."

"Did you show your ID to purchase the drinks?"

She nods. "I showed mine, and even though I was paying, the bartender wanted to see Bryant's, too."

"Did he do so?"

"Yes."

"Did the bartender serve Mr. Halpert?"

"Yes."

"How many drinks did you and Mr. Halpert have that first night?"

"Just the one."

"Can you tell us what happened after your one drink together?" Selena asks, her tone neutral.

Color rises to Teagan's cheeks. "I invited him to come home with me."

"For what purpose?"

She squares her shoulders. "To have sex."

"Who drove to your home?"

"I did."

"Did you ask, or did he volunteer, as to why he couldn't drive?"

She nods. "If I recall, he said that he'd ridden to the bar with a friend because his car was in the shop."

"Did you and Mr. Halpert engage in sexual intercourse?"

"Yes," she answers quietly.

"At any point prior to having sex with Mr. Halpert, did he inform you of his age?"

She shakes her head. "No."

"So, how did you know he was over eighteen?"

"I assumed."

"What would lead you to believe that Mr. Halpert was over eighteen?"

"The bar where we met was—is—a college bar. He showed his ID to the bartender and I assume, the bouncer. He was well over six feet tall and physically large. He told me he was studying business," she states, her tone cool.

"How long did you have a relationship with Mr. Halpert?"

She splays her hands. "A few weeks, maybe."

"Were you dating? That is to say, were you in a monogamous relationship?"

"No."

"How often would you say that you and Mr. Halpert met for sex?"

"Once or twice a week."

"Who would initiate the contact?"

She clears her throat. "He would be at the bar and we'd run into one another."

"The same bar as the first time?"

"Yes."

Selena nods. "Where would you go to have sex with him?"

"My place."

"Who drove?"

"All but the last time, it was me."

"When did your relationship with Mr. Halpert end?"

Her jaw clenches. "His real ID fell out of his wallet just as he was getting dressed to leave my apartment."

"What did you do?"

"We argued. I told him that he'd lied to me and we couldn't see each other again. I also made him give me his fake ID."

"What did you do with his ID?"

"I destroyed it."

"Why?"

"Well, I didn't want him to be able to go right back to the bar. I didn't want him to deceive anyone else the way he had me. I didn't want him to jeopardize anyone else's future like mine possibly was."

"What happened after that?" my lawyer asks.

Teagan shakes her head. "Nothing."

"Did you ever see Mr. Halpert again? At the bar, at your home, in public?"

"No."

"Were you ever arrested?"

"No," she answers quickly.

"Were any charges ever brought against you?"

"No," she says again.

"If you had known Mr. Halpert's true age, would you have approached him at the bar?"

"No. Never," she replies emphatically.

She nods. "And to your knowledge, have you ever engaged in sexual acts with a minor on any other occasion?"

"No."

"No further questions, Your Honor."

The judge nods at Brooke's lawyer. "Mr. Givens, would you like to cross-examine?"

"Yes, Your Honor." Demille motions as if to say, *take it away*, and Givens stands to walk to the middle of the courtroom.

"Miss Roth, when did you and Mr. Briggs get married?"

"Objection, relevance?" Selena asks, her tone tired.

Brooke's lawyer nods. "I promise, I have a point, Your Honor."

"Overruled. Let's make it a quick point, Mr. Givens."

He nods again and looks to Teagan, who squares her shoulders. "May thirtieth."

"Can you tell this court why you married Mr. Briggs?"

My heart starts to pound. If she's dishonest, she'll perjure herself. If she's honest, it could come back to bite us in the ass.

My wife smiles. "I asked, and he said yes."

Well, sure, let's break it down to its most basic parts.

"Do you recall when you asked Mr. Briggs to marry you?"

She squares her shoulders. "After attending my best friend's wedding in Tennessee."

"What prompted you to propose?"

"Again, Your Honor. Relevance?" Selena objects.

"Mr. Givens, my patience is wearing thin with this line of questioning. It's already been established that the validity of Mr. Briggs's and Miss Roth's marriage is not in question; nor is it relevant to these proceedings."

"I'm almost there, Your Honor," Givens promises.

The judge nods curtly, but glances at Teagan for her answer. My wife sits up straighter, her eyes sliding to mine. "He's my best friend. I wanted to be there for him; support him."

Brooke's lawyer frowns. "You asked him to marry you so you could be there for him?"

She nods, returning her attention to the lawyer. "Yes."

"You asked him to marry you so you could be there for him?" he repeats, seemingly confused.

Selena sighs. "Your Honor, asked and answered."

The judge's nostrils flare. "Mr. Givens, do these questions have a point? Miss Sato is correct. The question has been asked and answered. Either ask a different question or move on."

"Yes, Your Honor." The lawyer shifts his weight from one foot to the other. "Are you close with Gus, Miss Roth?"

"Define close," Teagan prompts, her brow furrowing.

"Do you love him?"

My wife's expression softens. "As if he were my own son."

"Is that because you can't have children of your own?"

"Objection, Your Honor. Relevance," Selena remarks, her tone harsh.

"Sustained, Mr. Givens."

The lawyer nods. "Was your reason for marrying Mr. Briggs so that you could gain access to Gus?"

"I'm not sure I understand your question," Teagan replies.

"Are you hoping if this trial is granted in favor of your husband, you'll have a prominent place in Gus's life?"

"I have a prominent place in Gus's life, regardless of how this trial goes."

Givens's brow tics up. "How do you figure?"

"I've been in Gus's life since he was born. I babysat him and have watched him grow up. His parents trusted me with his wellbeing on countless occasions; trusting that I would keep him safe. Like I said, I love Gus as if he were my own child. I was a part of Gus's life before his father and I were married. Regardless of how this plays out, I will still be in Gus's life because my relationship with Gus is separate from my relationship with Joel."

Her eyes slide to mine for a beat. "Even if his father and I were no longer married, Gus would still be important to me. I believe, barring any legal or moral reason, even if Joel and I weren't together, he would still allow me to have a relationship with his son."

"Is your goal in this to usurp his mother?"

Teagan huffs a laugh. "No. I respected Brooke. I believe she's doing what she feels is right in her mind for Gus; same as Joel."

"But you no longer respect her?"

"No. Not as a person. I respect her as Gus's mother."

"Did the fact that you inherited a large estate from your late aunt factor into your decision to marry Mr. Briggs?"

"Objection. Relevance, Your Honor," Selena calls.

"Sustained."

Brooke's lawyer's jaw clenches. "No further questions, Your Honor."

"You may step down, Miss Roth," the judge instructs.

Teagan breathes a sigh of relief as she climbs down from the witness stand. I follow her with my eyes, and as she rounds the partition to the outer section of the courtroom, my gaze snags on my father. His expression is forlorn and full of regret and I simply clench my jaw as I stare him down, my expression cold.

The judge clears her throat. "Does either party have any additional statements they'd like to make?"

Having discussed this earlier with Selena and knowing there's no reason I should speak, she shakes her head. "No, Your Honor."

Brooke and her lawyer seem to be engaged in a heated discussion, but she shakes off a hand that Givens places on her shoulder and stands. "Your Honor, I have something to say."

"Very well, Mrs. Briggs. You may proceed."

"Thank you. My entire goal in this was simply so I could have more uninterrupted time with my son. I've seen him so little over the past year and have missed him so much. He has a baby sister now and I want them to have a good relationship. I miss my son and deserve to be with him. I am his mother." Her jaw clenches. "That woman has no right to my son and shouldn't be within five hundred feet of him; let alone living under the same roof. She is a pedophile and should be locked away where she can't infect anyone else with her loose morals."

It's all I can do to keep my seat as Brooke continues her tirade. But continue it, she does. "I will never stop fighting for my son. He deserves to be with parents who will raise him right; teach him right. I want my son with me. I deserve to have him with me."

She drops into her seat, and I'm just thankful it's over as

silence descends. The judge's face is free of any emotion as she nods, slipping off her reading glasses. "We will take a two-hour recess for lunch, after which time, I will have a ruling." The gavel bangs against the bench and I nearly jump.

Brooke storms out before I've even stood, my father trailing behind her, his posture resigned. I'm emotionally exhausted and am not sure if I want the next two hours to fly or crawl.

CHAPTER TWENTY-FOUR

Joel says something to his lawyer that I can't hear and, after sharing a nod, my husband comes around the partition to pull me in for a hug. "I'm so sorry, Joel. I had no clue they'd dig that up." My voice grows shaky as tears fill my eyes and he hugs me tighter.

"Tee, it's not your fault." He pulls back to takes my face in his hands. "Let's go get some lunch, okay? We'll get out of here for a bit and feel better. There's nothing else we can do one way or another to sway the judge." I close my eyes, resigned, and he gives me a gentle shake. "Look at me." When I open my eyes, he's shaking his head. "No matter what happens, you are not to blame. Even if we lose, you are not to blame. Brooke fought dirty and even if she wins, it won't be a fair outcome.

"You did good, sweetheart. I couldn't love you more if I tried right now. You could've crumbled up there and you didn't. You were amazing and I'm so proud to be your husband."

"I didn't know how young Bryant was. I swear. I was so sick after I found out, I threw up," I tell him, tears rolling down my face. "I'm so sorry if I messed this up for you. I will never forgive myself if you lose because of me."

"Teagan, stop. We are fine. I'm not upset with you, okay? I swear, regardless of the verdict, I know we did our best."

With a final nod, I let him pull me out of the courtroom and we head to lunch. It would seem that neither of us have much appetite, so we mostly pick at our food for nearly an hour before finally giving up and going for a walk. We stroll hand-in-hand in the vicinity of the courthouse, simply being together. We don't really talk and just seem to take comfort from the other's presence.

Ten minutes before we're due back in court, I start to grow anxious. Just before we get to the door of the courtroom, he pulls me to a stop. Turning to face me, he takes both my hands in his, bringing them to his lips to press kisses to the backs of them. His expression is resolved and calm as he looks into my eyes. "Regardless of this outcome, we are fine. No matter what happens, we can always keep fighting."

He swallows, his eyes softening, and lowers his voice so only I can hear him. "I can't thank you enough for everything you've done for me and Gus. And I don't only mean for this. Thank you for loving me and helping me heal. I love you so much and know that whatever happens, we'll make it through it because we have each other."

I nod, and he gives me a sweet kiss. Then, after a deep breath, we walk into the courtroom. He leaves me in the audience with a last squeeze to my hand before retaking his earlier seat next to Selena. The lawyer turns to look at me over her shoulder. "You did good earlier. Even if this doesn't go our way, you still did great."

"Thank you. And thank you for fighting so hard for Joel."

"Anytime. Hopefully, this'll be the last time we have to do this."

"Amen to that," Joel mutters.

The door opens loudly behind us, but I don't turn to watch Brooke, Clive, and her lawyer enter and take their seats. I keep my eyes fixed on the bench as I pray for a favorable outcome.

A few minutes later, the bailiff is instructing us to stand as the judge enters from the back to take her place on the bench. She motions for us to sit and slides her reading glasses up her nose, clearing her throat before looking out to the crowd. "I've been doing this job for a long time. When a custody case is being determined, there are a lot of factors that come into play. First and foremost, you have to take the child's wellbeing into consideration.

"By all accounts, Gus is a thriving, intelligent, rambunctious little boy. It's clear from this court's research that he has a positive relationship with both of his parents. Honestly, I'm happy to see that."

She directs her attention to Brooke. "Mrs. Briggs, in the months since the previous custody hearing where primary custody was granted to Mr. Briggs until you relocated back to Florida—a period of a little over one year—you had seen your son a total of eight times. All but one of those visitations was no more than four hours at a time and always at the behest of Mr. Briggs. The only exception was the trip where Gus spent nineteen days with you at your home in Tennessee, beginning in May. I understand that visit had to be cut short as well.

"I'm willing to concede that since relocating to the residence next door to Mr. Briggs and Miss Roth, you seem to have spent considerably more time with your son. But overall, it appears that you've shown very little initiative in spending in-person time with Gus until just recently, even though records show that you resided in Florida at least half the year, within reasonable driving distance of your son."

Her gaze shifts to Joel, and I nearly hold my breath. "Mr. Briggs, although it's not relevant to this trial, you should know that committing marriage fraud simply for the sake of collecting an inheritance is punishable by law and carries a sentence up to five years in prison and a $250,000 fine. Just throwing that out there."

The judge rests her elbows on the bench and steeples her fingers. "Mrs. Briggs is seeking sole legal and physical custody of the minor child, Augustus Clive Briggs. Mr. Briggs is counter-suing for fifty-fifty joint legal and physical custody with the current child support agreement in place.

"I'm not in the habit of essentially tearing a child from its parent. I understand the original custody agreement was put in place when Mrs. Briggs moved to Tennessee. Seeing as you have returned to Florida and are in such close proximity to Mr. Briggs's residence, I am hesitant to grant sole custody to either party.

"Mrs. Briggs, during your closing statement, you spoke of 'loose morals'. In my experience, people in glass houses shouldn't throw stones," she says with a lifted brow and I blink in surprise. "Fifty-fifty legal and physical joint custody is granted, along with the current child support agreement already in place. A proposed parenting plan must be agreed upon by both parties within thirty days, or this court will determine an appropriate schedule. Also, Mrs. Briggs is to maintain a permanent residence in Duval County until such time as future hearings rule differently." The judge bangs her gavel, and Brooke makes a sound of disbelief in the back of her throat. Her lawyer leans over and whispers something to her.

My mouth falls open in shock. *We won?* We won. Tears of relief and joy burst from my eyes and I nearly sob with how happy I am. Joel stands, leaning over the partition to grab my face, planting a huge kiss on my lips. "We did it, Tee."

I nod. "I know. I can't believe it."

"Neither can I," Brooke snarls from the aisle next to me. I stand, taking a preemptive step back. Clive attempts to put his arm around her, but she shrugs him off. "This isn't over. It won't be over until you are gone from our lives." She points a finger in my direction.

Selena stands up straighter. "Mr. Givens, I sincerely hope your client isn't making threats against mine. In open court. Right this moment."

The other lawyer's nostrils flare. "Of course not. Let's go, Brooke." He tugs Brooke along and Clive follows behind, but shoots a look at Joel over his shoulder, his expression sad.

Despite how thrilled I am to know that Joel isn't losing custody of Gus for a mistake I made, I still can't stomach knowing that he could have. Even though I have no desire to confront who I suspect provided the information to Brooke, I still wake up early the morning after the trial and, after leaving a note for Joel, head to Tallahassee.

Two-and-a-half hours later, I pull my car to a stop in my parents' driveway and steel myself for the confrontation as I climb the steps to their house. When I was a little girl, I always thought the large Victorian we lived in was a castle, and I'd pretend I was a princess. Now, I see it for what it is: a shrine to excess.

We were a family of three. No one needs seven bedrooms for a family of three. No one needs three luxury vehicles, two boats, and a heated driveway. In Florida.

Thankfully, I've moved past needing my parents' acceptance, approval, or even love at this point. Suspecting what I do, I realize this will probably be the last time I ever speak to my parents again, let alone see them.

Squaring my shoulders, I knock on the door, not bothering to pretend I'm familiar enough with this place anymore to just walk in. Footsteps sound behind the thick wooden door and when it opens, I'm greeted by my father, a sneer pulling at the corners of his mouth. "Oh, it's you."

He looks the same as he always has. He's always had gray hair, even from the time I was a little girl. Now, it's nearly all white. He's a few inches taller than me and thin, with a ruddy complexion. His eyes are blue, but different from my mother's, Tootsie's, and mine. His are a solid, pale blue. As usual, he wears dress pants and a button-down, even during his leisure time. He's barefoot, though, and his toes peek out from under the hem of his slacks.

"Sure is. Where's Mom? I need to talk to you both. Now."

"You don't get to make demands of me, little girl. Not after everything we did for you."

Rage simmers in my chest, and I blow out a breath. "And what exactly did you do for me? Honestly, I can't think of one thing except use and exploit me and attempt to ruin my husband. I know it was you or mom who told Joel's ex-wife about Bryant Halpert. Do you have any idea what you could have cost Joel? He nearly lost custody of his son because of you."

"You should've given us the money, Teagan. Your mother tried to warn you that you'd pay; you didn't want to listen."

I shrug. "It doesn't matter now. Your plan didn't work. Joel was awarded joint custody and all the stuff you dragged out didn't work. Like I told you on the phone, I'd rather watch Tootsie's estate burn than let y'all ever see a dime. Goodbye, Dad. I hope you and Mom can live with yourselves. I hope you're proud of the fact that you almost ruined a good man's life."

I pivot to start down the steps, but my father calls my name, saying something I don't quite hear. "What?" I ask, turning to face him once again.

"I tried to warn Teresa that no good would come from taking you. Tootsie didn't want you, but she didn't want strangers to raise you, either."

I blink. "What?"

"If Tootsie had put you up for a private adoption like I suggested, none of this would've happened. She would've left everything to us. It's all your fault. Yours, and Tootsie's shitty sense of obligation to you."

"What are you saying?"

"What do you think I'm saying? You can write Teresa and me off all you want; you're already an orphan, girl." He considers his statement. "Well, that might not be entirely true. Who the hell knows who your father is." His lips curl into a disgusted frown. "Like mother, like daughter, I tell you. She may have been an even bigger slut than you," he says with a snort.

My chest grows tight, and I have trouble breathing. "Are you telling me Tootsie was my mother?"

"Looks like all those brains she had didn't trickle down to you, though. Jesus, are you stupid? Yes, Tootsie was your mother. Why do you think she wanted to spend summers with you? She only wanted to have fun with you, not parent you. *We* took care of you. *We* clothed you. *We* fed you. *We* raised you. We are owed for taking her bastard. She promised."

My father's—or, I guess, *not* my father's—words might as well be physical blows. I flinch with each statement and the venom in his tone. I don't want to cry. I want to be strong and not be affected, but I'm heartbroken, and my tears stubbornly spill down my cheeks despite my best efforts to blink them back. "So all I was to you was some sort of eventual payday?"

He smirks. "Why else would we agree to take you?"

Feeling even more disgusted now than when I arrived, I nod. "Thank you for telling me." I turn on my heels and return to my car, ignoring the hatred and curses my father spews at my back. Sliding behind the wheel, I ignore the ache in my chest and gnawing in the pit of my stomach as I pull out of the drive-way. I try to tell myself that I'm better off and deserve more than *them*. I try to remind myself that I have a family waiting for me at home who loves me.

Even knowing those things doesn't stop the pain. Tootsie was my mother, and she gave me to *those* people? How could she do that? My mind flashes on an envelope currently still sitting inside another envelope full of a giant—in meaning, if not size—legal document that changed my life. Hoping for some sort of closure, I drive faster toward home.

CHAPTER TWENTY-FIVE

JOEL

Rolling over to find Teagan's side of the bed empty is a bit jarring. She's such a naturally late sleeper, I can't recall a single morning when she's gotten up before me. Frowning but not actually concerned, I rise to make the bed, only then noticing the note on her pillow.

Had to take care of something.
Be back this afternoon.
Love you,
Tee

Feeling a bit better about things, I go through my typical Saturday morning routine of making coffee after letting Jethro out to do his business before going through a quick workout.

Gus ended up staying at his friend's house last night, so today, it's only me at home.

I'm reminded that had Teagan and I not gotten married and Brooke won full custody, this would be my life. I'd be all alone. And not that I struggle to be by myself, but God, am I thankful I don't have to be. I have a wife I love and a great kid who I hope is always as happy as he is right now.

My phone dings with a text, and I pick it up to read the screen.

> Selena: Brooke's lawyer already submitted a proposed parenting plan for the split custody. Check your email and let me know what you want to do. Try not to laugh when you read it.

I shoot her a thumbs-up emoji before navigating to my email, where sure enough, there's an email with a ridiculous schedule that I nearly do laugh at. Brooke's proposed schedule states she would get every spring and fall break from school, along with Thanksgiving and Christmas morning. Her schedule also has him going from house to house nearly every other day as if this is truly her idea of "fifty-fifty".

Running through possible schedules of my own in my mind, I sip my coffee. I pick my phone back up to compose a response to Selena's email when a knock sounds at the door. Unsure who would be knocking at—I glance at the clock on my phone—eight-fifteen on a Saturday, I still set my coffee down and stride over to the door, not bothering to put a shirt on.

A look through the peephole has me groaning and I hang my head just as another, more insistent, knock rattles the door. Rolling my shoulders, I brace myself for whatever's about to happen. Who knows when it's Brooke, right?

I keep my expression neutral when I pull the door open

and she doesn't wait for an invitation, just walks right in. "Why yes, come on in, Brooke. To a home that's not yours anymore." My ex-wife simply rolls her eyes as she strides over to the coffeemaker to pour herself a cup of coffee. "And yes, help yourself to my coffee."

"We're out," she replies, her tone flat, as if this is even a remotely valid excuse.

"You know, Starbucks is right down the street." When she pivots to lean against the counter, sipping her coffee as she blatantly ignores my statement, I pinch the bridge of my nose. "What can I do for you, Brooke?"

She looks around as if assessing the space. "So, since you got what you wanted, Teagan's gone now? You got her help and money, and whatever deal you struck is done since you won? Let me guess, she's going to take all that money she inherited and disappear?"

Narrowing my eyes, I fold my arms across my chest. "How did you even find out about the inheritance?"

She shrugs, the action nonchalant and dismissive. "My lawyer had some great investigators. Turns out, Teagan's parents aren't real happy with her. They told the P.I. all sorts of stuff."

"So, that's how you dug up the stuff about the kid who testified?"

She shrugs again. "Seemed like a good idea at the time."

I nod, considering. "And yet, it didn't work. I hope you're happy with yourself; for how low you were willing to sink. All that bashing of Teagan's integrity and playing dirty, and you still didn't get what you wanted."

"I've never gotten what I want," she spits out, all her previous flatness and placidness suddenly gone.

"What are you talking about?"

She slams her coffee mug to the floor, shards of ceramic and coffee flying in all directions, and I flinch as she stalks toward me, her eyes blazing. "All I ever wanted was you, Joel."

I can't bite back the shocked laugh that falls from my mouth. "You sure as hell had a funny way of showing it. You slept with my father, Brooke. You basically abandoned your kid."

Tears fill her eyes. "You were supposed to chase me. You were supposed to fight for me, Joel. For us. For our marriage. I only wanted to get your attention. I only wanted my husband back, but all you cared about was Gus."

I blink in disbelief. "What?"

"All you cared about was him. It was like once I got pregnant, I ceased to be your wife. I was only the mother of your child. You didn't even see me anymore. And when he was born, all your devotion, time, love; all of it was for him."

I stare at her, gobsmacked. "Is that truly what you think?"

"What else was I supposed to think? You were only ever at Gus's disposal. You never paid me any attention after he came along. You loved him more than you loved me."

Bitter tears fill my eyes. "How can you think that? You're pissed at me because I was a good dad? Because I love being a dad? After he was born, you were sick and one of us had to step up to be his primary caregiver. I took care of you, too. Jesus, Brooke, I loved you more than my own sanity. Had it been anyone but my father, I probably could've forgiven it. That's how much I loved you.

"What would you have had me do, not care for Gus? Not love him? Neglect him so you could always feel like my top priority? He's a kid, Brooke; and you gave him to me. He will always be the best thing I've ever done in my whole life and was created out of our love. I'm sorry if I ever made you feel less important to me than you were. I swear to you, that was never the case."

"We can start over," she says, her eyes wild as she steps closer, reaching for me.

I bat her hands away. "No, we can't. You're with my father. I'm with Teagan. I love her. The best thing we can do is be good coparents for Gus. *He* should be our priority."

"Please, Joel," she pleads, her expression now full of anguish.

I shake my head. I must truly not have any love left for her if I can't feel anything other than pity for her in this moment. "Go home, Brooke. To your husband. To your daughter."

Her eyes harden. "You know, at least your father actually sees more than a mother when he looks at me. He is completely devoted to me. I never have to question who comes first for him. I never have to wonder if he'll choose to play with the baby instead of holding me. I never have to worry she'll be more important to him than I am. He treats me like a queen."

It should bother me to hear her tell me all the ways she perceives my father to be a superior husband than me. It doesn't. Again, I only feel pity for her. "I'm glad, Brooke. I'm glad my father treats you the way you prefer. As you are Gus's mother, I truly want nothing but happiness for you. Because if you're happy, he'll be happy."

"So that's all I'll ever be to you now, huh? Gus's mother?"

I nod. "Yes." Again, she reaches for me, but I deflect her touch. "Go home, Brooke."

Her eyes drag down my bare torso. "God, I miss you. It was so good between us. Don't you remember? It can be good again, Joel. I promise. We can be a family again."

Angry for everything this woman has put me through in the past two years, I can barely keep the edge of rage out of my tone as I usher her toward the door. "I have a family. Teagan and

Gus are *my* family. Clive, Lily, and Gus are *your* family. *We* are not a family. We ceased to be a family the second you fucked my father. I will tell you one last time: go home." The last words come out like a low growl and I slam and lock the door as soon as she's back onto the porch.

Once Brooke leaves, I take my time cleaning up the coffee and mug shards from the floor, countertops, and even twenty feet away from where she threw it down. Part of me thinks I should tell my father to keep an eye on her. With her drastic shifts in mood while she was here, along with her history of severe post-partum depression, it's likely she has it again. But is it my place to be concerned about her anymore?

I've switched to beer a little after noon when Teagan's key slides into the lock on the front door. Gus was dropped off about an hour ago and immediately went to his room to crash. Apparently, kid sleepovers consist of staying up until way past dawn.

As the weather is a balmy seventy-five this late in October, Jethro is still enjoying the pool, so I toss his ball into the water and don't bother even looking over my shoulder as Teagan moves around the house. Ten minutes after she's walked in the door, she comes out to the deck, dropping onto the end of the lounger where I'm sitting. She has a thick envelope in her lap and I nearly startle when I see her face.

Immediately forgetting everything that's happened this morning, I devote my full attention to her. "What happened? What's wrong?"

She drops her gaze, her eyes puffy from crying, down to the envelope. When she speaks, her voice is thick with emotion. "I went to see my parents."

"Your parents?" I confirm.

She nods, still not looking up from the envelope. "They were the ones who told Brooke's lawyer about Bryant Halpert. My mom was the only person who knew. After it happened and I learned the truth, I was freaked out and confided everything in my mom. Then I waited. I waited for the police to show up and arrest me and label me a sex offender. I just knew I'd be taken away and locked up for years, and I was terrified. But she was the only one I ever told.

"So, I went to confront my parents because of what that information could've cost you. I was so angry at them because I knew without even having to ask them why they did it. They were pissed at me for the inheritance and me not giving it to them. But, it turns out, they're not even my parents."

I blink. "What?"

Her eyes lift to mine as she shrugs. "Tootsie was my mother. She asked my parents to raise me. They assumed if they did it, they'd get some sort of payday when she died. My dad said that it was Tootsie who insisted I visit during the summers so we could spend time together. He said he tried to talk my mom into not taking me, but because Tootsie was her sister, she felt obligated."

I grip the back of her neck, tugging her to me as I press my forehead to her temple. "I'm so sorry, Tee."

She doesn't respond, just flips the envelope over, lifting the flap to dig around until she fishes out another, smaller envelope with her name on it. Extending it to me, she asks, her eyes pleading, "Will you read this for me?"

Confused, I frown. "You want me to read it?"

Nodding, she blows out a breath. "Out loud?"

"Are you sure?"

"Yeah. I don't know if I'm up for it."

Taking the envelope, I gave her a soft smile. "Of course. Now?"

She shrugs. "No time like the present and all that, I guess. Is Gus home from the sleepover?"

"Yeah. Although, there apparently wasn't much sleeping because he came home and went straight to bed. I'll probably get him up in about an hour."

"Alright. Then, yeah. Go ahead and read it."

I work the flap open and peer down into the envelope, where something glints in the light. Plucking out a small metal key, I offer it to Teagan, who accepts it, holding it in her palm. Looking at it more closely, it appears to be a safe deposit box key. I don't comment and simply withdraw the folded sheets of paper. I clear my throat as I unfold the pages and, after a final glance at my wife, I begin to read.

> Teagan,
> If I know you, and since you're so much like me, I feel as though I do, you will wait until some ungodly time after you've decided whether to accept the inheritance to read this letter.

Teagan snorts a watery laugh, and I continue.

> If I were to guess how you reacted to finding out the conditions of receiving your inheritance, you got good and sloshed and wanted to

bring me back to life simply to throttle me. How close did I get?

Also, if I know you, you might consider asking that sweet friend of yours, Jonas, to marry you simply because you say the sex is really good and you're friends. I can honestly think of worse foundations for marriage, so if that's the case, I'm not mad about it.

Although, I also remember you telling me about that neighbor—you know, the one with the "crazy gorgeous eyes" as you put it—who's going through the divorce.

I look up at Teagan and she shrugs. "I was worried about you," she says matter-of-factly, and I give her a small smile before returning my attention to the letter.

You talk about his son as if he's the most amazing child ever and I know you've always said since your diagnosis that you don't "want" kids, but I think we both know that was never the reality of the situation. I think if you could have a child like Gus, you'd jump at the opportunity.

To hear how you also speak of Gus's father— is his name Joel? Anyway, that's what I'm going to call him since I can't remember for sure. To hear how you talk about Joel, it's always about how grumpy he is, but you say it with such affection, I know you secretly love that he's grumpy. Because you are sunshiny and love nothing more than making grumps a bit less grumpy. Truthfully, I think someone like that is much better suited for you.

But I digress.

I'm sure you're wondering why I left everything to you and in this envelope is the key to the safe deposit box I left you. In that box, you'll find further explanation. But we both know you have to accept the inheritance to gain access to the box, so you have a choice to make about how much you want the information.

I will tell you this. I left my estate to you because you are my daughter. I don't pretend to make any excuse for not raising you myself. I can only say that I was selfish and self-centered and thought you'd be better off with Teresa and Ted. They'd just lost Teddy, and I'd lost things, too. I felt like it was the best solution for everyone at the time.

I can't say I regret this decision because you've turned out to be the most amazing human imaginable, with the most selfless heart. I'm not sure, if you'd been exposed to my influence full-time, that I'd be able to say that. I will say, my summers with you were the best days of my life.

When we talk, you share about how you never want to get married or that you believe you're not made for love. As someone who also felt that way a lot of the time, I can promise that when you find that "one," you'll see exactly how made for love you are.

I can't resist leaning over to press a kiss to the side of her head as I'm reminded that I told her nearly the exact same thing weeks ago. She leans into my kiss, breathing a contented sigh as I return my eyes to the paper.

I know my conditions are drastic. And unorthodox. Call it mother's intuition or some sort of gut feeling, but I think this is just the thing you need.

I'm fully aware you may shun my conditions and the inheritance. It's a chance I'm willing to take because the charities I've chosen are also worthy causes. Truth be told, though, I think you'll find one that's even better.

Whether or not you take it, this inheritance— along with the memories we've shared—is all I have to offer you. I was never good at much more than making money and I'm sorry I couldn't be the sort of mother you deserved.

With all that being said, if I know your parents—and I do—they'll be less than thrilled by the contents of my will. They've long assumed I'd leave everything to them as some sort of payment for taking you off my hands. I didn't see that at first, but I do now. Learning the people I trusted to carry out the most important task imaginable—raising my child—could have those sorts of motives fills me with unending shame.

Although, if you decide to give your parents any of the inheritance, that's up to you. My recommendation would be to see if they show their asses before you make your decision. Something tells me you'll do the right thing where they're concerned and they'll get exactly what they deserve.

Teagan, you will always be the accomplishment I am most proud of. I'm even prouder that your accomplishments are all of your own making. You are incredible. I admire your spirit and your intelligence and your sass. You also underestimate yourself and what you're capable of. You, my sweet, amazing, gorgeous daughter, are capable of so much love.

I think, above all else, I want you to see that more than anything. I know if you decide to honor the conditions of your inheritance, you will choose someone worthy of you. You will find a man—or woman or person—who will show you exactly how well you can love. You will find someone who, on their worst day, is still the person with whom you'd want to share your life. You will find someone who thinks you are perfect, exactly as you are.

Because you are, my girl. You are so much more than you allow yourself to believe. You are the sun and your light is life to those who you choose to shine down on.

As your "Tootsie", I will forever be that old, eccentric hippy lady who wanted nothing more than to show you a good time. As your mother, I want nothing more for you than a lifetime of happiness and fulfillment.

I am so unbelievably proud of the woman you have become and will forever cherish the gift your life is to the world; especially mine.

Love,

Tootsie

Teagan sniffles before clearing her throat, and I fold the letter, returning it to the envelope. She wordlessly takes it, hanging her head for a beat before letting out a deep breath.

"Looks like Gus wasn't the only one trying to play match-maker," she says, a soft smile on her face.

"You did say Tootsie was wicked smart. Maybe she was also clairvoyant."

She snorts a laugh. "Maybe."

I tap my finger against the fist currently still curled around the key. "What are you going to do about that?"

"I'm not doing anything today. I think I'm truthed out today."

I nod. "I know what you mean." I spare a glance at the house next door. "I had a visitor this morning."

"Yeah?"

I nod again. "Brooke came by."

One of her dark brows tics up. "And?"

Huffing an uncomfortable laugh, I shake my head. "It's almost absurd to even tell you what she said."

Teagan rolls her shoulders. "Let me guess; she's still in love you and everything she's done was to get your attention."

I frown, shocked. "How the hell did you know that?"

My wife splays her hands. "She said something at Gus's birthday that struck me as odd. She said if it came down to it, who would you choose, Gus or me. But the way she said it, it was almost...wistful, I guess. Of course, I told her you'd always put Gus first, and your love for him and me wasn't a competition. I realized that for her, it probably was.

"You thought she assumed you'd chase her. It hit me that even negative attention is attention, and what better way to get your attention than to sleep with your father, have his baby, and then try to take Gus away? I hoped maybe I was jumping to conclusions or being a bit delusional about things."

I shake my head. "You weren't. That's exactly what she was doing. She was jealous of Gus. Honestly, I think she's got post-partum depression again, because she had some wild mood swings while she was here. I'm tempted to tell my father, just so he can be aware, but is it my place?"

"Yes," she says automatically. "As she is the mother of your son and he's going to be there with her, you have to do what's best for him. Even if it's talk to your dad. Because it's for Gus."

I sigh. "Yeah."

Turning her body, she runs her hand up my jaw. "I'm sad. Take me to bed and make me feel better?"

"Of course."

CHAPTER TWENTY-SIX

TEAGAN

Leaving Jethro outside to dry off in the shade, we quietly make our way into the house, mindful of Gus's presence as we shuffle toward our bedroom, kissing along the way. Even with the revelations of today and the inner turmoil I feel about what my parents said, Tootsie's letter, and what Joel said about Brooke, it only takes seconds of my husband's mouth on mine to drive away every thought except him.

After he silently shuts and locks our bedroom door, he yanks me back to him, his mouth claiming mine in a hungry, needy kiss. I return it with greedy kisses of my own as we hurriedly undress. It takes less than a minute for both of us to be naked and panting. As Joel breaks his lips from mine, a sweet smile on his face, he sits, tugging me between his knees. He lifts his hand to cup my face as he looks deeply into my eyes. "God, I love you."

I grin, unable to keep the pleased blush off my cheeks. "Oh? I had no idea." He chuckles, and I lean down to kiss a line down his neck and over his bare shoulder. Threading his fingers through the hair at the base of my skull, he lets out a slow breath. "I love you, too," I say between kisses to his collarbone and across his chest.

I glance up at him as I trail my mouth down his sternum. "I love your brain, your surly attitude, and your big heart." He hisses when I tug his nipple between my teeth. "I love how you think I'm good, when most of the time I doubt myself." I kiss my way down his abs, loving the way the muscles flex under my lips. He reclines a few degrees, but leaves his hand in my hair. "I love how free you are with your love for Gus." I let my eyes come to his. "I love how unconditional it is." I can't stop the tremor in my voice, and he gives my scalp a supportive squeeze. I lower my head to nip at the skin next to his navel, making him huff a quick breath. "I love what a good man, good husband, and good father you are."

I plant my hand in the middle of his chest to encourage him to recline farther as I drop to my knees. Pressing a kiss to his hip, I make my way down his thigh. "I love how you feel inside me and how you make me feel when we make love." Running my hands up his inner thighs, I look at him again, his beautiful eyes darkened with hunger. "I love that you are the first person I ever felt anything with. I love that the love of my life also happens to be the best sex of my life."

He grins, a soft laugh falling from his mouth that dies as soon as I wrap my fingers around his shaft. I swipe the bead of pre-cum off the head, and Joel groans when my grip tightens around him. I bend to lick a line up the underside of his cock, making him inhale sharply when I flick my tongue over the tip. "I love the way you taste."

I wrap my lips around the crown to give it a hard suck. He grunts, his grip turning nearly painful in my hair. "Fuck, Tee." I huff a laugh as I sink my mouth lower to take him deep, bringing my hand in to work his length. When I return to the head and hollow out my cheeks to suck him again, his hips buck. I nearly gag, but I relish the low growly sounds he makes, the way his fingers massage my scalp, and the curses and filthy words of praise he mutters.

I could lose myself in this; the giving of pleasure. God knows I enjoy giving it to Joel. But as grumpy and surly as he is a lot of the time, selfish he most definitely is not. Even if I were determined to make this only about him, I could almost guarantee he'd figure out how to still make it about me.

Although I'd love nothing more than to feel him spill down the back of my throat, I'm not a bit surprised when he yanks me off of him before I'm anywhere near done. I attempt to protest, but he claims my mouth, pulling me to him, my mind going blank with anything I was about to say. Because in the next second, he's got me flipped on the bed, both of my hands pinned to the mattress with one of his.

Without my sense of touch, his kiss becomes more intense, his groans against my skin more acute, his fingertips skimming over my breasts and plucking at my nipples become sharper. Even as I moan his name and roll my hips, encouraging him to enter me, he doesn't; seemingly content to drive me into a frenzy.

He teases my clit with the tip of his dick, his grin cocky as he peers down at me. I know if I actually struggled against his grip, he'd release me. Lucky for us both, I don't want him to release me. I want him to *take*. I want him to lose control. I want him wild and possessive. I need it.

I let my head fall back on a moan, but he grips my face with his free hand. "No, I want your eyes, Tee. I love to look into them when I fuck you. I like to know you're right here with me."

"I am," I promise.

Hands down, the easiest promise I've ever made.

"Good." He punches his hips forward, and I gasp with the

delicious invasion as I keep my eyes on his. "That what you wanted?"

"Yeah. Fuck, you feel good."

He groans as he grips my thigh, his fingertips digging in. "You're one to talk." I rock my hips, wanting him even deeper, and he grunts through gritted teeth. "Shit."

He shifts to brace my calf on his shoulder and I nearly scream at the change in angle as he pounds into me, but I clamp my mouth closed. "You're trying so hard not to scream, aren't you? Can't let anyone hear how well your husband fucks you; how deep he hits you."

"No," I croak. "Oh, God. Shit."

His jaw clenches, and he groans before he quickly pulls out and giving me a swift smack on the backside. "I want your ass in the air for me."

I scramble to obey, enjoying how much he's taking control of things. After everything that's happened today, I think we both need to be mindless for even a few minutes. I know I do. He brackets my knees with his own, running his hand up my bare back to fist my hair. "I said I want your ass in the air. Drop your arms, Tee."

The words, spoken in a deep, husky scrape, make goosebumps rise on my arms as I drop down on my forearms. "That's it. Jesus, look at you, all spread open for me, ready to take exactly what I'm willing to give you."

The hand not currently still in my hair squeezes my hip possessively. My chest heaves, my heart racing, as I try to be patient. Truth be told, I'm not all that patient. Today, I'm feeling even less so. I snake my hand between my thighs, needing *something*, and Joel lets out a deep, rumbly chuckle that makes my breaths come quicker.

"You needing something, Sweetheart? Can't wait any longer?"

My answering moan has his grip on my hip tightening and in the next second, all the air whooshes out of my lungs as he slams into me with a groan. I drag in a lungful of air as he withdraws to drive back in, the fronts of his thighs slapping against the backs of mine.

He drops his forehead to my shoulder blade, his breath hot on my skin as he takes and takes and *takes*. And fuck if I'm not here for it. It feels like it lasts for hours, but I know in my brain it's probably only a few minutes. He was so close before, and with him, it always feels like I am, too. Still, it seems to go on and on and on. When his hand snakes around my hip to cover my fingers with his as we both work my clit, I am wrecked, my strangled sob muffled by my pillow.

His thrusts turn even more frantic, his breathing labored, his grip on my hair verging on painful as he buries his face in the back of my neck. His body goes rigid, a choked grunt working its way up his throat as he comes.

My husband is gentle as we come down, slowly pulling out and lowering us both to the bed. He tugs me against him, his fingertips gently sweeping over my shoulder and down my back, his eyes never leaving mine. "Sorry, I kinda lost myself there for a second."

I huff a laugh, shaking my head as I tilt my chin to press a soft kiss to his lips. "Are you kidding? That was sexy as fuck."

Blushing, he drops his forehead to mine. For several long moments, we just lie there, content. Eventually, though, he pulls back to look at me. "I'm sorry about your parents being the ones who gave Brooke possible ammo during the trial."

I ignore his statement in favor of a question of my own. "How does what Brooke said make you feel?"

He considers, blowing out a long breath. "Sad. Sad that she ever felt like I didn't love her enough. Angry that she ever felt like I didn't love her enough. I also wonder if there was any truth to what she said. Do I put Gus first—to the detriment of my other relationships?"

I hurriedly shake my head. "No. I've never felt that way. I honestly can't say how she feels because I never knew you before Gus was in the picture. But you love with your whole heart and it's one of my favorite things about you. Seeing how devoted you are to him made me love you more. I can't speak for her, though. I'm sorry if her visit drummed up a lot of feelings for you."

He gives me a slow, deep kiss, and *damn*, I already want him again by the time he breaks it.

"All it did was make me see that I truly don't love her anymore. All I felt for her was pity."

Nodding, I swirl my fingertips in his chest hair as I look up at him. "Still, it's got to be hard to process knowing how much you loved her at one point. I wish I could empathize with you. I'm sorry I can't."

Sweeping a stray hair off my forehead, he presses a kiss to it. "I'm glad you can't. I'm glad you don't know what it feels like to have your heart broken like that. Although, your parents broke your heart, so I wouldn't say you can't empathize, even if it's a different kind of heartbreak."

"Maybe," I admit.

Jethro barks, and I sigh, making to rise from the bed. Joel gives my hip another squeeze. "I'll get him. Let me think you need to recover for a little while longer."

I laugh as I pull the covers up around me. "Deal."

CHAPTER TWENTY-SEVEN

JOEL

The following day, after finding enough consideration for Brooke as the mother of my son, I call my father to give him a heads up about my suspicion that Brooke has PPD again. When he doesn't answer, I'm not sure whether to be disappointed or relieved, but I figure I can try again later. So while Teagan and Gus take Jethro to the dog park for some socialization, I head over to the high school to do some work on the dugouts.

As I'm putting some finishing touches on painting the bench in one of them, I freeze mid-brushstroke when I hear a voice say, "A little early to be starting on maintenance, isn't it? The season's months off."

Taking a couple of deep breaths, I place the paintbrush on the edge of the roller tray and pull myself to my full height to face my father. He's dressed casually in jeans and a button-down as he stands in the dugout entrance. I don't move any closer to him and simply lean against the wall on the opposite end of the space. "There's a youth league that uses the field for fall ball. A return call would've been sufficient, you know; I didn't actually need to see you."

He splays his hands as if to say, *and yet, here I am.* "I went next door and Teagan said I could find you here."

"So you have," I deadpan, folding my arms across my chest.

My father pinches the bridge of his nose. "You were the one who called me, Joel, so don't act like I'm somehow imposing on your time."

"Forgive me if it takes me a moment to work up the gumption to even look at you, let alone speak to you in person." I inhale a deep breath, blowing it out as I try to be mindful of the whole reason I wanted to talk to him in the first place. "I think Brooke has postpartum depression again."

His brow furrows. "She's fine."

"No, she's not. She's exhibiting the same sort of mood swings and erratic behavior she did after Gus was born. I mean, can you honestly say that the outburst she had at court was rational? And then, she came by yesterday and—."

"You saw her yesterday?"

I sigh. "Yeah. Plus with the ridiculous parenting plan she submitted to the lawyers, there's no way she's okay. Like I said, she was having some wild mood swings within a very short period of time. You need to keep an eye on her."

"I already told you; she's fine."

I nod. "Whatever you say; she's your wife. I'm just speaking from the experience I had living with her for years. I don't really give a shit about either of you, but she's my kid's mother, so that's the only reason I'm able to show an ounce of concern. But sure, ignore my warning."

He's quiet for a long moment, turning to look out toward the field. "I want to say I remember every one of your games that I attended. Truth is, I can only recall a few of the big ones." I don't respond because I'm not sure why he's bringing up my playing. "Your mom could remember, though. Her memory was like this vault. She could recall a conversation from our first date like it was yesterday. Sometimes, I think she might've had some sort of photographic memory or something because it was so good."

I look down at my feet as my chest begins to ache. Why is he talking about my mother? Does he think it's remotely okay? I'm not even sure I've ever been able to properly grieve her because all I can see is Brooke and my father standing in her hospital room.

"I never meant for it to happen, Joel; any of it." His voice is full of anguish, but I can't bring myself to care. I still can't even look at him. "The first time, it was right after the funeral and we were so drunk that it wasn't until after that I even realized what happened."

Bile rises up my throat as I finally raise my gaze to his. "I don't care how or why it happened. It never should've fucking happened. I—."

"I know that, son. There's never going to be a valid excuse I could give for how things happened. I was in such a terrible place and I think Brooke was, too. We used each other to deal with our grief. Then, we both had to grieve you, too. I truly didn't plan on falling in love with her, Joel. She's not your mother, and I'll never love her the same way, but I do love her. I'm also not you for her. She's never going to be over you, and that's something I'll have to live with for the rest of my life. That for her, I'm a second choice."

I ball my hands into fists at my sides to keep from walking across this dugout to put my hands around his neck to choke the life out of him. "Is all that supposed to make me feel better about things? Does you unburdening yourself make you feel less guilty in the hope I'll ever forgive you and Brooke for what you've done to me and to my son? It's never going to happen.

Like I told you that day at the airport, you are dead to me. For the sake of my son, I will try to remain as civil as possible, but I will never give any thought to you and Brooke except where it concerns Gus."

Turning my back on my father, I bend to resume painting.

"Joel, I—."

"I've said everything I have to say to you. You can get the fuck off my field."

I'm not sure I take a full breath until I hear him walk away and start his car. By then, the tears have started and I'm thankful no one is around to see me sob for the next half-hour. Because even though I'm happy with my current life and I love Teagan with my whole heart, I hate that because of his and Brooke's betrayal, I've lost my relationship with my father. I hate that any part of this has touched my son and we may not know for years what sort of impact it's had on him. I hate that I can't think about my mother's last days and not be reminded of my father and Brooke. I hate that because of all of this recent mess, Teagan's now been traumatized and has to learn to live with her parents' betrayal.

I just fucking hate it all.

<hr>

A few days later, Teagan and I are leaving work. As we climb into my truck, she asks, "Gus has basketball practice, right?"

"Yeah, until five. Why?"

"I think I'm ready to go find out what's in the safe deposit box. I haven't been able to get Tootsie's letter off my mind and I need to know. Since we have time, I figure why not."

I nod. "Alright. Do you want to go home and come back out, or do you want me to go with you?"

"Will you go with me? There's no telling what I'm going to find, and I just really don't want to be alone."

Taking her hand in mine as I pull out of the school parking lot, I give it a squeeze. "Of course."

She shoots me a grateful smile before breathing a relieved sigh. "Thank you."

"Anytime. I'm kinda curious about what's in it, too. I'm feeling sort of like Brad Pitt in *Seven*."

She snorts, rolling her eyes. "I sincerely doubt it's going to be a severed head."

"One can only hope," I agree.

"So, how are you feeling about everything your dad said at the field the other day?"

I side-eye her. "Nice segue, Tee."

She shrugs. "What? I gave you days to bring it up, so that should probably earn me some sort of medal for my patience." Squeezing my hand again, she lifts it to press a kiss to the back of it. "You know I worry about you and we both know you like to bottle it all up. We also know how well that's worked out for you in the past. I'm just giving you the opportunity to let it out before it builds up pressure and I'm forced to replace the bathroom mirror again. I really like this one."

For a long moment, I don't say anything, and she doesn't push. But knowing my wife and how right she is about most things where feelings are concerned, I finally roll my shoulders as I blow out a breath. "I feel like he didn't believe me about Brooke's PPD. Who knows; maybe I'm wrong and she really is fine, but I don't think so. Of course, that just makes me worry about Gus and even Lily, even though she's not my kid."

"No, but she is your sister. And Gus's."

"Don't remind me."

"I don't have to remind you, Joel; it is what it is. Even if you never interact with her more than in passing for Gus's sake, she is still your sister. She's going to know that, too. She didn't ask to be born, so none of this is her fault. So while I understand, in theory, you wanting to resent her, she's just a baby and doesn't deserve it."

"I don't resent *her*," I argue, my voice rising. "I resent the fact that there was even an opportunity for her to exist. Her existence is proof that my father didn't just sleep with Brooke that first time. It happened over and over and over and it's still happening. It's like fucking salt in an open wound."

"I can understand that," she says calmly. "But you and Brooke were no longer married when she got pregnant. You had divorced her, and even if you didn't know it at the time, she was already remarried. I'm not saying that you shouldn't have divorced her. Infidelity is a choice, and it is choosing to willfully hurt the person you swore to love. But the fact remains that because of everything that's happened, you now have a sister.

"I'm never going to ask you to forgive them because I'm not sure I could forgive it, either. All I'm asking you to do is look into the future. In ten, fifteen, or twenty years, when Lily is older and she knows you are her brother, imagine what that will be like for her to know that you don't acknowledge her because of your hate for them. Is that something you can live with? Is that something you want Gus to see?"

"Dammit, Tee, you know I hate it when you make me examine myself."

"Sorry, pal. I love you, but I don't want you to someday, when the wound isn't so raw, wish you'd been better for kids who are in the middle of all this by no fault of their own. Plus, you have to admit, she's pretty cute."

"Yeah, she is," I say with a sigh. I pull into a parking spot in front of the bank before turning to look at her. "What would I do without you dropping all these logic bombs on me?"

She smiles. "I don't intend to let you find out." Glancing at the bank's entrance, she shakes her head. "Here goes nothing, I guess."

We step out of the truck to walk into the bank, and Teagan requests entry to her box. After she shows her ID and signs in, we're escorted to the vault where she and the clerk, a young man with warm, light-brown skin, both insert keys into the correct box. The clerk pulls the box out before leading us to a private room within the vault, setting the box on a tall table.

"When you're done, you'll just replace the box and it will automatically lock. Let us know if you have any issues or need assistance."

She nods, and he steps out, leaving us alone with the box. It's not very large, probably ten inches by twelve inches and three inches deep—only big enough for documents or smaller items. For a long time, Teagan just stares at it, her hands flexing on the table where she planted them after the clerk set the box down.

"Well, I don't think it's big enough for a severed head anyway," I offer, and she huffs a laugh.

"Probably not. But this is it. After this, I don't have any other mysteries from Tootsie. Truthfully, I'm not sure what I'm hoping to find."

I cover her hand with my own. "Whatever it is, I'm here with you. No matter what, you're still Teagan Roth, badass wife, stepmom, and dog mom. You're still the woman who helped me heal and loved me when I'm not sure I loved myself anymore. You're still the woman who's always loved my kid like he was your own, even before he was. You're still the best friend I've ever had. Nothing in this box changes any of those facts."

She blinks back tears and nods, swallowing thickly. After taking a steadying breath, she flips open the lid of the box.

CHAPTER TWENTY-EIGHT

TEAGAN

Joel and I peer down into the black metal box. As I've never been sure what I'd find in this thing, I don't know how I'm supposed to react. Nevertheless, I fish the items out to spread them across the tabletop.

There are a couple of things I recognize immediately. One is a chunky sterling silver ring that Tootsie wore for as long as I can remember. I slip it onto my middle finger and it fits like a glove. There's also a gold pocket watch I've never seen before, but appears to be in pristine condition, along with a wide gold band that's seen better days. It's scuffed and weathered and appears to have a lot of miles on it.

"Holy shit," Joel says as he picks up the watch.

"What?" I ask, alarmed.

"This is a Patek Philippe."

"Is that supposed to mean something to me?"

"It should if you know anything about watches."

"Assume I don't," I deadpan.

"Okay, so Patek Philippe is one of the most prestigious watch manufacturers in the world. They are credited as having created the first Swiss wristwatch and, out of the ten most expensive watches ever sold, nine of them have been Patek Philippe. The other was a Rolex. You'd have to have it appraised, but there is no telling how much this thing is worth."

"How do you know anything about luxury watches?"

He shrugs. "I read stuff."

"So, you're not only into astrophysics, but luxury timepieces?"

"I like to be well-versed in a multitude of topics. You never know when something might come in handy during a game of Trivial Pursuit."

I can't help but laugh. "Touché." He flips it over, making a noise in the back of his throat. "What, does it have some sort of cryptic inscription or something?"

"Not cryptic, just a little cheesy. 'Time stops when I'm with you,'" he says, reading the back of the watch.

"You're right; that is cheesy."

I hold up the band. "I wonder who this belonged to."

"Tootsie was never married?"

"Not that I know of." I check the inside of the ring finding only a jeweler's stamp stating that the ring is eighteen karat gold. Returning it to the table again, I pick up one of the several manilla envelopes spread out on the table. It's about six by nine inches and about an inch thick. When I work the brad through the flap, I reach my hand inside, realizing that it's a stack of photos.

Joel rounds the table to look at them with me as I flip through the stack. Most are of a place I don't recognize; some green, mountainous location with lush evergreen trees and a crystal clear river. They're gorgeous and almost artistic in a way. Honestly, there's no telling when the photos were taken until I'm about halfway through the pile and my breath catches.

There's a picture of a pregnant Tootsie dressed in a flowy white sundress in the middle of a meadow of wildflowers. Her blonde hair is long and wavy and a crown of flowers sits atop her head. She's also not alone.

Standing behind her with arms wrapped around her, their hands joined over her belly, is a tall man with tan skin in jeans and a black T-shirt, dark hair cut short in an almost military cut. I can't make out much of his face since it's buried in Tootsie's neck as her head is thrown back in a laugh. But from what you can see, he's grinning. He also has a ring on his left hand; they both do. Hers is the one I now wear on my middle finger.

I turn the photo over, hoping to see something written regarding the name of the man or the location where it was taken. There's nothing. I set that specific photo to the side while I flip through the rest and while there are plenty of photos of Tootsie, as well as nature, there aren't any of the man. Maybe he was the photographer?

Hoping to find more photos, I open the other envelopes. One contains some documents about the patents Tootsie held, while another has the deeds to both the Del Mar house and my own. The third envelope makes me stop short because it contains what must be my original birth certificate—where no father has been listed—as well as the adoption agreement between Tootsie and my parents.

As I pull the documents out, something falls to the floor. I bend to retrieve it, my eyes immediately burning with tears when I see what the item is. It's a photo of Tootsie and me. It must've been taken right after I was born because Tootsie's in a hospital gown and I'm wrapped in a blanket and have a tiny hat on.

"You look like her. A lot," Joel comments.

I nod. "I always thought it was one of those weird family

things." Placing the photo with the others, I return the documents to the envelope after giving them a quick once over.

Lifting the final, largest envelope, I brace myself for whatever might be in it. The envelope is heavy for its size and when I open it, I see why. There are two thick leather journals and a small stack of about ten photos.

Immediately, I begin flipping through the photos, which appear to mostly be of an increasingly pregnant Tootsie, the last one gives me pause again. It's the same man from the meadow, but I can see all of his face as he and Tootsie stare into the lens of the camera, their joined hands once again resting on her enormous belly. Again, they both wear rings on their left hands.

He's handsome, with classic good looks and chiseled features. He would definitely draw the eye if you passed him on the street. Deductive reasoning would tell me this is my birth father and he and Tootsie were, in fact, married. But looking at the photo, I don't see anything of myself in the man's face. He appears to have kind eyes and a warm smile, but it's one nanosecond from an entire life. For all I know, he was a terrible, horrible man. For all I know, he may not be my father. For all I know, he may not be someone to whom Tootsie was married. I only know what I see in the two photos of a woman who I now know to be my mother and a man who was obviously someone of importance to her.

Picking up the journals, which are tied together with a length of white grosgrain ribbon gone dingy with age and handling, I work the knot loose and proceed to open the top book. Seeing the words, "Dear Baby" in Tootsie's handwriting has me slamming it closed again a split second later.

"What is it?" Joel asks, concern in his tone.

"Tootsie wrote letters or kept a journal or something. It

says, 'Dear Baby,' so I'm not quite up for that just yet. I think I'll wait until I get back home."

"Sure," he agrees. "What do you want to do with this stuff?"

"I guess take it with us? There's not that much, and I don't really have a reason to leave it all here."

"Sounds good."

As we begin gathering items, I turn to face Joel. "Thank you for coming with me."

His brow furrows. "There's nowhere else I would choose to be right now. I love you and supporting you in this is the least I can do for everything you've done for me." He pulls me into his arms and I willingly let him hold me for a long moment, my chest aching with a mix of gratitude and love for him, along with a sense of trepidation about what I'll read in the journals.

After supper, Joel and Gus decide to go grocery shopping, so I'm left home alone with Jethro and the journals. Like a siren song, the small leather tomes call to me from where I've stashed them in my nightstand. Knowing there's no way I'll get through this sober, I pour myself a giant glass of wine before heading to discover my truth, Jethro trailing right behind me.

I down half the glass before I even work up the nerve to open the drawer, but Jethro keeps giving me the stink eye, so I finally set the glass down to pull out the books. With a final bracing breath, I open the first book.

Dear Baby,
That sounds really cheesy and generic and like

what all normal people say when they find out they're going to be parents. I'd like to think I'm none of those things. So maybe we can call you something else. I don't yet know if you're a boy or girl, so for now, I'll just call you Spud.

I snort a laugh, shaking my head. When I was little, Tootsie always called me Spud. Now I guess I know why.

I haven't told your father yet, but knowing him as I do, he will feel like I do already; that you are the best thing to ever happen to us. If I'm honest, I never imagined this would be my life. I've never felt that maternal tug that most women talk about; the yearning to carry a child and hold it in their arms.

No offense, Spud, but I wasn't asking for this. For the first few weeks after I found out, I debated whether this was actually something I could do. I'm not anti-baby or anti-motherhood or parenthood. I simply know myself.

I've discovered, though, letting yourself be loved has a way of making you see things in a new light. I now know my heart is big enough for this and so is my life.

A little background about myself. I have a

sister who's a bit of a pill, if I'm honest. But she is my sister and I love her. She and her husband have a little boy named Teddy, and I'm excited about the prospect of us raising our children together.

I'm an inventor by trade and not to toot my own horn, but I'm sort of a big deal in the computer world. Probably by the time you're my age, I predict we'll have computers small enough to fit in your pocket. Hopefully, I'm right.

Your father, Nigel Devney, is the kind of person who is able to brighten even the most dark day. His good heart, gentle nature, and fierce loyalty are just a few of the many reasons I fell in love with him. I can't deny he's quite the looker, too.

He's a journalist from England who enjoys photography as a hobby and is the most talented person I know. I expect as I expand, Nigel will find any excuse possible to put me in front of the camera. We met in San Francisco at a gallery that happened to be showing a couple of his images in a showcase for amateur artists. I actually ended up buying one of his pieces, a huge print of the Golden Gate Bridge at sunrise with lots of fog, giving it this almost ethereal feel.

I gasp because I know the picture she's talking about. It was one that had hung in my house for as long as I've been there. Tootsie actually gave it to me as a housewarming gift. She gave me a photo my *father* had taken? I return my attention to the journal.

When I came to pick up the print, he happened to be there, and we struck up a conversation. A conversation turned into drinks, drinks turned into dinner, dinner turned into love. God, I think I loved him from the first night we met. Not that I'd ever admit that to myself.

Love was something for saps and fiction. I was much too analytical for mundane and pedestrian things such as feelings. Of course, Nigel being the ray of sunshine and absolute force he is, I didn't stand a chance. We were married a month later.

In reality, the last year has been the happiest of my life. How I ever thought I wasn't meant for love is a mystery I'm thankful every day that Nigel was able to solve.

You are loved more than you could ever know already. You are the dream I never knew I would want. You were created from the most beautiful love this world has ever known.

Love,

Mom? Mommy? Mama?

We'll work on the title.

Tears pour from my eyes as I close the book, unable to read any more right now. Every part of me is screaming to read the remaining entries *right the fuck now* so I can find out what changed from that point to Tootsie giving me up for adoption. Instead, I simply set the book on my nightstand and lie down, sobbing into a pillow for *this* Tootsie. I never knew *her*; this woman who was obviously happy and in love and looking forward to becoming a mother.

CHAPTER TWENTY-NINE

JOEL

When Gus and I return from the store, Teagan is nowhere to be found in the common areas of the house. After taking a few minutes to get everything put away, Gus retreats to his room to get a head start on his required reading for school, so I check my bedroom when I hear Jethro whining behind the door. He darts out as I open the door, immediately scratching at Gus's. I can't help but smile as my son opens his door to allow the dog entry.

As I step inside, I see Teagan lying on the bed in the fetal position, a soft snuffling coming from her direction. I hurriedly cross the room to kneel next to the bed, brushing her hair off her face. She appears to have been crying for a while. "Tee, what's wrong?" I ask, worry flooding my chest.

She shakes her head and sits up, clutching a pillow to her chest. "I read some of Tootsie's journal," she says between hiccups.

Rising to sit on the bed beside her, I take her hand in mine. "Was it bad?"

Again, she shakes her head. "No. It was beautiful. She told

me about my father. He is—was—British. His name was Nigel, and he was a photographer. He took the photo that hung in my living room. The one of the Golden Gate Bridge?" I nod, and she continues. "They met when she bought the print. She said he had a good heart and was gentle and loyal."

"A lot like someone else I know," I offer, swiping her tears away with my thumb.

"They were married and really, really happy. She never believed in love until him."

"I'm sure it was difficult to read all that. Did you find out what happened?"

"Not yet," she says, mopping her face with her shirttail. "Hopefully, I will."

"I hope you get all the answers you're looking for."

"Would you mind if we go get that photo out of storage and hang it somewhere in the house?"

I shake my head. "Of course. Tomorrow?"

She nods. "Okay. I'm tired; I think I'm going to turn in."

"Sure. Get some sleep." I stand and drop a kiss on her cheek as she gets settled under the covers. "If you need anything, just holler, alright?"

"I will. Love you."

"Love you, too." I switch off the bedside lamp and quietly exit the bedroom. While I'm glad she's possibly going to get answers about her birth parents, I can't help but worry she might end up disappointed if she doesn't get all the information she's searching for.

After looking in on Gus, who's curled up next to Jethro as he reads *The Lightning Thief*, I head to the kitchen, pulling a bottle of beer from the fridge. Since it's such a nice evening, I step out onto the deck, dropping onto one of the loungers to stretch out. I take a long drink of my beer as I watch the stars begin to come out.

Sometime later, I wake with a start, realizing I must've fallen asleep on the deck. It's cooled considerably and I almost shiver as I rise to my feet to head back into the house. I've nearly made it to the back door when the sound of breaking glass drifts over from next door and I can't help but look that direction.

Listening more intentionally, I recognize not only the sound of shattering glass, but raised voices. It's not that my house and Teagan's old one are so far apart, but they're definitely not right on top of one another, either.

I almost ignore it. Brooke and my father's problems aren't mine to interfere with. If they're fighting or whatever's going on, good for them. But the conversation I had with Teagan on our way to the bank the other day nags at me.

Do it for the kids.

Waiting a few more seconds to see if things calm down, I stand stock still and simply listen. Half a minute goes by with no additional sounds of chaos, so I assume everything's calmed down and I won't need to interfere. I turn once again to go back into the house, but then more glass breaks. Following that is the sound of the front door opening and a baby wailing. Before I even register I'm on the move, I'm halfway to the deck gate before taking off at a sprint toward the house next door..

By the time I make it to the driveway, Lily's cries have turned into near shrieks. I run around to other the side of Brooke's van. "Everything okay over here?" With how quickly I've jogged over and the adrenaline currently dumping into my system, my heart rate is up and my breathing is a bit labored.

Brooke is bent over, attempting to get the baby into her car seat, and since she hasn't acknowledged me, I call her name. She still doesn't react, so I touch her shoulder. She recoils, snapping her head in my direction, and I nearly gasp at the sight of her. Her eyes are wild and the nightgown she wears is covered in blood.

"Brooke," I say calmly. "Are you okay?"

She doesn't appear to be injured, and her bare arms, legs, and feet don't look to have any cuts or scrapes. I steal a glance at Lily and she, too, seems uninjured.

"I'm fine. I have to go."

"It's late, and it seems like Lily's a bit upset. Want me to try to calm her down?"

She practically lunges toward the baby. "Don't you touch her," she hisses.

I hold my hands up in mock surrender. "Okay. Well, how about we go back into the house and I can get you cleaned up? Are you hurt?"

"I'm fine."

I nod, trying to think of any way possible to get her and the baby back into the house. At least if they're in the house, I can assess the situation better. Considering my father hasn't come outside, I'm also beginning to get concerned about his whereabouts.

"Alright. Can I go inside and fix you a cup of tea? I bet you've got some of that great lavender kind you always liked. You remember how you always wanted me to fix it for you to help you relax? I can do that now, too. Let's go into the house, okay?"

"No." She takes a step toward the driver's door and I do, too. "Like I said, I have to go."

"What about a diaper bag? Don't you need to get Lily's things?"

"No."

"Brooke, come on. Can't you hear Lily crying? She doesn't want to go anywhere. We can go in the house, okay? I'll help you get her put to bed and we can you get you taken care of."

"Brooke?" My father's voice, weak and sounding a bit disoriented, streams out the still-open front door.

She whips her head around, her eyes even wilder than before. I take the opportunity, with her being distracted, to quickly wrap my arms around her, turning our bodies so I'm between her and the baby. She shrieks, flailing her limbs, as she tries to escape. I simply hold on tighter, bringing mouth next to her ear. "Hey, it's okay; I've got you."

My ex-wife continues to struggle against me for a few more seconds before all the fight seems to leave her. She slumps, her body shaking with sobs. At this point, I'm not sure who's crying louder, her or Lily. Somewhere in my mind, it registers that my father has stepped past me to retrieve the baby from her car seat and is quietly shushing her as he carries her back inside.

"Let's go in the house, okay? We'll get you taken care of."

Brooke's sobs have turned to whimpers, but she doesn't fight me when I loosen my grip on her to usher her back toward the porch of the house she shares with my father and their daughter. Pushing away the bitterness that still threatens to bubble up at that thought, I guide her into the house and toward the bedroom.

Along the way, I ignore the broken glass on the floor until I realize Brooke is barefoot, so I pause to scoop her up. She makes no noise and her eyes don't seem to actually see anything. She also doesn't make to hold on to me. I simply continue on to the bedroom to lay her on the bed before tugging the covers up around her.

She curls up on her side, staring blankly ahead, her eyes red-rimmed and puffy. I squat down to examine this woman who I used to love more than my own life, only feeling sad for her. I'm reminded of how often she was in this sort of state before she got help after she miscarried and after Gus was born. Tears burn my eyes once again for the loss of our family.

Much like an actual death, I've mourned the loss of my marriage, my relationship with my father, and the fact that I'll probably never be able to grieve in a healthy way for my mother since everything is all jumbled up together.

Although I'm not sure I'll ever be over what happened, I don't hate Brooke. I'm not sure I ever could. If for no other reason than she gave me Gus, a part of me will never regret everything. I guess, in a way, she also gave me Teagan, and I'd never wish to give her up; not for anything in the world.

Footsteps falling behind me pull me out of my thoughts, but I don't take my eyes off Brooke. "Do you need to go to the hospital?"

"No," my father replies. "It's only a small cut."

"Is Lily okay?"

"Yeah. I've also called a colleague of mine who's going to come examine Brooke. She's a psychiatrist."

"Brooke already has a therapist; she's familiar with her. She'll be more comfortable with someone who knows her history."

"Don't talk about me like I'm not here," Brooke says, her voice flat and low.

I nod, waiting for her eyes to focus on mine. "You want us to call Dr. Lambert?"

"Okay," is all she says, curling tighter into herself as she closes her eyes.

In a few moments, her breathing levels out. I let out a slow exhale, relieved that she's asleep.

"I'll take it from here," Dad says, stepping up beside the bed.

Wordlessly, I stand to look at my father. He has a cut over his left eye and I have to bite my tongue to keep from showing concern. Truth is, I'm all out of concern for today. But then my mind flashes to Lily. None of this is her fault.

Do it for the kids.

"If you need any help with Lily until Brooke's back on her feet, let me know."

My father blinks in shock. "What?"

I clench my jaw as I roll my shoulders. "If you need someone to babysit or pitch in until you all are in a better place, Teagan and I are happy to help."

The man I used to look to for my entire moral code and example of what a good father and husband should be examines my face. I imagine he sees himself in me. How can he not? We're nearly identical. Briggs genes are a force to be reckoned with. But what does he see now? Hate? Loathing? Indifference?

"I can't ask—."

"Yes, you can," I cut in, insistent. "It's not a favor to you or her. You were right; Lily's my sister. None of how I feel about you or Brooke has anything to do with Lily, and I won't resent her for shit that's not her fault. So, if for no other reason than because it's what Teagan and Gus—and Mom—would expect of me, I will."

The mention of my mother makes Dad flinch and all the color drains from his face, but I continue. "Because God knows she was better than any of us and she would tell me I'm better than this. I'm not, but I loved her for always thinking the best of me. So yes, if you need help with Lily, call me."

For a long moment, he simply looks at me before finally nodding. I pull my phone out, navigating to my contacts to share the information for Brooke's therapist with my father before turning to leave.

I'm nearly out the door when he says my name. I pause, but don't turn around. "Your mother would've been right. You are better than this. You're a lot better than me, that's for sure. I know you got that from her; that big heart of yours. I'm sorry we broke it, son."

I blink back tears as I walk out of the house. I barely make it to my back patio before I drop onto a lounger, unable to go any farther. Burying my face in my hands, I sob, thankful Gus and Teagan can't hear me.

I don't love Brooke. I also don't hate her, though. As the mother of my child and someone who will always be in my life, I want her to be healthy. Part of me even wants her to be happy. Otherwise, what was all this pain, sorrow, and betrayal for?

The back door opens and I clamp my mouth shut, mopping my face in case it's Gus. "Joel?" Relief floods me hearing Teagan's voice. She wastes no time dropping onto the chair beside me, examining my face. "Hey, what's all this? You okay?"

I shrug, clearing my throat as my tears subside a moment later. Looking out toward Brooke's house, I sigh and relay the events of the night. Teagan loops her arm through mine before swiping her thumb over my cheek.

"I'm sorry I volunteered us to babysit without talking with you. If that's not—."

She puts her finger to my lips to shush me. "Of course we will. You did the right thing. I'm proud of you."

"Did I wake you up?"

My wife shakes her head, pressing a soft kiss to my lips. "No. I woke up, and then read more of Tootsie's journal. I got up to get a drink of water and heard you out here. I'm sorry you had to face all that stuff next door by yourself."

"Maybe it was something I needed to do alone to know I could do it."

She nods. "I understand that."

"What did the journal say?"

"So far, it's mostly about her pregnancy cravings and their

life in San Diego. Not too much about my father except that it's clear they were in love. Part of me wants to skip to the end to find out, but I also like getting to see this side of her that I never knew."

"Enjoy it, Tee. It's like having her with you. I wish I had something like that from my mom."

Teagan places her hand over my heart. "You do. You love like she did; big and with every part of you. She'd be so proud of what a good man you are."

I lift her hand to my lips, pressing a kiss to her palm. "Thank you for believing that I'm a good man. There were a lot of days I wasn't sure anymore."

CHAPTER THIRTY

TEAGAN

A few weeks later, I'm curled up on the back deck under a blanket, starting on the second of Tootsie's journals. To this point, she's continued to talk about her cravings and symptoms, as well as her relationship with my father. I've learned he went to Cambridge for college and studied English, but always wanted to do something creative; thus the phenomenal photography. I learned he was an only child and his parents died before he met Tootsie. That part made me especially sad since I hoped I'd be able to track down some of my other family. But I guess that's par for the course as far as my luck goes.

Jethro's bark from where he lies next to my lounger has me looking up from the page I'm currently reading about the first time Tootsie felt the baby kick. I blink, unsure I'm seeing what I actually am. Brooke is standing just inside the gate, a tentative smile on her face. When our eyes connect, she gives me a small wave.

I shut my book, dropping it onto the small table next to my chair. "Brooke," I say in greeting, not bothering to hide my uncertainty as to her presence. "Gus is at the park with Joel if you're looking for him."

She nods. "I know. Clive took Lily to meet them."

I blink. "I didn't know that."

"It was sort of last minute. He caught them as they were heading out, and Gus invited him. And for Gus, Joel won't say no; even if it means spending time with Clive."

I immediately bristle at her comment since it reminds me of what she said the day of Gus's birthday. She must see it in my face, because she pushes ahead, holding up her hands to ward off the retort I'm getting ready to lob. "I didn't mean that as a jab. I only meant that Joel doesn't have it in him to deny Gus when it's something he can do; even if it means he's uncomfortable for a little while. I actually came to see you."

Unable to hide my surprise, I open my mouth, only to close it again before I finally confirm, "Me?"

She nods, gesturing to a nearby chair. "May I sit? Please?" Her tone and expression are a bit pleading, and after a beat, I finally nod. Brooke gives me a quick, small smile, dropping onto the lounger next to mine. Jethro eyes her, but other than a dismissive huff, doesn't seem to be bothered by her presence. I choose to take that as a sign that she might not actually be here with any sort of hostile intent. If Joel can grow and be the bigger person for the kids, so can I.

For a long moment, she doesn't say anything and neither do I. After a solid two minutes of silence, I open my mouth at the same time Brooke says, "I'm sorry."

I blink, thinking for sure that I've misheard her. "What?"

Her cheeks color, and she clears her throat, fidgeting with her large diamond engagement ring. "I'm sorry. For the trial— for Bryant Halpert."

Unsure what to say, I simply stay quiet, since she looks like she's just getting started. "I'm not sure if Joel told you that I have a history of depression." When I nod, so does she. "Not that it's any excuse, but when Laura died, I didn't handle my grief well." The mention of Joel's mother has my hackles rising again, but I still keep my mouth shut.

"I was closer to Laura than I've ever been to my own mother, so losing her was like losing a mom and best friend in one. And, well, my depression manifested in a way that it cost me my marriage and Clive his relationship with his son.

"Like I said, I'm not trying to make excuses because I still made choices, but I never set out to destroy my entire life. Then, when I got pregnant with Lily and gave birth, a lot of my depression was compounded further because of the hormones and the divorce and my guilt. But I couldn't see it. That's the thing about depression. Sometimes you can feel it coming and sometimes it's this sudden shift. When you've been depressed for so long that it becomes your new normal, you can't see exactly how bad it is."

She tucks her dark-blonde hair behind her ear as she blows out a breath. "I'm back in therapy and on my meds. I probably never should've left therapy after my depressive episode following Gus's birth, but I thought I was better. Turns out, it's something I'll need for the long-term. As I'm realizing the damage I caused, I know I can't change my actions or the repercussions of those actions, but I can—and want to—attempt to make amends.

"You have no reason to forgive me and every right to tell me to fuck off. I wouldn't be able to blame you, but I wanted to offer a sincere apology for the harm my actions caused you. The things I said and did were unjustified and hurtful and I am so, so sorry. I understand if hate me, and again, I couldn't blame you. But I want to thank you for being there for Joel and for Gus when I threw my life away."

I swallow against the lump forming in my throat.. "They're

my favorite people and there's nowhere I'd rather be than by their sides."

She gives me a sad smile as her green eyes grow glassy. "Are you familiar with any show tunes?"

I frown, confused by her abrupt change in subject. "I'm not sure. Why?"

"There's this one Broadway show called *Waitress*. Have you ever heard of that one?"

I think for a beat. "I think there was a movie by the same name a while back."

She nods. "Yes, it's based on the movie. Sara Bareilles wrote the music they used in the Broadway show. That's not really the point, just an informational thing, I guess. Anyway, there's a song in the show called 'She Used To Be Mine'. There's a line in the song that talks about how life's nothing like she planned and when she sings the song, her character is pregnant. She talks about how it wasn't what she asked for and if she could, she'd go back and rewrite her story."

Brooke swallows, looking down at her hands. "I love Lily and I love Clive and I know I can't take anything back, but most days, I want to. Most days, I wish I could turn back the clock and make different choices." She huffs a soft, sad laugh. "The thing is, Clive and I both know we've settled. I'm not Laura and he's not Joel. We also both know we hurt the best man we've ever had the privilege to love and there's nothing either of us can do to repair his broken heart."

When her gaze returns to mine, her expression is pleading. "Please promise you won't hurt him. He's been through enough. They both have."

I shake my head. "I couldn't hurt him if I tried. I'd have to break my own heart to cause him intentional pain. Because that's what he is to me: my heart. They both are. I'd never try to be you or replace you, but I love your son as much as I could any child of my own; I hope you know that."

"I do," she says quickly. "As much as I hate knowing I'm the reason Gus even has the opportunity to have a stepmother, I'm glad it's you. And again, I'm so sorry for how I've treated you and the things I said. I know I'm not completely back to an even keel yet, but I'm far enough out that I'm horrified by the things I did."

I don't think I'm anywhere near ready or able to forgive Brooke outright, but I can understand and appreciate how hard even coming to have this conversation with me must've been for her. Once upon a time, she and I were very close, and this might be the closest thing to *that* Brooke I've seen since before Joel's mom died.

"Thank you for your apology. I'm sure it wasn't easy for you to work up the nerve to come over and offer it. I don't know what's going to happen, but I can promise you that I will never speak ill of you to Gus. You are his mother and without you, he wouldn't exist. As he's my favorite kid, I can't imagine a world without him in it, so you will always have my respect and appreciation simply for bringing him into the world. You have my word."

She heaves a relieved sigh. "Thank you. And Joel should be receiving a call or email from his lawyer, but I've agreed to the schedule he wanted."

My brows rise in surprise, and she shrugs. "Since we're next door, I can appreciate Gus having some autonomy and choice in the matter about where he spends his time. Maybe as I improve, we can all communicate better. While I know we'll probably never be one of those sickeningly perfect blended families, maybe we can try. For Gus. I mean, I know you and Joel have been trying this whole time, but I'll try, too."

"I'd like that. I think he would, too."

"Good. Well, I'll get out of your hair. Thank you for letting me get all that off my chest."

"Sure." I give her a small, hopeful smile as she exits the gate. Although I know things will probably never be as good between Brooke and me as they once were, I can appreciate the olive branch she extended. Like I told her, I'm sure it took guts to come over and apologize. The least I could do was hear her out, right?

I turn my attention back to the journal in my lap and reopen it to the page I was reading. As I flip to the next page, I frown, confused by what I see. Or rather, what I don't see. There's another entry, sure, but several pages have been ripped out between this entry and the last. I run my fingertip down the gap where jagged fragments of pages are left.

Although I unsure what it means, I start reading.

> Dear Baby,
> I have no clue if you will read this someday. I want to say that I'll be brave enough to let you, but I'm not brave. I'm a coward. Because I'm too scared to do this alone.

I blink in shock. *Alone?* What the hell? I glance at the top of the page for the date, but there's nothing there. Blowing out a breath in an attempt to dislodge the dread settling into my gut, I pick up where I left off.

They say it's better to have loved and lost than never to have loved at all, but I'd rather never know what this feels like. I'd rather never know what it's like to hand your heart over to someone and then watch it shrivel at the same time the light leaves their eyes. Because without Nigel, I have no heart. And if you don't have a heart, you can't be alive, right?

Although—judging by how active you are—I'm physically alive, I'm dead inside. What good will I be to you as a dead person? You deserve so much more than that. You deserve to have two parents who will love you and never look at you with anything but affection and hope.

I can console myself that I'll always know where you are and who you will become and I will always make sure you're taken care of, but I can't be the one who takes care of you when I can barely take care of myself.

You need more than I can offer you and in truth, I think they need you more, too. Right now, it's a chore for all of us to simply survive, but I think you'll heal their broken hearts. Like I said, I no longer have a heart, so I can't heal.

If Nigel was still here, I'm sure this letter would be completely different. But he's not here. He'll never be here again. He'll never laugh with me again. He'll never hold me after a trying day *again. He'll never tell me that I'm being cheeky and ask me if I'd like a cup of tea. He'll never again be there when I fall asleep or wake up.*

He'll forever be the best and worst thing that ever happened to me. So will you. Because if I didn't know what it was like to love you both, I'd never know what it was like to lose you both. This loss is suffocating. In truth, I'm not sure I'll survive it. At least I'll know you will be okay, even if I never will be again.

-Tootsie

I frown at the page before flipping to the next one, only to find it blank. I continue flipping, but the remainder of the book is also empty. Slumping back against the lounger, I reread the entry, attempting to glean information I know I won't find in these pages.

A few minutes later, Joel walks out the backdoor and Jethro's tail wags, thudding against the metal leg of my chair. He stoops to scratch the dog behind the ear before giving me his full attention. "What's with your face, Tee?"

I extend the book in his direction as I heave a frustrated sigh. "Read this."

His brows rise in mild surprise, but he drops onto the lounger with me. "Okay. But you don't look too happy, so should I prepare myself?"

I shrug. "I'm not sure."

He nods, accepting the journal, holding it away from his face in an attempt to find a good distance from which to read it without his glasses. Once he's found one he deems acceptable, he squints at the page. His eyes drift over the book for the few minutes it takes him to read it.

Once he's done, he blinks a few times as he turns to look at me. "Okay, so it looks like something major happened between her and Nigel and she couldn't handle it?"

"I think so, but that's the last entry, so who actually knows? Is he still alive? Did they have a massive falling out, and he abandoned her? From the way she talked about him in these journals, I can't see that. They seemed utterly devoted to each other."

"Okay, so look online. If he's still alive, you can find him. If he's not, you can probably find out how and when he died. If he died, it would make a lot more sense for this type of thing; that she was so depressed about losing him, she felt you'd be better off with your parents." He takes my hand in his. "It won't change anything that's happened, but you might get closure."

I nod. "Yeah. Probably."

"Well, whenever you're ready, if you want support, you know I'm here. Although, if it's something you feel like you need to find out alone, I understand that, too. You just let me know what you need, okay?" He leans over to press a kiss to my forehead. After a beat, he pulls back, his expression excited. "Oh, yeah. Guess what? Selena called to say Brooke finally agreed to the custody agreement. Can you believe it?"

I smile, loving how much more relaxed he looks in just the ten seconds since he's spilled the news. "I know."

He frowns. "You do? How?"

I glance over my shoulder toward Brooke and Clive's house. "She came by." His eyes go wide and he opens his mouth, but I shake my head. "No, I'm fine. It wasn't hostile. She actually apologized. For everything."

"Everything?" he asks, his tone incredulous. "Like, *every-thing* everything?"

"Yeah. She and I are good. I mean, I don't know if we'll ever be besties or anything, but I think we can all agree to be good, if only for the sake of the kids. I think she's going to be okay, though. She said she's medicated and back in therapy, and I'm sure it took a lot of courage for her to come and own up to her mistakes. We're not going to hold it over her head," I say meaningfully. "We're hopefully going to put all of this behind us and try to peacefully coexist."

Joel huffs a laugh. "Well, I'll be damned. Alright. Sure. Let's try to...*coexist*."

"Atta boy," I say with a wink and give him a quick kiss.

Later that night, once Gus has gone to bed and Joel is taking Jethro out one last time, the curiosity finally becomes too much for me. Honestly, I'm shocked I lasted this long before deep diving into Google, but supper and deciding as a family what sort of holiday card we wanted to send out this year took precedent, I suppose.

But now, as I sit in bed alone with my thoughts, I can't help but reach for my phone to type my father's name into the search engine. Bracing myself for what I might find, I hit enter and wait. Truthfully, I'm not sure I'll find anything since, if he died, it was over thirty years ago. And if he's still alive, I'm not sure I want to know. A split-second later, an ancient article from a paper in San Diego tells me everything I need to know.

Local Photographer Succumbs to Injuries

I sigh, clicking on the link. According to the article, dating a few months before I was born, Nigel was walking across a busy intersection when he was struck by a driver who had ignored the traffic light. He was taken to the hospital and survived a few days following the accident, but wasn't able to recover. The article doesn't mention Tootsie, only the gallery showing he had planned for the following week. It does, however, mention that the driver was taken into custody and charged with vehicular manslaughter.

I suppose that should bring me some comfort, but what about the comfort and justice for Tootsie? What about how this one incident completely changed her? What about the fact that at one time, she was full of hope and love and it was ripped away? What about what this incident cost *me*?

Even knowing I can't wish for things to be different than they were, I still feel the loss of what might have been if Nigel had lived and Tootsie had allowed herself to be my mother. She was right. She made sure I was taken care of, but truthfully, I think I would've rather had her and not her money.

I wish I could say I sob for hours over this revelation, but the loss feels abstract. I didn't know Nigel except through Tootsie's journal entries. I didn't know them as a couple. Truth be told, I probably didn't even know the real Tootsie. I've already mourned the one I lost.

When Joel finally comes to bed, I roll toward him. He does the same, sweeping my hair off my face. "Nigel died," I say, my tone flat.

He's quiet for a beat. "You looked it up?"

"Yeah. He was hit by a car while he was walking across the street."

"Wow. And how do you feel about that?"

I nearly want to laugh at the idea of Joel asking me about my feelings, but this is what we do now. Instead, I smile at how far he's come. "Thank you for asking me how I feel. I'm not sure I'll ever get used to that, but I love you for it. I'm not sure, honestly. I didn't know him, so it doesn't really feel like I have a right to be torn up about it. I'm sad for how it affected Tootsie and how she probably never fully recovered from the loss. I could never want things to have turned out differently. You and Gus are my entire world, and if they had, I might've never met you all. I do wish I could've seen how happy and in love she was. I think that would've definitely been something."

He nods. "I'm sure. Are you alright, though? Do you need anything?"

I lay my head on his chest, breathing him in. "I already have everything I need."

He huffs a laugh, pressing a kiss to the top of my head as he wraps his arms around me. "Me, too, Tee."

"Are you sure I didn't go overboard? He's not going to be embarrassed when he gets here and sees all of this?"

Joel laughs as he pulls me to his side. "It's a little late for that since it's already a done deal. But you only graduate from Yale once, right?"

"So they say. Do you think he's going to like it?"

"Tee, it's a house. I'm pretty sure he's going to shit himself."

"Yeah, but is it too much?"

My husband rolls his eyes. "I think you need to go chill out. Go hang out with Callahan or something. Don't y'all have some gossip to catch up on? Send Jonas over here to help me with the ribs. Have a drink and chill."

"Hey, Tee?"

I swivel to see Lily standing behind me and I smile. "Yeah, honey?"

"When's Gus coming?"

"Soon. Your mom and dad went to go pick him up at the airport."

"Okay. Can I swim until they get here?"

Nodding, I tug her braided pig tail. "Sure. I think Tucker and Lyla are over in the pool. I'll walk over with you."

Joel drops a kiss on my cheek and waves at his little sister. "Thanks for giving Tee something to do besides worry she went overboard with the party, Lil."

"Well, y'all did buy Gus a house, so it's probably justified."

I scoff. "Excuse me? Are you twelve or twenty? Besides, we didn't *buy* him a house, we're simply giving him one we're not using. It was a great first house for me, so we wanted him to have the same experience. It's not like you won't be there all the time, too."

She smiles. "I know. You think he'll let me keep my old room?"

"Probably. He's a pretty good guy."

"Yeah, both my brothers are pretty cool," she says matter-of-factly. It never ceases to amaze me how Gus and Lily have always just accepted their lives as "normal". Although, I suppose for them, it is their normal. We should all strive to be so well-adjusted.

"Hear that, honey, a tween thinks you're cool," I call to Joel as we make our way over to our house so Lily can swim with Jonas and Callahan's kids.

"My life's purpose has been fulfilled. I can now die a happy man," he deadpans, making me laugh.

Once we're onto the deck, Lily wastes no time taking off toward the pool. "Hey, Jonas, Joel wanted to know if you could come help with the ribs?"

"Sure." He drops a kiss on his wife's cheek before jogging next door, where the grill and picnic tables are setup under a large tent to provide a respite from the already sweltering late May Florida sun and heat.

Callahan lounges nearby, her strawberry-blonde hair braided over one shoulder, a battery-powered fan in one hand

and a cold beer in the other. As I get closer, dropping onto the seat next to hers, she pulls a drink from a cooler, handing it to me. "Thanks."

"Anytime. So, are you excited to finally have Gus home?"

I nod as I sip my beer. "So glad. It's been too quiet without him. I mean, I probably could've done something a bit more constructive than gotten a rescue puppy, but she's just too cute."

"And not a bit spoiled, I'm sure. Are you getting any sleep, though?"

I snort. "You know, they say puppies are like having a new baby and I would probably assume they're correct. For weeks, I was up twice a night until she finally started sleeping longer stretches."

"Pretty much," Callahan agrees.

"So, how's everything with Maddie's divorce? Last we talked, they were in the home stretch."

She nods. "It's finally final and I think she's more relieved than anything. Even though she's spending the entire summer away from the kids, I think the time and space will be good for her to reflect and heal."

"Weren't they supposed to go to Isle of Palms and stay in that big house on the beach?"

"She's already been there for a week. It was already paid for and her house is being renovated, so she didn't really have a reason to stick around. Truthfully, I'm just hoping she has some fun." Her smile widens, and there's a wicked gleam in her eye as she lowers her voice. "She called me last night to say that she got flirty with a twenty-something bartender. She was freaking out a little, but she was planning on meeting him after he got off work. I'm sincerely hoping she gets some good dick out of the deal."

I snort. "Wow. Twenty-something? Can you imagine?"

Callahan shrugs. "She said he looked like Nathan Scott from *One Tree Hill*."

"Well, then. Who can blame her?"

"Right?"

Her phone dings in her lap, and she picks it up as it dings again. She examines the screen, laughing before extending the phone to me. "I guess she survived."

I take it to read the texts.

> Maddie: I'm alive. Holy. Fucking. Shit. There are no words.

> Maddie: Actually, I have lots of words, but my brain is glitched from the best night of my life and I can't form them. 24?! Who even am I???

I laugh as I hand the phone back. "Go, Maddie."

"That's exactly what I say."

A car horn blares from the driveway, and I hop up. "Keep an eye on Lily?"

"Of course. Go see your kid."

I can't keep the smile off my face as I make my way around the house, joined by Joel, as Gus climbs out of the backseat of Clive's Tahoe.

My stepson is still a miniature version of his dad; except he's not so miniature anymore. He's over six feet and stocky, with his father's smile and his mother's eyes. And while his first hug is for his dad, he has a long one for me, too. "Welcome home, kid."

"Thanks, Tee. Although I gotta admit, I definitely don't miss this humidity."

I nod as we part. "I know what you mean. Did your mom and Clive take you to see the new house?"

"Yeah. We drove by, anyway. They said Dad was making ribs, so I was eager to get here. Lil's in the pool, I'm guessing?"

"Of course. You know she's a water bug." I exchange a glance with Joel, Brooke, and Clive. After they all nod, I turn Gus to face the house—my old house. "And we hope that just because you now have a place of your own, you won't be a stranger. I mean, we all know where you live, so good luck trying to hide from us."

He blinks, confused, and looks at us all. "What? What's happening?"

Brooke steps forward. "We all agreed we wanted you to have a nice graduation gift, but this was all Teagan's idea. Clive and I pitched in on some repairs and updates that needed to be done, but we all figured that since you'd be working here and you were used to having your own space, you wouldn't really want to live with any of us."

Joel offers him a soft smile. "I'm sure it's lame to live next door to your parents, but we hope you'll still want to hang out with us and watch ballgames and stuff."

Gus's mouth still hangs open, and he finally shakes himself. "This is really mine?"

I nod. "Some of the best days of my life happened in that house. I got to watch you grow up from there and would love to watch you make it your own place."

"So, this is for real? It's not some prank?"

We all laugh, and Joel pulls a set of keys from his pocket, extending them to Gus. He doesn't take them, and instead grabs his dad in a big hug, followed by the rest of us.

"We're all so proud of you," Clive adds.

It's the wee hours of the morning before the party winds down. When Joel and I finally fall into bed, it's only for a certain six-month-old fluff ball named Patsy to jump up onto the mattress, worming her way between us. "This is all your fault, you know," Joel argues as he tugs off his reading glasses.

I scoff in disbelief. "I'm sorry, wasn't it you who said that 'we can't just let her cry all night; it's inhumane?'"

"Yeah, but I didn't mean for this to become a nightly thing."

She snuggles up under his arm as he absentmindedly runs his hand down her back. She's snoring in about thirty seconds.

"You have to admit, she sleeps better in here and we get better sleep when she does."

He sighs. "I suppose. But I'd rather snuggle up next to you," he says, wiggling his eyebrows.

"We're empty nesters, so we can snuggle anytime we want. Plus, it's summer break, so you know what that means. *Snuggling* at all hours of the day and night."

He laughs. "That does sound appealing. Do you think Gus liked the house?"

"I think he's still in shock. I predict by tomorrow, the shock will have worn off and he'll already be roping you and Clive into different projects."

He's quiet for a beat, a contemplative smile on his face. "Can you believe this is how our lives have worked out?"

I run my hand down Patsy's back. "It does seem pretty surreal most days. Especially considering where we began."

"Yeah. But I guess, if it all got me this—you—I can't be upset, right?"

I let my eyes drift to the photo of the Golden Gate Bridge on the wall opposite our bed. "Yeah. I'm not one for signs, but I can't help but think that everything worked out the way it was supposed to."

"Probably. It's been a long road, though."

I snort, leaning my head back against the headboard, and turn my face toward his. "You're telling me. It's good now, though. You and your dad have mostly found your way back to something like a relationship, even if it's never going to be like it was. You and Brooke are civil. The kids are amazing and loved by everyone in their lives. Your son is a college graduate and headed for law school. And you still have your good looks," I add with a grin.

He leans over to give me a quick kiss. "I'm pretty sure that's because your goodness keeps me young. You wouldn't let me be all bitter and stuff. I probably would've turned into this shriveled, mean old man whose kid didn't want to be around him. I would've sat on the front porch and yelled at people to get off my lawn."

I huff a laugh. "I suppose you have a lot to thank me for, huh?"

"Oh, so much, wife." He trails kisses down my neck and I let out a slow breath. "Let me show you my appreciation."

ABOUT THE AUTHOR

For as long as she can remember, Rachael has been a voracious reader. At the age of eleven, she discovered her grandmother's stash of clench-cover romance novels and she was forever changed. A lover of many, many fictional men and one very non-fictional one, she strives to write real and emotional characters who always get their happily ever after. Rachael lives in East Tennessee with her husband and two sons on their family farm. When she's not tackling her endless TBR, she can be found drinking all the coffee in existence.

ALSO BY RACHAEL OGLE

<u>Until Duet</u>

Until August and onto Forever (Until Books 1 & 2)

<u>Summer Lovin' Series</u>

Fake it to Forever (Summer Lovin' Books 1 & 2)

<u>Knox County Series</u>

My Ada Mae (Knox County Book 1)

Not Your Girl (Knox County Book 2)

Change My Life (Knox County Book 3)

Crash Into Me (Knox County Book 4)

<u>Talk of the Town Series</u>

Talk of the Town (Talk of the Town Book 1)

Hell for the Holidays (Talk of the Town Book 2)

9 789899 195764